TEAROOM
mysteries

Dear Reader,

Writing this piece of Jan and Elaine's story was such a fun departure from real life with all its demands and busyness. I enjoyed getting lost in a world with good friends, delicious baked goods, and a little bit of mystery to keep things interesting. I loved dreaming up this story, their adventures, and all the twists and turns the mystery could take to lead them to its end.

Though my life is very different from that of these two cousins, it was easy to imagine buying and renovating an old Victorian home with my own sister or cousin one day and all the fun we might have drinking tea, working on puzzles, and maybe even getting caught up in the latest mystery. Though I'm not sure I'd be as good at solving these as Jan and Elaine are!

Something about this setting, this town, this slower-paced life instantly drew me in and made me want to be one of the homeowners on the same block as Tea for Two. That neighborly kindness and small-town camaraderie is often too rare these days. I especially enjoyed infusing Jan's world with a little bit of my own by writing an outing at the local theater, a place that's near and dear to my heart (and a place where I spend an awful lot of my own time!).

I hope you will continue to get wrapped up in this small-town story and that it will be a lovely escape from the rigors of everyday life.

Sincerely,
Rebecca Adams

Tearoom Mysteries

Tearoom for Two
Tea Rose
To a Tea
Crosswords and Chamomile
Burning Secrets

TEAROOM mysteries

Burning Secrets

REBECCA ADAMS

Guideposts

New York

Tearoom Mysteries is a trademark of Guideposts

Published by Guideposts Books & Inspirational Media
110 William Street
New York, New York 10038
Guideposts.org

Acknowledgments

Every attempt has been made to credit the sources of copyrighted material used
in this book. If any such acknowledgment has been inadvertently omitted or
miscredited, receipt of such information would be appreciated.

Scripture quotations are taken from *The Holy Bible, New International Version*.
Copyright © 1973, 1978, 1984, 2011 by Biblica, Inc. Used by permission of
Zondervan. All rights reserved worldwide. www.zondervan.com

Cover and interior design by Müllerhaus
Cover illustration by Ross Jones, represented by Deborah Wolfe, Ltd.
Typeset by Aptara, Inc.

Printed and bound in the United States of America
10 9 8 7 6 5 4 3 2 1

Burning
Secrets

CHAPTER ONE

J an Blake opened her warm oven, smiling as she inhaled the aroma of cinnamon, nutmeg, and banana.

She'd worked all week perfecting the recipe for her mini banana loaves, and even she had to admit she'd succeeded. The secret was the buttery streusel topping. Jan's mouth watered at the memory of the many tastings it had taken to perfect the recipe.

"Something smells delicious." Jan's cousin, Elaine Cook, appeared in the doorway of the kitchen, already dressed in her emerald-green Victorian gown.

Jan closed the oven door and added two more minutes to the timer. "Really? Oh, I hope so. I want everything to be just right."

The women of Lancaster Community Church had decided to host an event at Tea for Two and the cousins had worked hard to ensure everything went according to plan. Jan hoped they could provide a truly memorable event for such an influential group within their community. It could mean a good deal of future business for their tearoom. Many of these women were visiting the tearoom for the first time, and Jan wasn't about to waste their chance to make a good first impression.

"It will," Elaine said. "But you should go get dressed. We only have a few minutes before they arrive."

Jan glanced at the clock above the sink. Three o'clock had snuck up on her. Too much last-minute tinkering with her recipe. "Can you take these out of the oven for me when the timer goes off?" Jan asked Elaine as she removed her apron and hung it on the hook next to the door.

"Of course," Elaine said. "Now go."

Upstairs, Jan pulled her burgundy Victorian gown from the bedroom closet. It had recently been returned from the dry cleaners and had that crisp, clean smell to it. She dressed quickly, and glanced at herself in the mirror above her dresser to be sure she hadn't missed a button. One look at her reflection and she had to laugh at the thin dusting of flour on her nose.

An occupational hazard, she supposed.

As she wiped the powder away, something outside her window caught her eye. In the distance, black smoke billowed from a building near the lake.

What on earth?

It looked like more than your standard leaf-burning fire—the smoke was thicker, blacker.

Jan watched for a few moments trying to determine where the fire was coming from, to no avail. At this distance, it was hard to say. She imagined it wouldn't take long to find out. In Lancaster, word spread quickly.

It was time to open the tearoom. She took one last look at the smoke, silently prayed that no one was injured, and then walked down the winding staircase and into the entry hall, where she saw Rose Young, one of their employees, greeting the church women with her usual charming smile.

Jan glanced briefly into the east parlor off to her right as she stood facing the door. She took a moment to admire the Victorian-style curtains hanging from the windows, which were the loveliest complement to the lace tablecloths on every table in the tearoom.

A collection of mix-and-match tea settings graced each table. While they'd initially settled on a variety of mismatched teacups, saucers, and teapots for financial reasons, it had turned out to be one of Jan's favorite happy accidents. They'd found that unique cups and saucers at each place setting sparked interesting conversations as their guests dreamed up stories about the history of the pieces.

In fact, every time they purchased another teacup or teapot from a flea market or estate sale, Jan let her own imagination roam free, inventing a provenance for each. How exciting to think their little tearoom was filled with history.

"Jan, everything looks lovely," one of the women said, pulling Jan from her daydream. Jan thanked her and began to usher the women to their tables. As she did, Maureen Oakley appeared at her side. A friend and regular at Tea for Two, Maureen had been kind enough to organize this little gathering with the help of Sarah Ryder, the pastor's wife. The women of Lancaster Community Church had certainly welcomed the cousins and their little business with open arms, and Jan was grateful. Entertaining friends with a special high tea hardly felt like work at all.

"Thank you so much for having us today, Jan," Maureen said with a smile. "It's a wonderful way to introduce some of our younger women to this delightful tradition you all are carrying on."

"Thank *you*, Maureen," Jan said. "We're thrilled to share our tearoom..." Jan stopped before finishing her sentence. Something wasn't right.

"Jan? Are you okay?" Maureen laid a gentle hand on Jan's arm. "You look a little pale."

She gasped. "My banana bread!" Jan would know the smell of overcooked baked goods anywhere. She rushed to the kitchen and found her cousin standing beside the oven holding a pan of burned mini loaves.

"I didn't hear the timer," Elaine said, her face full of apologies.

"Oh no." Jan wanted to cry at the charred streusel topping.

Elaine frowned. "I was distracted, Jan. I'm so sorry."

"Don't worry," Jan said. "We'll whip something else up. No use crying over burned banana bread." She smiled. "Now, you go entertain our guests. I'll need about twenty minutes. Do you think they'd like to hear a story about one of our more exotic teas?" Jan asked.

Elaine smiled. "Good thinking." She disappeared into the parlor and moments later Jan heard music—one of her favorite Mozart piano concertos. Jan looked at the burned loaves.

"I can do this." Jan gave herself a little pep talk, but she couldn't ignore the way her heart raced as she ran through a list of ingredients in the refrigerator. She had leftover finger sandwiches and the chilled dough for her miniature maple croissants. Those could work with the other items on her menu. She could still save this tea. She'd simply have to keep her wits about her.

Jan moved around her kitchen with ease, her baking station set up for convenient access to the ingredients she used most often. With everything at her fingertips, Jan found it easy to create the pastries and desserts their customers raved about. She worked at the island in the center of the large kitchen, assembling her croissants. They were a sure crowd-pleaser and something she could finish quickly and from memory. She was humming along to the concerto as she worked, lost in her own world, when the back door opened. She hadn't even realized it was unlocked.

Jan stopped stirring and turned toward the door just in time to see Macy Atherton slip in.

"Goodness, Macy. You gave me a scare!"

"*Shh!*" Macy hissed as she entered the kitchen. "Are they already here?"

Jan cracked an egg into a glass bowl to make an egg wash. "The women from the church? Yes. Why aren't you out there with them? You could've used the front door, you know. It's much nicer out that way."

Macy paced in a circle around the kitchen, making it difficult for Jan to stay focused on her recipe. Jan glanced up at her and noticed her brow was even more furrowed than usual.

"Macy? Is everything okay?" Jan set her whisk down. When Macy didn't respond immediately, Jan grew concerned. It wasn't like Macy to be quiet for too many minutes in a row.

Macy turned toward Jan. "Why does it smell in here? Did you burn something?" Macy sniffed loudly. "It smells like something burned."

"Just a little burned bread," Jan said as she fished a brush out of the drawer and began applying the egg wash to her croissants. "Feel free to join the other women in the parlor, Macy. I think they're enjoying a presentation on the exotic teas of India at the moment."

Macy shook her head and sat on a stool across from her. "I need your help, Jan."

Jan's eyes darted to the other woman. Several years her junior, Macy Atherton had been a constant supporter of the tearoom since they opened, but her show of support had often been encased in criticism, making her one of those personalities that challenged Jan's goodwill. She'd always tried to see the good in people, and she supposed if Macy needed her help she would find a way to give it.

Jan still remembered the first time Macy visited Tea for Two. Elaine had interacted with her, but she told Jan later Macy had complained about her scones being too dry. Jan was thankful her cousin had been on high alert and sent Macy out with a small bag of ginger cookies on the house. Despite her initial complaint, Macy had sent her daughter-in-law to the tearoom with a rave review.

As owner of Green Glade Cottages, Macy had sent many of her guests their way ever since. Proof that you should never judge a book by its cover.

"Believe me, if I could go to anyone else, I would," Macy said, nearly scoffing. "You aren't exactly my first choice for a private investigator."

Jan inserted two sheets of croissants in the oven and then closed the door and turned to Macy. "I suppose that's good, since I'm not a private investigator."

Macy frowned. "What do you call it then?"

"I'm the co-owner of this tearoom, and I bake some pretty delicious desserts, if I do say so myself." Jan waggled her eyebrows for effect.

"Don't be coy, Jan," Macy said. "I know all about you and your cousin and your side business getting to the bottom of things that need gotten to."

Had they really developed such a reputation around town? Something about the idea excited her. She'd never have thought of herself as a master sleuth, but she and Elaine did seem to have a knack for putting puzzles together. Jan *had* always loved a good puzzle.

"Well, there's no 'side business,' but we have found ourselves in the middle of a few mysteries lately. How do you think we can help you?"

"Someone started a fire in one of my cottages this morning," Macy said, unmistakable fear on her face.

Jan stilled. So that's where the smoke had originated. How awful. "Is everyone okay? Are *you* okay? And why are you here—shouldn't you be with the police or the fire marshal or somebody?"

Macy began pacing again. "I'm fine. Everyone is fine. It was a relatively small fire—I mean, thank goodness, it's been put out—and the building is still intact. That's not the problem."

It sure sounded like a problem to Jan. "Then what is?"

Before Macy could answer, Elaine appeared in the doorway. Behind her was Arnie Sheffield, one of the Kennebec County sheriff's deputies. Elaine's eyes darted back and forth between Jan and Macy, confusion spreading across her face.

Macy turned away.

"There you are, Mrs. Atherton." Deputy Sheffield's voice cut through the muffled melody of the distant concerto playing in the other room. He held his campaign hat with both hands in front of his chest, revealing his neatly trimmed, wavy brown hair. The man was likely just thirty years old, and yet he clearly commanded authority in this room. "We have some talking to do."

CHAPTER TWO

Jan's pulse kicked up as if she was the one the deputy was there to see.

"And there you are, Deputy," Macy said.

"Saw you leaving Green Glade and thought I'd see where you were off to in such a hurry," the deputy said. "Can't say I expected you to leave the scene of a possible crime for a cup of tea."

"What crime?" Elaine asked.

"I didn't realize we were calling it a crime," Macy said, moving away from Deputy Sheffield.

"We can't rule anything out just yet, which is why you shouldn't have left."

"I'm sorry, Deputy Sheffield," Macy said. "It upset me to see one of my cottages in that condition. Green Glade is my whole life."

"All the more reason to stay put, don't you think?" The deputy whipped a notebook out of his back pocket and flipped it open. "Did you see anything suspicious at all? Last night or this morning?"

Macy continued pacing. "No, but I wasn't exactly looking for prowlers. Especially not in the middle of the day." She smoothed her hair with her hands, a worried look painted on her face.

"I see." The deputy scribbled something in his notebook. "Was the electrical up to date in that cottage?"

Macy stopped and wrung her hands together before answering. "I believe so."

"When was the last time you had an electrician out to inspect your cottages?"

The timer on the oven went off, and Jan scurried over to retrieve her croissants. Elaine met her beside the oven. "What is this all about?" she whispered.

"One of the cottages at Green Glade caught fire," Jan whispered back. "Sounds like the deputy is trying to get a fuller picture of what's going on."

"We heard reports you've had some financial troubles lately," Deputy Sheffield said.

Macy tossed a look over her shoulder and Jan and Elaine quickly looked away. "I think you're asking the wrong questions, Deputy Sheffield. Of the wrong person."

"Financial troubles?" Elaine whispered. "Macy?"

"Why would he bring that up unless..." Jan kept her voice low. "You don't think Macy would've burned down her own cottage, do you?"

Elaine helped her position the warm croissants on a serving tray. "Of course not."

"Right. Of course not," Jan said. So why did Macy avoid the deputy's question about her supposed financial troubles?

"Where were you at the time of the fire, Mrs. Atherton?" the deputy asked.

Macy lifted her chin staunchly. "I was home."

"Can anyone confirm that?"

"No, sir. I was alone."

Jan and Elaine exchanged worried glances.

The deputy closed his notebook. "I see." He studied Macy for too many long, silent seconds. "Why don't we continue this down at the station?"

"Oh, I doubt that's necessary," Elaine interjected. "Deputy Sheffield, Macy is a valuable member of our community. You can't believe she would commit a crime."

"I'm not arresting her, Mrs. Cook," the deputy said. "I'm simply trying to get all the facts." He started for the kitchen door.

"Wait, Deputy Sheffield," Jan said. "Go through the back door, please. We're entertaining." And all of her—and Macy's—friends were out there. From the looks of it, the last thing Macy needed was a roomful of prying eyes to speculate about her innocence.

"Of course," he said. "Mrs. Atherton?" The deputy held the back door open, waiting for Macy to pass through.

Macy turned to the cousins before she followed him out the back door. "Can I count on the two of you to help me? Please?"

They watched Macy disappear through the door, and after she left, neither Jan nor Elaine said a word for several long seconds. While the deputy had been quick to point out he wasn't arresting Macy, his questions certainly suggested he was suspicious of her.

The only question was why.

"What did she mean by counting on us to help her?" Elaine asked.

Jan turned back to her croissants, remembering they had two parlors of hungry church women to feed. "It's why she came here in the first place. She said we've gotten a reputation around town. She called us private investigators." Jan stifled a giggle as she spoke the words.

Elaine's eyes widened with what Jan could only describe as delight.

"And, if our friend is in trouble and it's our help she wants, I suppose we should oblige. It's what private investigators do." Jan smiled.

"Let's not get carried away," Elaine said. "We have to consider one thing before we agree to help her."

"What's that?" Jan asked, picking up the tray of croissants.

"What if our investigation leads us back to Macy?"

ELAINE HAD SPOTTED the deputy in the entryway next to Rose. She'd assumed the guest had been a latecomer, but she never would've predicted law enforcement. Not at a high tea specially prepared for the women of Lancaster Community Church. She and her cousin had looked forward to this event for weeks, and it would seem everything was intent on going wrong from burned bread to the arrival of the police.

Elaine had turned the tea over to their employees, Archie Bentham and Rose Young, with a few quick instructions, then excused herself, hopeful she could scoot the deputy into the other room unnoticed.

The church women didn't seem to mind, as conversation was never difficult for them. Within moments, the room was alive with chatter and Elaine felt her worries dissipate.

That is, until she had opened the door to the kitchen.

Now Elaine and Jan still stood in the same spot they had moments ago when the deputy had escorted Macy out for questioning, Elaine's question still hanging in the air, unanswered.

"We don't really believe Macy could be guilty, do we?" Jan broke her stunned silence. "We have to help her."

"I'm not sure this is the right kind of case for us." An uneasiness had settled inside Elaine. She could admit that it had excited her when Jan informed her they'd gotten a reputation for their sleuthing, but getting involved in this case could be a mistake. Macy was their friend and a loyal customer, after all. Heaven forbid their investigation turned up something unflattering, or worse, criminal. Elaine didn't want to be the one to have to share that news with the authorities. "Maybe we should let the professionals handle this one."

Jan set the tray of maple croissants back on the counter. "I understand it might be difficult, but she was practically begging for our help. It doesn't feel right to abandon her."

"And we won't, but she hasn't been charged with anything. At this point, we don't even know if a crime has been committed." Elaine smoothed the front of her green Victorian gown, a special costume for their special guests, women who very much deserved their full attention. "Now, would you mind helping me with our guests?"

Jan sighed, still troubled, Elaine could tell. But she followed Elaine into the dining room with her delicious croissants, cream puffs, macarons, and the most adorable petite sandwiches. It wasn't her planned menu, but it would more than suffice. Jan had such a knack for putting together the kind of refreshments that turned first-time visitors into regular customers. Their tearoom was on its way to becoming a beloved part of the Lancaster community and they'd only been open about six months.

Elaine let the thought sink in for a moment. It was hard to believe how much her life had changed since her husband, Ben, had passed away just about a year ago. She never would've imagined moving back to her childhood hometown to start a business with her cousin, but now that Tea for Two was a success, she couldn't imagine anything she would rather be doing.

As the door to the kitchen swung closed behind them, the sweet maple aroma drifted into the parlor.

"Whatever you've cooked up in there smells absolutely amazing," Maureen said to Jan.

Elaine couldn't be sure, but she thought a blush of pink warmed her cousin's cheeks. Ever modest, Jan usually demurred at a compliment to her talents, so Elaine saw to it that she was properly bragged upon. After all, she still felt responsible for the change in menu given that it had been her fault the banana bread had burned in the first place.

"This is one of Jan's most requested recipes," Elaine said, loudly enough for the entire room to hear. "Exclusive to Tea for Two, these mini maple croissants are our best-kept secret."

Elaine didn't miss the grateful smile on Jan's face. It was always nice to be appreciated, and she certainly appreciated her cousin's talents.

"What did the officer want?" Rue Maxwell's innocent question quieted the room, as if everyone wondered the same thing. Rue was always perfectly put together, even in her most casual attire, and while her question was innocent, Elaine had hoped to avoid it. Jan tossed Elaine a worried look as she set her last tray down at the center of one of the tables.

"I thought I saw Arnie sneak in here. Is everything all right?" Maureen wore a look of genuine concern.

Elaine paused for a long moment, desperately wanting to change the subject. "He was here for a brief moment. But he's headed out now. Who's ready for...?"

"Where is Macy?" Rue cut in, looking around. "We'd made plans to talk a little business today at the tea. It's not like her to not show up for a social event." The two women often discussed the joys and trials of owning a tourist-dependent business. Rue and her husband's Northwoods B and B didn't compete with Macy's Green Glade Cottages, but there were enough similarities that they had much to talk about.

"Is Arnie still here?" Maureen asked. "I didn't see him leave."

"Oh my!" One of the younger women across the room waved her phone in the air. "My husband just texted me. There's a fire at Green Glade."

A collective gasp raced across the room as the chatter picked up.

Elaine stepped forward, not sure exactly what to say. "Ladies, Macy is okay."

"You've seen her?"

"Yes, she was here," Elaine answered. "She's fine. She simply needs to answer a few questions for Deputy Sheffield and then she'll be home safe and sound."

A pause hung in the air, and for a moment Elaine thought she may have appeased their curiosity.

Seconds later, however, the questions started.

"What kind of questions is he asking? Does Macy know something?"

"Is Macy a suspect?"

"Why is the deputy investigating at all? And why does he have Macy?"

"He doesn't *have* Macy. He's...," Elaine started, but was quickly interrupted.

"Did someone burn the cottage down on purpose?"

"Was anyone hurt? Was it arson? Do we have an arsonist in Lancaster?"

The barrage of questions continued until the women had assembled a number of possible explanations for Macy's current situation, and Elaine was helpless to stop the speculation. In the end, the truth was that no one knew what had really happened.

And while Elaine still maintained this might not be the best case for them to take on, she couldn't deny she was curious about what had happened at Green Glade that morning and how Macy was involved—if she was.

After their guests left an hour later, Jan and Elaine cleaned up the parlors and kitchen with Rose and Archie's help. Once their two employees had gone, Elaine hung her Victorian gown back in her bedroom closet and dressed in a pair of casual pants with a soft pink blouse. With the tearoom closed for the evening, Elaine looked forward to a few hours of reading on the back porch—and perhaps giving Earl Grey, the cat who took up shelter on their front porch, a well-deserved scratch behind his fuzzy ears—despite the cool autumn temperatures. She'd grown to love their porch and the deck below it, the views of Chickadee Lake and the feeling of being home. She'd moved around so much in her life that having a place that made her feel settled was exactly what her soul needed for this season.

There was a light knock on her bedroom door.

"Come in," she called. She didn't need to see Jan's face to guess what her cousin had come to discuss, but one look at her told her she was right. "I know what you're going to say," she said.

Jan crossed the room and stared out one of the three large windows in Elaine's room, this one overlooking Chickadee Lake. The afternoon sun had just begun to dip down in the sky, casting a sweet orange glow on the bedroom.

"I think we should take a quick run out to Green Glade and see the cottage for ourselves," Jan announced.

Elaine removed the emerald earrings from her ears and set them safely in her jewelry box, the one her late husband Ben had made her early in their marriage. It wasn't long after Jared was born, and he was stationed in South Korea. Ben always knew what Elaine was feeling, often even before she did, and at that time, she was homesick.

Oh, she'd put on a brave face, and she was thankful she had Ben and her new baby, but she missed home. One night, only moments after she'd gotten Jared to sleep, Ben came home wearing that smirk—the one that told her he was up to something.

He'd wrapped the jewelry box in a grocery bag, but inside, she found a beautiful locket with Jared's photo on one side and her and Ben on the other.

Ben had been so proud to give her that gift. "I just wanted you to know how much I love you," he'd said. "It's a 'just for being you' gift."

When she found out he'd made the jewelry box himself, it meant all the more to her. In all their travels, it had been one of the few things she'd packed in her suitcase. She wasn't about to risk it being lost by movers.

"I can tell by your silence you disagree," Jan said, pulling Elaine back to the present.

"I don't like the idea of, well, spying on our friends," Elaine said. "I would feel funny poking around Macy's cottages."

Jan seemed to consider it, but only for a few seconds. "Doesn't it seem strange to you, though, that Macy left the cottage before the police could talk to her?"

Elaine turned to her. "Maybe she was overwhelmed and didn't know *what* to do."

"Maybe." Jan shrugged. "But there was something about the way the deputy questioned her. He seemed to be getting at something."

Elaine headed out the door and down the winding staircase that deposited them in the entry hall. Jan followed her. "What could she possibly gain by setting fire to her own cottage?"

Jan thought for a moment. "It does seem far-fetched." She walked into the east parlor and began to remove the linens from the tables. "Macy can be challenging at times, but it's just about impossible to imagine she's an arsonist." Jan paused for a long moment, and Elaine could almost see her mind piecing the puzzle together.

"What is it?" She folded a soiled tablecloth and tossed it on the floor in a pile.

"Deputy Sheffield mentioned Macy had fallen on hard times financially," Jan said.

"He suggested it, but it sounded like conjecture to me," Elaine replied, retrieving a second set of linens from a small closet in the parlor. "And I hate to stick our nose in Macy's business." She gave her cousin a smile. She knew Jan loved her mysteries, but perhaps they'd have to wait for someone else to solve this one.

Jan didn't look convinced. She took one of the clean tablecloths and shook it out over the table, waiting for the air to disappear and allowing the linen to find its new home.

"Why don't we wait and see?" Elaine asked, covering another table. "There's a chance the fire was a complete accident, after all. I would hate to waste our time investigating something that may not even be a crime."

"I suppose so," Jan said. "I'm sure you're right. It's probably nothing."

The front door to their old Victorian popped open and Jan's daughter Tara appeared in the doorway of the parlor. Always fashionable, Tara wore a black trench coat with slick black pants and a sharp-looking pair of heels.

"Mom?" she called out as she closed the door behind her.

Jan turned, happiness on her face at the sight of her youngest daughter. A twinge of sadness skittered through Elaine's mind, but she quickly pushed the jealous feelings away. Sometimes she wondered if Jan knew what a blessing it was to be able to see her kids any time she wanted. Heaven knew she'd give anything to have that same blessing. Her two children, Jared and Sasha, lived out of town and she missed them desperately. Now that Ben was gone, her sense of loneliness had grown heavier. She was so grateful to have Jan by her side, and she didn't take that for granted. Of course she loved Jan's children, but boy, did she miss her own.

She pushed thoughts of Jared and Sasha out of her mind and focused on her beautiful young cousin. She shouldn't begrudge Jan this luxury, regardless of how it made her feel. Besides, she loved Tara too. The girl was more like a niece to her than a cousin, as she often thought of Jan more as a sister.

"This is a lovely surprise," Jan said, greeting Tara at the door. "What are you doing here?"

"I came for baked goods, of course," Tara said. "And to tell you my news."

Jan ushered her into the parlor, where Elaine gave the pretty girl a wide smile. "Is it a man?"

"Elaine," Tara said with mock indignation, "I'm a professional woman with my own business. I don't have time for romance."

Elaine hugged the tablecloth to her chest with a purposefully dramatic sigh. "There's always time for romance at your age. I miss those days!"

"There's time for romance at your age too," Tara said with a grin.

Elaine waved her off. "Don't be silly." Romance was about the last thing on her mind. Well, perhaps not the *last* thing. Never mind that she had the occasional fleeting romantic thought about her friend, Nathan Culver. She reminded herself the two of them were just good friends, though she found him to be very handsome.

"Anyway, this news is better." Tara's eyes sparkled, as if she could barely contain her excitement.

"Better than romance?" Jan asked with wide eyes. "I can't wait."

"I just came from a meeting with Faith Lanier. She's agreed to carry my jewelry at A Little Something."

Jan let out a gleeful squeal. "She did? Well, of course she did! Because Faith Lanier has impeccable taste."

"Congratulations, honey," Elaine said. Tara's custom jewelry designs were unique. They would do well during tourist season when people were out shopping for special trinkets and mementos of their time in Lancaster. Elaine couldn't think of a better place for Tara's jewelry than A Little Something. It was a perfect fit.

"I have just the thing to celebrate." Jan's eyes twinkled. "Leftover croissants." She ushered Tara toward the kitchen at the back of the house.

"The maple ones?" Tara asked, excitement in her voice. "I've always loved those."

Jan responded with a smile. Come to think of it, Elaine wouldn't mind a croissant or two herself. She'd worked up quite an appetite fielding questions and keeping the women from the church entertained. Many of those women were regulars, but there were several who'd never been in before. She hoped they'd won these new customers over.

In the kitchen, Elaine put the kettle on while Jan arranged a plate of the leftover croissants they'd only just packed away. "Why don't we treat ourselves in the dining room?"

Jan nodded in agreement. The dining room was often reserved for bridal showers and other special occasions, but it was one of Elaine's favorite places in their old Victorian home.

The crown jewel of the room was Jan's beautiful hutch, filled with unique treasures, including the Nanking teapots their grandmother had given them.

Ironically, sometimes the work of the tearoom made them forget the joy of slowing down to savor a good cup of tea and a great conversation. To appreciate the home and business God had provided for them. And after the hectic moments with Macy this morning, a little bit of downtime felt especially in order.

While they ate, Tara told them how her deal with Faith had come about. She showed off a few photos of some of her newer pieces—an interesting pair of silver bangle earrings and a lovely necklace with a pewter heart dangling off the chain.

Tara had just finished her third mini croissant when she dabbed the edges of her mouth with a cloth napkin. "Oh, did you hear the awful news about the fire at Green Glade today?"

Jan tossed Elaine a knowing glance across the table. And they were doing so well *not* talking about this.

"We heard," Jan said.

"Poor Macy." Tara took a sip of her peppermint tea. "It all seems so unfair."

"What do you mean?"

Elaine could see the concern on Jan's face.

"This isn't the first time one of her cottages has burned down."

Elaine straightened. Tara certainly had her attention.

"Years ago, she had a business similar to Green Glade in Augusta. Things were going wonderfully until there was a terrible fire that burned three of her cottages to the ground."

"Oh my," Jan said. "Three cottages?"

"Yes," Tara said. "A terrible loss. I can't imagine."

"Where did you hear about the other fire?" Elaine asked.

"Oh, you know how word spreads in a small town," Tara said. "When news of the fire got out, I was with Faith at A Little Something, finalizing plans for her to carry my jewelry, and she mentioned it."

"Sounds like hearsay to me," Elaine said.

"Oh, it is," Tara agreed. "But Faith seems to know a lot about everyone in town. I suppose that's what happens when you live here your whole life."

"I suppose," Jan said.

"Anyway, it's bizarre the same thing has happened twice, but I suppose it turned out okay in the end," Tara said. "If I understand correctly, she used that insurance money to start Green Glade. Seems a shame that here we are so many years later and the same thing is happening all over again."

Elaine frowned. "Yes, a real shame."

"At least this time, it sounds like they put the fire out before it was a complete loss."

"So the cottage is still standing?" Jan asked.

"Yes, mostly. At least that's what Faith said." Tara glanced at her watch. "I should get going. Thanks for letting me celebrate with a massive amount of calories."

Jan rose alongside her daughter. "Don't be silly. Calories don't count when you're celebrating something so exciting."

Elaine watched as Jan walked her daughter toward the door to see her out. When she returned, she avoided Jan's eyes. She had already wondered whether they should get involved in any of this. Still, the conversation with Tara had piqued her interest.

After several long seconds, Jan looked like she might burst.

Elaine shook her head, as if that could keep her cousin from speculating.

"Don't you think it's a bit fishy?" Jan blurted. "For someone to have two fires on two different properties seems, well, suspicious."

Elaine cleared the dishes from the dining room table and began carrying them to the kitchen. "It doesn't make sense for Macy set fire to her own cottage, especially since the cottage is still standing."

Jan followed Elaine into the kitchen and took the dishes from her, then began loading them into the dishwasher. "That's true. If she was having financial trouble and needed the insurance money, the cottage should've been burned to the ground."

"Unless something went awry," Elaine said. "No, forget I said that."

"You *do* think something feels off," Jan said, sounding a little exultant.

Elaine didn't want to say anything, not yet. But she couldn't deny the fact that something didn't feel right. "I don't know what the truth is, but I'm certainly intrigued."

"Maybe we could poke around a little?"

"Maybe." Elaine set her napkin on the table. "But carefully. Macy is our friend and a very good customer, despite her tendency to be ornery."

Jan gave her head a quick shake. "She does like to make it difficult for us, but somehow that's part of her charm." She smiled. "And besides, she did ask for our help." Jan closed the dishwasher.

"She did." Elaine agreed. "All right, Jan. Let's at least take a look around Macy's and see what we can find."

Jan nodded sternly, but as she turned away, Elaine could see the triumphant smile light her face.

CHAPTER THREE

The following afternoon, Jan sat in the passenger seat of Elaine's bright-red Chevy Malibu as they drove through Lancaster and out toward the edge of town.

"I'm still full from breakfast," Elaine said as she drove. "But it was worth it."

"Agreed." Jan had found a recipe for stuffed french toast and Elaine offered to taste-test it for her. It had been wonderful, though Jan might have indulged in one too many pieces. The way the cinnamon and cream cheese combined with the maple syrup had been even more delicious than she'd expected.

The Green Glade fire had been the talk of the morning at the tearoom, with much speculation from their customers as to what really happened. More than one person mentioned Macy as a possible suspect, which left Jan feeling uneasy about their impending visit. Somehow word had spread around town about Macy's previous fire and the resulting insurance settlement. Apparently Tara wasn't the only one who'd heard the rumor. Lancaster was a small town and by nature, its residents knew each other's business. According to their tearoom guests, the first fire was old news. Until now.

Because it was autumn and the tourist season was behind them, most of their customers that morning had been locals, including several who owned businesses right there in town. Jan and Elaine had fostered wonderful friendships with the others who worked and lived nearby, including Jo Murphy and Sylvia Flood.

Unlike some of the others they'd run into that morning, these women seemed to feel the same way about Macy that Jan and Elaine did, and none of them seemed interested in jumping to conclusions about what had happened.

"I feel sorry for Macy," Jo had said, once the crowd died down. She pushed a half-eaten cream puff around on her plate. "If she did start the fire, then things must be pretty dire, and if she didn't, how will she ever recover from all this chatter?"

Sylvia sipped her Russian tea, a special blend Elaine had made, with a swirl of cinnamon for a nice kick. "Oh, you know Macy. She always lands on her feet."

"That's true," Jo said with a smile. "Remember the time one of her guests accused her of taking his cat to the animal shelter without his knowledge?"

"Oh my," Jan had said, taking a break from her work to tune in to the rest of the story. "What happened?"

"One of the deputies showed up at her door with the angry man, who was demanding an explanation." Sylvia shook her head with a look of disbelief in her eyes.

"And Macy whipped out a written account, complete with photographs, detailing all the ways the cat should be charged as a criminal." Jo tossed her head back and laughed.

"The rumors around town were that Macy had lost her mind, but she showed up at the city council meeting with her visual aids, and by the end, she had the entire room on her side," Sylvia said, laughing.

"I suppose Macy is tough as nails," Jo said. "She can handle the Lancaster rumor mill."

Jan didn't doubt it. Macy could be difficult, but she was well respected, and underneath her tough exterior was a woman who was very kind. At least that's what Jan had decided to believe. While she didn't exactly consider Macy a good friend, she cared about her, and her quiet plea for help yesterday had left Jan feeling unnerved and sympathetic.

Still, she couldn't pinpoint why Macy had responded to the deputy's questions the way she did. Macy had been rattled, less than forthcoming, and almost defensive, and Jan knew that wasn't a good sign. Did Macy have something to hide? Or was she simply, and understandably, shaken by the fire and the way it repeated the earlier fires?

Jan thanked God she had never been in a fire, but she imagined it did a number on a person's nerves.

As they drove up to Green Glade, the faint smell of smoke still lingered in the air.

"We should've called first." Jan worried Macy would be taken aback by their unannounced visit. She'd likely comment on their bad manners, but folks around Lancaster were always dropping in on each other. Besides, Elaine had insisted they'd have a better chance of determining the truth if they didn't call first.

"We don't want her to tidy anything up. We want to get a peek at her home—and the cottages—just as they are."

"I'm glad to see you've changed your mind about getting involved," Jan said lightly.

Elaine, she could tell, was stifling a smile. "You know I have a hard time resisting once my curiosity is in play."

Yes, Jan had counted on it. Elaine had made her agree they wouldn't interfere with anything official. The last thing either of them wanted to do was become a nuisance in their new hometown, especially since they relied on the locals to keep their business going.

Elaine made the turn into the driveway of Macy's home on the outskirts of Green Glade.

The large, two-story home sat at the end of a long driveway with a circle drive at its front. The house fit in nicely in the cottage community of Green Glade, but it was much larger than its neighbors.

Now that Jan looked at it, Macy's home seemed lavish, given her chosen profession. Jan had always assumed Macy's family was wealthy, but she supposed it was possible that their apparent extravagance was only a façade.

After they knocked on Macy's door, they waited many long seconds before they heard any sign Macy was home. Elaine had lifted her hand to knock one more time when the door finally opened and Macy stood on the other side, glaring at them.

"I must say, I expected the two of you out here much sooner," she said. "Is this how you typically do business?" She turned and walked away, leaving Jan and Elaine on the over-size front porch.

"Are you coming?" Macy called from the other room seconds later.

Jan glanced at Elaine, who wore a confused expression that likely matched her own. They found Macy in her kitchen, a spacious room with a double oven Jan noticed immediately.

"Really, if you two are going to make a go of this private investigator thing, we should sit down and have a conversation about the way you conduct yourselves." Macy fetched a pitcher of iced tea from the refrigerator. "Waiting a full twenty-four hours before contacting your client seems a little lengthy to me."

Jan watched as Macy filled three glasses with ice. They certainly weren't official private investigators, but she knew she needed to pick her battles carefully with the woman.

Macy cut a lemon into three wedges. "But it's neither here nor there. I don't need your help after all."

Jan frowned. "Are you sure? You seemed pretty upset yesterday."

Macy filled the glasses and gave a soft shrug. "That was before the fire was ruled an accident."

"Oh? That was fast," Elaine said.

"It was an open-and-shut case," Macy said. "Let's take our tea in the sitting room."

As they followed her through the house, both Jan and Elaine surveyed the space. It was awfully large for one person, and from the looks of it, Macy was not having financial trouble. Unless, of course, her troubles were recent and she needed to find a way to keep up her lifestyle.

They passed an office with a partially open door. Jan lingered for a moment when she spotted what appeared to be a stack of bills next to a computer. If she could get her eyes on Macy's financials, maybe that would at least give them a clue if the woman had motive to burn down one of her own cottages.

Of course it wasn't typical for Jan to snoop around her friends' offices and it certainly wasn't typical to read their mail—but if she wanted to get to the bottom of this fire, she might have to bend her own rules. What was that old saying— you can't make an omelet without breaking a few eggs?

"How did they determine the fire was an accident?" Jan asked, catching up with the other two.

Macy motioned for them to sit in the two stuffed armchairs across from the sofa. She placed coasters on the coffee table between them and took a seat on the couch. "They determined it was an electrical fire due to faulty wiring."

"Wouldn't an inspector have found that in a routine inspection?" Elaine asked.

"Is the tea okay?" Macy asked, seeming to ignore the question. "It's not often I have tea connoisseurs in the house."

"It's delicious, Macy," Jan said. "When did you last have an inspector out to Green Glade?"

"I can't be certain," Macy said. "Last year? Maybe the year before. I can ask Shane and Zale. They're better at keeping records than I am."

Macy's son and his wife, Azalea, or "Zale," helped Macy run the cottages. If there were financial troubles, perhaps they should be considered suspects as well. Jan shook the thought aside. This could be nothing more than an accident, as the authorities said.

But then why did Jan have this nagging feeling there was more to this than faulty wiring?

"Has Shane been out since the fire?" Elaine asked.

Macy lifted her chin. "Why do you ask?"

"I'm just gathering facts," Elaine said.

"Your fact gathering sounds like accusation to me."

"I promise you it's not," Elaine said with a smile. "I'm simply trying to paint a clear picture in my head."

Macy didn't respond for a few tense seconds. Finally, she sipped her tea and looked away. "No, he and Zale are still out of town at one of their competitions. You can find their standings online if you still aren't convinced."

Perhaps the two weren't suspects after all.

"Macy, may I use your restroom?" Jan asked, standing. She couldn't ignore the nerves that seemed to be dancing a quick-step in her belly.

Making an omelet, she thought to herself.

"Of course, just down the hall and on your right."

Jan gave Elaine a knowing look and disregarded the warning glare her cousin gave her in return. Something wasn't right and Jan knew this might be their only chance to figure out what that was, so as much as she didn't like it, she had to dig around a little. Somehow, she didn't trust Macy to be forthcoming.

She left the sitting room and turned in the direction of the office, sneaking down the hallway like a prowler in the middle of the night. One look over her shoulder and another one down the hall and Jan disappeared inside the office, where Macy's paperwork waited for her.

The computer was sleeping and Jan gently toggled the mouse to wake it up. She could hear the low hum of conversation coming from the next room and figured she had least a few minutes before she was missed. While she waited, she thumbed through the stack of bills. Nothing out of the ordinary. Nothing marked past due.

Oh, she didn't like this snooping around at all. Yes, they were trying to get answers, but she wished there was another way to get them.

Hmm. Either the rumor of Macy's financial troubles was a false one or she was discreet about keeping it hidden.

The computer came to life showing an image of Macy's son and his wife posing in victory at least year's Jack and Jill Crosscut event. From the bits and pieces Macy had told them, Jan gathered the lumberjack events involved a team with one man and one woman cutting through a log with a saw in a matter of seconds. Shane and Zale were regulars in the area's Woodsmen competitions, and if this photo was any indication, they were pretty good at it.

And if Zale's muscles were any indication, she was the stronger of the two.

Jan clicked around for a few seconds, checking Macy's Internet history. Apparently Macy's time online was split between gardening sites and monitoring eBay auctions. Jan quickly moved across the desk, searching through stacks of paper and a pile of envelopes that appeared to be bills. On the front of one, stamped in big, bold, red letters were the words *Final Notice*.

Jan slipped the folded piece of paper out of the envelope and opened it, tossing a glance over her shoulder to make sure the coast was still clear. It appeared to be a bill for maintenance on one of Macy's buildings—and there was a strongly worded warning that if payment wasn't received, the company intended to turn her in to collections.

If Macy was behind on this bill, could there be others? She tucked the paper back inside the envelope and returned it to the middle of the stack.

She quietly left the office and moved down the hall toward the kitchen. She found the back door, which led to the garage, just as she'd hoped. Inside, she located a light switch to her right and flipped it on. Macy's garage looked immaculate with everything in its place. Jan hurried through the space, aware that it wouldn't be long before Macy missed her in the sitting room.

Jan surveyed the contents of the long workbench off to the right side. Everything was neat and in order. Macy seemed to have everything organized according to some sort of theme. One cabinet held pond supplies and fish food. Another held small tools, nails and screws. Another held grilling supplies, which were stowed away now that summer was over.

Jan moved around the car, but stopped when she nearly tripped over a box that seemed to be thoughtlessly discarded next to the tail end of Macy's Lincoln.

With everything else so clearly in its place, why would this one box sit out in the garage? Jan knelt down and sifted through its contents. The box was small and inside, she found an abrasive sponge, several rags smelling faintly of chemicals and a bottle of lighter fluid.

Jan picked up the bottle and held it up to the light. About half of the liquid inside was gone.

Her stomach dropped. *Oh no.*

Seconds later, she heard voices in the kitchen just beyond the door to the garage. She'd stayed away too long. Macy would find her out here and realize what she was up to.

As the voices got louder, Jan's adrenaline kicked up and she hurried out the back door of the garage, finding herself in Macy's backyard. She rushed around the house and back to Elaine's Malibu just as the front door opened.

"Jan, there you are," Macy said, stepping out on to the front porch. "What on earth are you doing out here?"

Jan held her gaze for an awkward second. Elaine had joined Macy on the porch and both women wore matching expressions, expecting her to answer.

Jan glanced down and saw her phone in the cup holder of Elaine's car. "I forgot my phone in the car."

Macy eyed her over the rim of her glasses. "Well, hurry up. Your cousin insists on seeing the cottage."

CHAPTER FOUR

Macy pulled her front door shut and started down the driveway with Elaine and Jan following close behind. "Aren't you going to bring your phone?"

Jan stopped. "Oh yes. Silly me." She looked flustered as she grabbed her phone from the car, and Elaine made a mental note to never let Jan go off snooping alone again.

Elaine knew it was a bad idea to get involved in this whole mess, and now that Macy insisted everything had been cleared up, they really should just go back home.

But Elaine couldn't help herself. Maybe the fire really was an accident, but now that law enforcement wasn't looking into it, they were free to do some digging on their own without upsetting anyone.

At least, she hoped so. They walked the property until they reached the cottage that still smelled of smoke. A sign near the front door read Escape. Macy had named each of her cottages with names that promised guests peace and rest during their stay.

Sadly, this one no longer lived up to its name.

Like the tearoom, Green Glade was positioned on the shores of Chickadee Lake. Guests of all stripes—sometimes the kind who loved fishing, boating, and water activities; sometimes romance seekers; sometimes writers and artists looking for a place to work in peace—would stay for a weekend, or a week or more. Many of the tourist guests at Tea for Two were also guests of Green Glade. She knew they had Macy to thank for that.

Indeed, the woman had made a point to inform them she'd decided to mention their tearoom on her "Great Things to Do in Lancaster" brochure, which was given to all guests along with the keys to their cottages.

Elaine couldn't help but smile at Macy's kindness. For whatever reason, the woman chose to keep her heart of gold a well-guarded secret.

Elaine could see why people found the place relaxing. It had a quiet charm, and while Macy's personality could be abrasive at times, she certainly knew how to turn a small home into a quaint getaway.

Macy unlocked the door and pushed it open, allowing Jan and Elaine to enter before her. Escape was more log cabin than cottage, or at least it had been before it became more tinderbox than home.

"I can't even stand to look at it like this," Macy said. Her distress seemed genuine enough, Elaine thought.

Inside, the walls and floor of the kitchen were black and charred, filling Elaine's nostrils with that deep, burned odor that still permeated the air. Off to their left she could see a small living room, its focal point being the fireplace encased in large stonework, reaching all the way to the ceiling. A dusting of dark ash covered the sofa, the rugs, and the curtains.

At their right, the open space had been sectioned off, but it led to the kitchen and dining area. This space had clearly been hit the hardest. The ceiling was black and charred and the rugs covering the hardwood floors, gray and damp.

Each of the cottages had the same basic floor plan with three bedrooms and a loft upstairs. Macy prided herself on being something of an interior designer, adding personal touches that made each guest feel special. In its current condition, however, Escape looked like anything but.

"I suppose you can look around, but I don't know what it is you think you're going to find that the authorities didn't," Macy said with a tone much more confident than it was yesterday. "They were very thorough."

Elaine thought it odd that yesterday Macy had been desperate for their help, but now that the authorities ruled there had been no indication of foul play, she seemed to want them to stay out of it altogether.

"Do you have those photos of this cabin? Of what it looked like before the fire?" Elaine asked Macy.

Macy nodded. She opened the drawer of a small chest in the entryway and pulled out a file folder. "I keep photos of each room in each cottage, with copies in my office. Partly for insurance, partly to help the staff. Besides, I like things a certain way. The photos make it impossible for my employees to say they didn't know where something was supposed to go."

That didn't surprise Elaine at all. She and Jan opened the folder and spread the photos out on the table situated in the dining area just outside the kitchen. This room had also suffered from the fire, its walls badly damaged and the hardwood floor underneath them black and fragile.

Elaine glanced outside through the large picture window, which showed a screened-in porch at the back of the house as well as a long walkway leading right down to the lake.

She turned her attention to the photos, watching as Jan flipped through them, stopping when she found the ones for the room they stood in.

"This seems to be where most of the damage is, correct?" Elaine asked Macy.

"Yes, they said the fire likely started here in the kitchen." Macy motioned to the smaller room at her left, open to the dining area and living room. "Because of the damage to the ceiling here, one of the bedrooms upstairs now has an unsafe floor, but the other two are in fairly good condition. They were able to extinguish the fire quickly."

"That's a blessing." Elaine watched Macy for any kind of reaction.

"Yes." Her sigh was heavy. "But we will still have a great deal of work to do to repair Escape. We stand to lose significant income if it's not done by spring. This cottage is booked all the way through next fall."

An insurance settlement might cancel out that shortage, but if she did start the fire and expected the house to burn to the ground, she'd likely have received a larger settlement. Was that what she was counting on? Perhaps someone had noticed the smoke and called it in before the fire had time to do its job?

Elaine picked up a photo of the kitchen and held it up, comparing it with the scene in front of her. She glanced at the photo, then at the space and back again.

"Anything?" Jan asked.

Elaine shook her head.

"Like I said, it was an electrical fire," Macy said. "Besides, I thought you were only here for educational purposes."

Jan gave her cousin a puzzled look. She'd been off exploring the house when Elaine convinced Macy to let them take a look at the partially burned cottage. "Educational purposes" seemed as valid a reason as any. Plain curiosity might not have gone over as well.

"It's helpful for us to study scenes like this in order to improve our skills," Elaine said. "We've never walked through the scene of a fire before."

It wasn't a lie. Elaine found the whole scene in front of her fascinating.

Macy narrowed her gaze. "Then why do I feel like you're looking for something incriminating?"

"What do you mean?" Jan asked.

Macy scoffed. "You know what I mean. But I certainly don't know how this happened. I'm the victim here, remember?"

Elaine held up the photograph, turning her attention to the living room and comparing the scene before her with the one in the picture. Sofa. Armchair. Coffee table. Fireplace. Jan hovered behind her, probably comparing the two like a "spot the differences" puzzle in the back of a magazine.

"Wait."

Jan took the photo and walked into the living room.

"What is it?" Elaine asked, following her.

Jan turned and looked at them. "Macy, I think it's a good thing you came to us yesterday."

"Oh, really? Why is that?" Macy questioned.

"Because I'm not sure this was an accident after all."

CHAPTER FIVE

Jan studied the photo she'd taken from Elaine with a peering Macy close behind her. She could feel both of them straining to see what she had seen, and she waited a few long seconds hoping one of them spotted it.

"What is it, Jan?" Macy finally asked. "Do I need to be afraid?"

Jan paced a few feet into the living room, then turned to face them both in a dramatic fashion. "Look at the mantel."

Jan watched as Elaine's eyes scanned the busy mantel, a number of knickknacks and collectibles still neatly in place. She thought it a miracle the fire had been contained to the kitchen and dining area. While the living room had certainly seen better days and would need a great deal of restoration and repair, it wasn't difficult to imagine what it had once been. Much of the room was still intact, including the mantel.

Elaine squinted as she looked back and forth from the photo to the mantel. It was a small detail, and yet not so small...

Macy gasped, derailing Jan's train of thought. "It's gone."

"What is?" Elaine glanced at Jan, who stood quietly beside the fireplace as Macy made her realization. "What's gone?"

"My vase." Macy took the photo from Jan and held it up so Elaine could see what the mantel was supposed to look like.

"Oh my," Elaine said. "How did I miss that?"

Probably because the mantel looked anything but empty. With its antique framed photographs, handmade pottery, candles, and figurines, Jan thought it might be the one spot in the cottage that didn't look professionally decorated. Instead, it looked like someone couldn't decide what to leave and what to take away.

But sure enough, there was an empty spot in the center of the mantel where a tall vase was supposed to be.

"Why would somebody steal a vase? And then start a fire to cover it up?" Elaine compared—a little more closely it seemed, now that she could zero in on the mantel—the photo to the scene in front of her.

Jan continued to survey the room. "Macy, look closely. Is anything else missing?"

Macy took several long minutes going over every nook and cranny of the room. Once she was sufficiently convinced nothing else had been stolen, they did the same in each room of the house.

"I can't believe I didn't see it before," Macy said, after they'd finished checking each room in the cottage. "I love that vase."

"Can you tell us a little about it?" Elaine asked. Had someone started the fire with the purpose of stealing it?

Macy sighed, and then the cousins followed her outside and on to the porch. Elaine was thankful for the cool, fresh air after being cooped inside the smoky cottage for too long.

"It's not especially valuable." Macy locked the front door. "At least not that I'm aware. But it was priceless to my family. It's been with us for years." She leaned against the railing at the right side of the front steps. "I can't imagine anyone stealing it."

Jan's brows drew together in a tight line. "Who else knew it was there?"

"Besides Shane and Zale and me?"

"Yes," Jan tried not to think about the past-due bill, the previous fires, or the lighter fluid she'd found in Macy's garage. She didn't have an explanation for any of those things, but given Macy's forlorn expression, she simply couldn't imagine the woman had anything to do with any of this.

Macy led them off the porch and through the front yard, letting out the occasional *"hmm"* and "maybe," but her thoughts were disjointed at best.

"Who else would know that the vase was in the cottage?" Elaine asked.

Macy gave her an incredulous look. "We can start with any guest who has stayed in Escape, but it's a fairly long list."

"True, but I suppose you can start with the people who stayed there fairly recently," Jan suggested. "Do you think we could get our hands on a list?"

"Yes, I can get it for you," Macy said. "The fire department didn't know the vase was missing. What if someone is stealing our family heirlooms for some reason? Could this be something personal?"

Jan thought for a moment. "Can you think of anyone with enough of a grudge against you that they would do something like this?" She thought of the catnapping incident Jo and Sylvia had described. She had to imagine there were others with similar stories. What if one of them became truly angry with Macy?

Jan reminded herself this was Lancaster. Quiet, calm, peaceful Lancaster. The residents of their small town were kind. And while they may become frustrated with others on occasion, it seemed unlikely any would have reason to start a fire. But what if this had been done by someone who wasn't a resident? An out-of-town guest of Green Glade?

"I can't think of anyone." Macy bristled. "I'm very well liked around town."

Jan avoided eye contact with Elaine, who was likely as amused by Macy's proclamation as she was.

"Do you have other heirlooms we need to check on?" Elaine asked.

Macy nodded. "Every cottage has its own unique family piece like this one."

"What kind of pieces?" Jan tried not to imagine all the potential burglaries.

"Every cottage is different," Macy said. "But I include a little story about what makes it special to my family with their check-in paperwork. It's just one of the things that separates Green Glade from other establishments."

Jan didn't miss the pride in her voice. "It's a lovely touch, Macy." She gave Macy's shoulder a little squeeze. She couldn't imagine how the woman felt about all of this, but it had to be troubling. Jan could see Green Glade was very important to her, and knowing someone had done this on her property likely felt like a terrible violation.

"I like to make my guests feel like part of the family. That vase may not look like much to the average person, but it's special to me and my family because of its history."

"You're right, Macy. Perhaps we should check some of the other cottages," Elaine said. "The ones that are currently vacant, at least."

"I never thought anyone would take advantage of my good intentions. Our family history is priceless to me." Macy's expression was sad. "I would hate to stop sharing it with our guests."

"Don't worry, Macy," Elaine said. "We're going to try to get to the bottom of this. Why don't we look around and see if anything else is missing?"

Macy turned and walked toward the cottage next to the one that had been damaged. The collection of porcelain figurines was still on the table in the hallway, so they moved on to the next unoccupied cabin. A tattered quilt with a lifetime of stories still hung on the quilt rack in the master bedroom.

The search gave them enough confidence to determine that probably nothing else had been stolen from Green Glade. The vase seemed to be the only item missing, as far as they could tell.

"That's good, right?" Macy locked the door to the last cottage at Green Glade.

"Yes, it does help us narrow things down," Jan said. "It appears that the key to this whole thing is that vase."

They started the trek back to Macy's house. A couple of small animals scurried in the distance, rustling the autumn leaves, and the air was filled with the high-pitched, rhythmic tweeting of the warblers. Lake Chickadee held an undeniable charm in the autumn, with its crisp air and the sun glistening on the clear water the way it had when Jan and Elaine were kids.

Jan could still remember the days they'd spent fishing and swimming on the lake. Their childhood had been filled with such joy, and as she walked through the woods at Green Glade, it was as though she was transported back to those days instantly. This little cottage community Macy had created preserved those simpler times perfectly. It gave the busy families of today a little slice of the good old days. Jan had done her best to do that for her own kids, and now wanted it more than anything for her grandchildren.

The memories brought her to a sudden realization. Green Glade was more than just a local business—it represented so much of what she loved about Lancaster.

How could somebody come in and try to destroy that?

She knew the world was different now than it had been when she and Elaine were growing up, but somehow Lancaster had managed to remain untouched—or at least it felt that way. If there was anything Jan could do to make sure that didn't change, she was going to do it, starting with figuring out everything they could about that vase.

CHAPTER SIX

They reached the long driveway that led back to Macy's house. "Why don't you come back inside?" Macy said. "I don't have any burned bread or dry scones, but I'm sure I can scrounge up something for us to eat."

Elaine glanced at Macy as they entered the front door, looking for a sign that the woman was cracking a joke, but her face was impassive. Elaine hoped Jan wouldn't let the barb dig in too deep. They had both learned to take Macy's criticism with a grain of salt. Besides, Jan should be quite confident in her baking skills.

Elaine looked over at Jan, who seemed to be trying desperately to suppress a laugh. She was taking Macy, and her complaining, in stride.

"It's okay, Macy, you don't need to feed us," Jan said. "We had a big breakfast."

Macy almost looked relieved. "So then where do we begin?" Macy asked, motioning for the cousins to take their seats in the living room.

"Why don't you start by telling us what you know about the vase?" Elaine suggested.

"For starters," Jan said, "are you certain it was there just before the fire? I mean, between the time the photo was taken and when the fire started?"

"*Hmm.* Well..." Macy seemed to reflect for a moment. "I don't think I can say so with one hundred percent certainty, but I feel reasonably sure I saw it quite recently."

Jan nodded. If the vase had been gone for a long time, it might have nothing to do with the fire at all.

Macy took out the photo of the vase and stared at it for a long moment before setting it on the coffee table between them. "As I said earlier, there is no monetary value to this vase. At least not that I know of. To me, it was simply something that had been passed down through our family. It's the story that makes it important to me."

Elaine watched Macy for any sign of insincerity, and found none.

"It must mean a lot to you," Jan said.

"It does." Macy leaned forward and touched the photograph, the hint of a smile playing at the corners of her mouth. "It was always important to my mother that she share her stories with us when we were children, and I suppose having something to hold on to made the stories more memorable."

"What is the story behind this vase?" Elaine realized she was excited to find out more about it. From the photo, it didn't look very large. It was rounded with some sort of design on the front of it, protruding from the glass. Elaine most likely wouldn't have looked twice at it, but apparently someone else did and thought it worth stealing.

Macy settled back into her chair. "When my mother gave me that vase, she told me it had been given as a gift to my grandmother from my grandfather. He fought in World War II and they were married the day before he shipped out. About two months later, she found out she was pregnant with my mother. She had the baby on her own and spent two long years wondering if she would ever see him again."

Elaine understood the plight of a military wife all too well. How many nights had she had to comfort herself with prayers for her Ben? Even in seemingly peaceful times, there was an element of danger to his job—and that could be torture for a wife. Many times her imagination had tried to run away, entertaining her worst nightmares, but she'd eventually learned to trust Ben to the Lord. She wondered if Macy's grandmother had that same peace.

"She tried to keep busy, but mostly she worried about her husband, wondering whether or not she'd ever really know what it was like to be his wife. It was a very difficult time for her. Finally, one day, she received this vase filled with daises, her favorite flower, along with a note that said 'I'll see ya soon, Val.'"

Elaine swallowed a lump of empathy that had formed in her throat. What a joyous day that must've been for Macy's grandmother. When Ben traveled, he sometimes sent small trinkets or gifts for the kids home before he arrived, just to let them know they were on his mind. Elaine had saved every single one, so it was easy for her to understand the sentimental value of this vase.

"My grandfather said he found the vase in a little shop in Warsaw and it made him think of her—his sweet Valerie. Sending them ahead of him was the perfect way to let her know he was coming home from the war." Macy paused abruptly. "The flowers made it home, but he did not."

Jan let out the tiniest sound, as if the declaration had stolen her breath. "Oh, Macy, I'm so sorry."

"I can't imagine how difficult that must've been."

Elaine had imagined it too many times to count. Losing Ben had been one of her greatest fears. Now, here she was on the other side of it, and though she missed him terribly even all these months later, she saw the way God had taken care of her, leading her here, to Lancaster, to Jan and the tearoom.

"Did you worry about the safety of your vase?" Jan asked. "When you put it in the cottage, I mean?"

Macy's face softened. "I probably should have, but I didn't. The vase was likely a cheap trinket from a flower shop, but it was important to me. I've written out the story behind every piece I've added to my cottages and each guest receives the story as part of their check-in procedure. And I guess I wanted our guests to feel like they were a part of our family. That feeling is what keeps people coming back to Green Glade."

"I never took you for a sentimental person, Macy." Jan fished a tissue from her purse and handed it to her.

"I'm full of surprises." Macy's mouth drew into a tight smile.

Elaine reached across the table and squeezed Macy's hand. It was too bad her kindness in sharing this special piece of family history had backfired on her.

"Is that all you know about the vase's history?" Jan asked.

Macy nodded. "Unfortunately, yes. I didn't see any reason to look into the vase. If it were valuable, wouldn't my mother have told me?"

"Perhaps," Elaine said. "Do you have any other photos of it? We can do some digging around and see what we find."

Macy thought for a moment. "Of course. When I wrote up the family story for each piece, I included a close-up photo. I think I have a copy in my office. Would you like me to get it for you? Oh, and you wanted a list of everyone who has stayed in Escape. How far back do I need to go?"

Elaine shrugged. "Maybe just the last six months?" That would take them back through Macy's most recent busy season, and it should be plenty to go on.

"Could we also have a list of your staff as well?" Jan asked.

"My staff?" Her brow furrowed.

"Good idea." Elaine brightened. "The staff also had access to the cottage, and they definitely knew the vase was there."

Macy's expression didn't change.

"Macy, what is it?" Jan asked, softly.

She stared at her folded hands in her lap. "I can't imagine anyone on my staff could've actually stolen from me."

"You're probably right, and we don't want to jump to any conclusions," Elaine said. "We just have a few questions to ask."

The sofa Macy sat on seemed to swallow her up, and her face turned forlorn. "The staff here is like family to me."

Elaine glanced at her cousin, who wore a concerned expression that most likely matched her own. She was surprised by Macy's unexpected sadness. The woman rarely seemed ruffled or emotional about anything. Perhaps the thought that someone she trusted had betrayed her was a trigger for Macy.

"We know this is difficult, Macy," Elaine said. "But giving us their names doesn't make them guilty. One of them may have seen something. They may not even realize it's a clue."

"That's true." Macy's countenance brightened ever so slightly. "Because I really don't think any of them would steal from me, let alone start a fire in one of my cottages."

"We just want to ask some questions," Jan said. "We'll be very nice."

"Okay. Then I'll give you a list of my entire staff, but there was only one housekeeper assigned to that cottage on that day. Her name is Sarah Clayton and she is as honest as they come." Macy stood. "I'll get you that photo and the contact list." She disappeared into the hallway, leaving Elaine and Jan alone.

"Can we cross Macy off the suspect list?" Elaine whispered, remembering their conversation and initial thoughts before they spoke with her. Certainly Macy wasn't a suspect now—nobody in Lancaster was that good an actress.

"Probably…" Jan moved closer and kept her voice low.

Elaine listened as Jan told her about a past-due bill she'd found in the office and the lighter fluid that seemed very out of place in the otherwise pristine garage. She tried to reconcile these findings with Macy's reaction to discovering her vase was missing and it simply didn't add up. Macy seemed personally affected by this theft, and Elaine couldn't find any reason to assume she'd been involved, even though Jan's findings did raise valid questions.

"I know we need to be thorough, but given what we've seen today, it seems like we should be able to clear her name." Elaine wondered if that was hopefulness she heard in her own voice.

"Clear whose name?" Macy returned with two folded sheets of paper just in time to catch the tail-end of Elaine's comment.

Both Jan and Elaine turned to face her. Elaine was certain they both looked like they'd been caught.

"What were you saying, Elaine? Do you have a suspect?" Macy inched toward them. "I haven't even given you my list yet."

"No, Macy, there's no suspect," Jan said quickly.

"Isn't there a rule that you two have to share your theories with your client?"

Elaine glanced at Jan, who wore a deer-in-the-headlights expression.

Macy's eyes darted back and forth between the two cousins as she moved even closer. "Me?"

Jan's eyes found the floor, and Elaine's quickly followed.

"You're considering *me* a suspect?" Macy put her hands on her hips and glared at both of them. "Do you remember I'm the one who brought you in here in the first place?"

"Of course, Macy," Jan said.

"Well, I wouldn't have done that if I was guilty," Macy said. "I certainly don't want you investigating *me!*"

"We didn't mean to upset you." Elaine said calmly. "We just like to talk through every possibility, no matter how far-fetched it seems. And you're right—this one is far-fetched."

"A fire is a terrible thing," Jan said. "I can imagine you're still shaken by all of this."

Macy looked like she was about to respond, but she didn't. Instead, she smoothed her hair as if to regain her composure. "You found out about the other fire, didn't you?"

Both Jan and Elaine stilled.

"We heard talk, yes," Elaine said. "But we don't believe everything we hear."

"I didn't start that fire," Macy said. "You can read the report."

A tense silence hung in the air until finally Jan spoke. "We believe you. Of course you didn't start that fire." She paused. "But is that why you left Green Glade the day of the fire? Were you afraid of being accused?"

Macy walked past them and sat back down on the sofa. "Yes. I know it's hard to believe, but even I get scared sometimes. I wasn't thinking clearly, but I assumed it would be a matter of hours before the police learned this wasn't the first time one of my properties caught fire and then I would've ended up a suspect."

"Oh, I don't know," Elaine said. "The people here in Lancaster want to believe the best about everybody, and you said yourself you are very well loved." At least, she was in her own way. Macy Atherton and Green Glade were knit into the fabric of this community.

Macy didn't seem to buy it. "Do you know how unlikely it is that two of my properties would be destroyed in the exact same way? I knew I would look guilty."

"But you aren't guilty." Elaine sat across from her.

"Of course I'm not. I love Green Glade." She lifted her chin, as if trying to decide if she should go on. "But I might've been a bit behind on my inspections. Shane mentioned the electrical probably needed an update, and I just haven't gotten around to it."

"So you *felt* guilty," Elaine said quietly. She understood the rigors of running a business better than most. While

Jan handled all the baking for Tea for Two, Elaine handled the bookkeeping, scheduled maintenance, and yes, set
up inspections. She kept meticulous notes; otherwise, she
might very well find herself in the exact same spot as Macy.
After all, their Victorian was old and required a good deal of
upkeep.

"I suppose I did." Macy sighed. "It's not easy for me to
admit that."

"I know this is a personal question, but I overheard Deputy
Sheffield ask you about your finances."

Elaine imagined Jan was thinking about the past-due bill
she'd found when she searched Macy's office.

"My finances are just fine, thank you very much," Macy
said. "Boy, you really don't miss a thing, do you?"

"We try not to." Jan smiled. "So you don't owe money to
anybody for anything?"

"Who said that?" Macy's entire face tightened. "Oh, I know
who it was. It was that good-for-nothing Bill Wyman, wasn't
it? He sends me past-due notices every single week, but he's
charging me for work he didn't actually do. I don't make a
habit of paying for shoddy craftsmanship."

It made sense to Elaine. That bill wasn't past due because
Macy couldn't pay it, but because she refused to pay it.

"Won't that go on your credit history?" Elaine asked, thinking she'd never had a bill go to collections and did her best to
pay every bill on time.

"If he turns me over to collections, he knows I will report
him to the Better Business Bureau. And I'll make a huge, public
display of my dissatisfaction."

Elaine didn't doubt it. Not for the first time, she made a mental note to never cross Macy. She certainly didn't want to end up on her bad side.

"Okay, so," Jan said thoughtfully, "since the fire was ruled an accident, they must not have found an accelerant or any sign of foul play," Jan said. "But if the fire was started to hide the theft, wouldn't it seem that there would be a trace of something?"

"Perhaps they found evidence of faulty wiring and considered it open-and-shut?" Elaine suggested. "If the thief was good, he may have known how to make the fire look like an accident."

"Assume for a moment that someone with access to the cottage did want to set it on fire—where would an arsonist look for an accelerant here at Green Glade?" Jan asked.

Elaine watched as Macy thought for a few long seconds. "I do have lighter fluid. I used it just the other day."

"It's awfully cool for a barbecue," Elaine said with a laugh.

Macy waved her off. "I wasn't grilling. I was cleaning."

"With lighter fluid?" Jan's eyebrows knit together. "Isn't that dangerous?"

"Little-known fact," Macy said. "Lighter fluid is an excellent remover of hard stains. Shane parked his Mustang in my driveway last week before he and Zale took off for their competition. That beast of a car leaked motor oil all over the pavement."

"And you used lighter fluid to remove the stain?" Elaine had never heard of such a thing, but she had a feeling Macy had all kinds of little tricks up her sleeve.

"I did." Macy looked proud. "It was unsightly. I didn't feel like waiting for Shane to come clean it up himself."

Elaine made a mental note to confirm that lighter fluid could clean hard stains, but she had a hunch it would check out. Certainly Macy hadn't expected Jan to ask about accelerants, and nothing about her response sounded dishonest.

"We should probably report the theft," Elaine finally said. "I can call the deputy and..."

"No." Macy stood. "I don't want the police poking around here. Not when they could easily make the same leap you two obviously did."

Elaine felt Jan's eyes on her. They knew they could never be a replacement for the police, and they certainly didn't want to make a name for themselves as troublemakers. But Macy was right. It wouldn't take long for the sheriff's deputy to uncover Macy's previous fire, if he hadn't already—and if he did consider her a suspect, they would all waste time clearing her name while the real thief seized the opportunity to disappear.

"I suppose it wouldn't hurt to keep it to ourselves for a little while," Elaine said. "But only until we know a little more about the vase."

For all they knew, there was a simple explanation. Maybe the vase had been misplaced. They couldn't claim the sky was falling just yet.

Macy paused for a few long seconds, then finally handed over the sheet of paper with her employees' contact information, and also a color copy of the image of the vase and a few paragraphs of text telling the story of how it came to be a part of Macy's family.

"Thank you both," she said. "I trust you'll keep me up to date when you find out anything."

"Of course," Elaine said. "But you may have to be patient. We have a lot of research to do."

Macy gave a stern nod, then walked them to the door. They said a quick good-bye and walked outside.

"Are we sure we want to keep this from the police?" Jan asked once they were safely inside Elaine's car.

"I'm not sure of anything yet," Elaine said. "But I don't mind digging around on our own to see what we come up with. If there has actually been a crime committed, then we can go back to Deputy Sheffield."

"But Macy's right. She'll be their first suspect."

"I'm afraid that's a chance we may have to take."

CHAPTER SEVEN

The following day, Jan woke early. The tearoom opened promptly at ten, but Rose always arrived early to set the tables and prepare for the day. They'd made such a good choice in hiring Rose Young, one of the sweetest souls Jan had ever met. Archie would be in later too, which gave Jan a feeling of comfort. Their tearoom could run smoothly even when she and Elaine weren't there, which was happening more often these days with mystery after mystery popping up. Jan felt like she was having her cake and eating it too, having two excellent employees, and she wasn't ashamed to feel that she and Elaine had earned it.

Thinking of her staff made her think of Macy and the way she'd bristled at the idea that one of her own employees could be responsible for the fire and the theft of the vase. Jan could certainly understand her sadness at the idea. She would feel the same way if someone had suggested Rose and Archie were capable of such a thing.

She picked up her Bible and read from Psalm 51, a long-time favorite of hers. No matter how many times she had read this passage, it never failed to speak to her in new ways. Today she homed in on verse 6: "Behold, thou desirest truth in the inward parts: and in the hidden part thou shalt make me to know wisdom." *Thou shalt make me to know wisdom,* she thought, making it a prayer for discernment about the situation with Macy, that she and Elaine could help Macy uncover the truth behind the missing vase and mysterious fire that could have destroyed one of Macy's cabins. But she expanded the prayer for wisdom in understanding the often-difficult Macy— to see her as God saw her.

When Jan had said her amen, she dressed for the day and made her way downstairs, thankful for the sunlight streaming through the windows on what appeared to be a beautiful autumn day. The leaves had long since changed, and the air was filled with the crisp freshness of the season.

Jan opened the front door and walked out on to the porch to retrieve yesterday's newspaper. She'd forgotten to bring it in the day before, and she made a habit of finishing the crossword with her morning tea.

As she bent over to pick up the rolled-up paper from the porch, she caught a glimpse of Faith Lanier sweeping the front walk of her shop next door. Jan stood and waved in Faith's direction, remembering her kindness toward Tara.

"Hi, Jan!" Faith called over. "You're up early this morning."

Jan met her halfway between Tea for Two and A Little Something and pulled the thin woman into a tight hug.

Faith laughed as she hugged Jan back. "You sure are happy to see me!"

"Yes, and I'm grateful to you," Jan said, pulling away. "I've always believed that Tara's jewelry is unique, but it's so wonderful to know that you saw it too. She's taking a big risk trying to make a go of this thing. It means the world to me that you would give her space on your shelves."

Faith leaned on her broom. "I couldn't be more excited about it myself. Her jewelry is just beautiful. In fact, we're thinking of having a little celebration at the shop soon, just to give her a bit more publicity and get folks excited about a local artist with so much talent."

Jan thought about her sweet daughter and what a boost this was for her. Tara had always been an artistic soul, but she'd had a few hard knocks that had hurt her self-esteem over the years, not the least of which was a college professor who told her she would never make it as an artist. Tara had been so crushed that Jan wanted to march straight into that man's office and give him a piece of her mind. She hadn't, of course, but she'd dreamed of it several times.

Now, though, Jan was thrilled to see Tara back on her feet doing something she was so passionate about. Besides, if she could make a good living here in Lancaster, she'd have no reason to go exploring other places to live, and that made Jan very happy.

"You let me know the details and Elaine and I will be the first ones to RSVP," Jan said. "And I'm happy to provide baked goods. Speaking of which, come on over if you get hungry later—I've got some raspberry tarts with your name on them." Jan smiled at her friend, grateful for her and the others on their block who had vowed to support each other as friends and business owners. What a blessing their little venture had turned out to be.

"Will do, Jan." Faith waggled a finger. "You know I can't resist your baking."

Jan smiled and made her way back inside, arriving in the kitchen just in time to catch Elaine by the back door pulling on a jacket. Last night, they'd decided Jan would use the morning to do some digging on the vase while Elaine had scheduled an appointment with the fire chief in Augusta, though there was no guarantee he would tell her anything about their findings at Green Glade.

"You're off early," Jan said. "And I see you've got our secret weapon."

With a grin and a twinkle in her eye, Elaine held up the Tupperware container Jan had set out for her last night. "Who could resist these? I'll be back before we open." Elaine paused. "Are you sure you'll be okay without me?"

They'd prepared nearly everything they could last night and called Rose in early, but Elaine was sweet to think of her. "I promise we'll be just fine."

Elaine nodded and made her way out to the garage as Jan pulled out the ingredients for her Southern-style lemon cake. She worked quickly as she still wanted to squeeze in a quick trip to the library in before Rose arrived.

About forty minutes later, Jan pulled her cake from the oven. The almond cream cheese frosting she'd whipped up was truly the star of this dessert, but even without it, the cake smelled delicious. Taste-testing all these baked goods could add inches to her waistline if she wasn't careful, but some days she simply couldn't help herself.

Certain desserts simply begged to be tasted—and this was one of them.

She set the cake on the counter so it could cool, stuck the frosting in the refrigerator, and left Rose a quick note with instructions and a promise she wouldn't be too long. She'd only have about an hour at the library, and she'd try to do her research in less time, but it was awfully difficult for Jan to hurry when she was surrounded by books that begged to be read. She could get lost in the Lancaster library for hours, she was sure, but she wouldn't. Not today, anyway.

With the air sharp but lovely, Jan decided to walk over to the library. As she passed by Murphy's General Store, she spotted Jo Murphy behind the counter and gave her a quick wave through the window. Jo smiled and waved back, then turned to help her husband, who was stocking shelves beside her.

She reached the library and smiled at the girl behind the front desk. Jan made her way back to the reference section and stopped at the computer to look up any books that might pertain to determining where the vase came from. She pulled the photo of the vase from her purse, just to keep it in front of her while she searched various titles that unfortunately seemed to be of little value.

In the original photo, the vase had appeared to be like any other glass vase a florist would use. It didn't seem to be particularly old or even special, but the close-up photo told a different story.

One side was graced with a pair of birds nested in a design of branches and leaves. The way it seemed to protrude from one side made Jan wish she could hold it for herself. She imagined it was sleek and smooth to the touch, and while Jan didn't know how valuable it was, she decided it was quite beautiful.

She read over the story on Macy's sheet and noticed a sentence near the end she hadn't read carefully before.

The vase has one notable distinguishing factor—a small mark engraved on the bottom with the letter E inside a triangle.

Jan reread the sentence. That must mean something to someone. A maker's mark? She jotted a note to herself to look into it later on and continued searching for reference books she could check out.

She wrote down the titles and call numbers of two books— one written for collectors of antiques and artifacts, and an antique price guide for glass vases. She located them on the shelves and pulled them down, then perused the books nearby.

She found a few others that looked promising, particularly one with a number of photos of what looked a lot like glass but was actually crystal—much more expensive than your garden-variety florist's vase.

She'd accumulated a small pile of books when the sound of someone clearing his throat near the end of the aisle caught her attention. She turned and her eyes fell upon Robert Claybrook. Her cheeks warmed at the sight of him. She was still getting used to the fact that it was perfectly acceptable to admit she found him handsome and distinguished. In some ways, even though it had been ten years since her Peter had died, she sometimes struggled with a sense that her affections for Bob were a betrayal.

Bob had been an unexpected blessing. A sweet surprise she could never have predicted. Sometimes she wanted to ask what a successful and charming lawyer saw in her, but she refrained. Insecurity didn't look good on anyone. She'd made up her mind to enjoy his company and be thankful for his friendship. After all, no one made her smile quite like Bob. He was outgoing and friendly—his personality like a magnet for many, including Jan.

"I stopped by the tearoom, but Rose said you were here," Bob whispered—an instinct given the fact they were in the library. "I almost couldn't leave. What was that heavenly smell?"

Jan smiled. "Southern-style lemon cake with almond cream cheese frosting."

"Do you need a taste tester?" He smiled broadly.

"I've made this one a hundred times," Jan said. "But I can save you a piece."

A comfortable silence fell between them, giving Jan a chance to study his brown eyes, which seemed to glimmer when he looked at her. "How've you been?" he asked, his gaze intent.

"I've been good. Not much has changed since I saw you last."

"Not true," he said. "You've gotten even more beautiful."

Jan knew her cheeks were flushed bright pink at the forwardness of his comment. Bob had a way of saying whatever he thought, though she hadn't gotten used to him thinking such things about her.

"You don't believe me," he said. "But it's true."

She laughed him off and tried not to act as flustered as she felt. "I bet you say that to all the girls."

He waited until she met his eyes, then shook his head. "No, just you."

It surprised her sometimes how very much she liked this man. When Peter died, she expected she'd spend the rest of her life alone, and she'd made her peace with that. When she and Elaine decided to buy their old Victorian house and open a tearoom together, she assumed they would live out their days, just the two of them. And while her affections for Bob were still very new, there was a part of her that hoped they would grow into something more.

Sometimes that thought scared her.

She reached for her stack of books, but Bob stopped her. "Let me."

Jan watched as he scooped up her selections, taking a moment to flip through them. "Do these have something to do with your trip out to Green Glade yesterday?"

"My, word sure does travel fast in this town," Jan laughed as she led Bob toward the end of the aisle.

"It sure does. What did you find?" They walked past the children's section, where the young girl who'd been sitting at the front desk now stood in front of a small group of children. Storytime at the library had been one of her own kids' favorite traditions. It made her thankful to know that children were still being taught the joys of reading.

"Some folks are placing bets on whether or not Macy Atherton tried to burn down her own cottage," Bob said only a few feet away from the front counter.

Jan grabbed his arm. "Are they really?"

"I suppose I made it sound a little more dramatic than it is, but I have heard talk."

"She didn't set fire to her own cottage," Jan said, still whispering.

"You're sure? Even seemingly normal people do crazy things sometimes."

"I'm pretty sure." Jan moved toward the counter where an older man took her books and her library card, checked her out, and sent her on her way.

Bob picked up her books, and they started for the door.

"So these books do have something to do with what happened at Green Glade?" Bob asked again.

They strode down the front steps of the library and on to the pavement.

"They do. I'm doing a little research about antique vases, specifically glass vases or maybe even crystal." Jan hadn't considered crystal. What else would her research turn up? "Do you know anything about antiques?"

"Very little, but if I know you, you're going to nearly become an expert."

"I do find it fascinating. There are so many possibilities." She explained how they'd discovered the vase had gone missing, then showed him the photo of it. "It's really quite beautiful, isn't it?"

Bob nodded. "It is, but if it was valuable, I doubt Macy would've had it on display in one of her cottages."

"Macy doesn't think it has much monetary value, but it meant a lot to her," Jan said. "It had been in her family for years."

"Ah, so she has a sentimental attachment to it."

"Exactly," Jan said.

"Seems odd someone would steal a family trinket," Bob said.

Jan hugged her books tighter to her chest. Perhaps that vase wasn't a trinket at all, but rather something much more valuable. Either way, she was determined to find out. "I should get going. I've got to frost my cake and get everything ready before we open for the day."

Bob stood, unmoving. "Can we have dinner this weekend?"

Jan met his eyes. "I'd like that."

He smiled, then leaned in and kissed her on the cheek, close enough for her to smell his woodsy cologne.

Her stomach somersaulted at his nearness.

"Until then."

After he'd gone, Jan stood in the same spot for several long seconds, wondering if Bob Claybrook had any idea how very much she liked having him around.

THAT NIGHT IN the upstairs sitting room, Jan took down the small box from the bookshelf. Inside was a sapphire ring that sparkled despite the indirect light from the lamps.

Its story was a strange one. The contractor the cousins had hired to redo their kitchen had found it behind a wall beneath an old flue cover. Who had put it there, and why? She and Elaine were not much closer to finding the answer now, several months later, than they'd been when they'd found it.

They did know that the design scratched into the ring's box was the Wood family's motto, "For Love and Blood," and the Wood family crest was etched into the flue cover.

"We at least know who the ring originally belonged to." Elaine spoke up from her chair, where she had been quietly sitting with one of her mystery novels.

"Were you reading my mind?" Jan teased. "Yes, we do know the name of the family. But we're not any closer to figuring out who put it behind the wall. Or why." Jan sighed.

Elaine stood and laid a comforting hand on her cousin's shoulder. "We'll find the answers to this mystery too," she told Jan firmly. "When we take on a case, we solve it."

CHAPTER EIGHT

Elaine checked the dainty gold watch on her left wrist. She was right on time for her early-morning meeting with Augusta Fire Chief Wilford Gillespie. He'd been on the scene at Green Glade and the investigation had been turned over to his department. Lancaster was too small to have its own fire department, though there were a number of volunteer firefighters in town.

The Augusta firehouse was in an old brick building that stood tall like two boxes stacked on top of each other. Two oversize garage doors faced the street, each with a black lantern overhead. The second story, with its tall, arched windows centered above each of the garages, gave the otherwise flat-fronted building a bit of small-town charm.

Elaine parked her car and made her way through the side door, which was where the chief had told her to enter in their brief conversation on the phone.

The man had made it clear he didn't have much time for her, something she'd expected. She couldn't blame the chief. After all, he was a busy man with many demands, and she was a tea shop owner with a list full of questions.

Her eyes fell to the box of freshly baked pumpkin muffins on her lap, her secret weapon, she hoped, for winning him over. Jan had whipped them up last night as a sort of insurance policy. Baked goods seemed to be the perfect icebreaker, and she knew the chief and his men worked long shifts. Certainly they'd appreciate something so delicious.

Elaine's thoughts turned to their conversation with Macy yesterday. They had lists of people to track down and a mysterious vase to research, but Elaine had tasked herself with learning what the fire chief knew about the actual fire itself. They'd reached the conclusion that the fire had been an accident so quickly that Elaine assumed it must've been obvious—but she wanted to know why.

She looked around the small office with its drab, off-white walls. She'd been ushered here by a young guy who'd been washing the fire engine when she came in the side door.

The door to the office flung open to reveal a rock-solid brick of a man wearing navy-blue uniform pants and a plain white T-shirt.

"Mrs. Cook?"

Elaine stood, clutching the muffins with both hands and collecting her thoughts after his sudden appearance. "That's me."

With the flick of his head, he motioned for her to sit back down. He sat down behind an age-old sturdy wooden desk that appeared to be more a catchall for piles of paperwork than a viable workspace. Behind him, two windows overlooked the garage showing a shiny red fire engine parked inside. On the wall were framed photos of Gillespie and a number of other firefighters. Despite his rough exterior, perhaps the man had a soft spot, at least for his guys.

"What can I do for you, Mrs. Cook?" The chief folded his hands on his desk. He looked at her, his gaze intimidating. His jet-black hair, eyebrows, beard, and mustache gave him a hard edge that instantly demanded respect.

"Please call me Elaine," she said.

"Elaine."

She gave him a soft smile, then remembered her peace offering. "My cousin and I run a tearoom in Lancaster. She's the best baker in town and she made these for you." She set the container on top of a wobbly pile of manila folders on his desk.

One of his bushy black eyebrows twitched. "She did?"

"Yes, to thank you for taking time to answer my questions."

Gillespie nodded his appreciation and pulled the container closer to him. As he cracked open the lid, the autumn aroma of cinnamon and nutmeg escaped. He inhaled. "Pumpkin?"

"Yes. Seemed perfect for the season." Elaine watched as the man reached in and took one of the muffins out of the container. He ate the entire thing in one bite and went in for another one.

"These are good," he said.

"I'll let Jan know." She marveled at the way he'd inhaled the muffin like a vacuum cleaner, wondering if he'd actually tasted anything at all.

"Did you come here to feed me muffins or do you have actual questions?" He took a bite from the second muffin, and Elaine tried not to be distracted by the crumbs falling into his beard.

"I'm here about the fire at Green Glade earlier this week," Elaine began.

"What about it?" the chief asked. He took another bite of the muffin, then took a swig from a mug that read World's Best Grandpa.

"I had the chance to walk through the cottage where the fire took place. The owner is a friend."

"She was lucky. A volunteer unit happened to be in the area, otherwise she could've lost a lot more than one cottage." Chief Gillespie stared at the muffins as if contemplating one more.

Elaine pushed the container a little closer to him. "I won't tell if you eat another one."

The corner of his mouth lifted ever so slightly, but he refrained from giving her a full smile. "Good to know." He pulled another muffin out and closed the lid on the container.

"I'd never walked through the scene of a fire before," Elaine said, thankful Jan's muffins seemed to be loosening the man up, if only a little.

"It's quite a thing to behold," the chief said. "A fire is an amazing animal."

Elaine didn't doubt it. She'd seen what it could do. "Macy said the fire was ruled an accident."

"Those are the preliminary findings. We haven't made that official, but it's pretty cut-and-dried with this one."

"Fascinating. I'm amazed by the science of it all. It's quite foreign to me."

"Most people know very little about fire." He tossed a muffin wrapper in the garbage.

"What do you believe caused it?" Elaine asked.

"Faulty wiring." He chewed. "Those cottages all need to be updated, especially the electrical. Your friend should've known that."

Elaine thought back to the guilty look on Macy's face when she admitted she should have had an inspection. She had known it needed updating, but Elaine wouldn't say so. "How was it determined that faulty wiring was to blame? I'm so curious how you can tell."

He studied her for a long moment. "Are you some kind of reporter or something?"

"No, just a lifelong learner. I enjoy discovering how things work and it's not often you get to see the effects of a fire up close and personal. It made me wonder how the cause of a fire can be determined because it all looked like a big mess to me. Everything was covered in soot and drenched in water, and it still smelled like the inside of a bonfire pit. To the untrained eye, there was no way to tell what really happened in that cottage."

Elaine knew that people liked to show off their expertise if given a chance, but she hoped she wasn't laying it on too thick.

Chief Gillespie fished through a number of files on top of his desk until he found one labeled "Green Glade." He opened it, pulling out a stack of photographs from the scene. She'd been hoping he'd do that.

The chief flipped through the photos until he found one of an electrical outlet in the kitchen. "See this here?" He pointed to the outlet box.

Elaine nodded.

"We believe this was the point of origin." He flipped to the next photo where the box had been removed from the wall to reveal what even Elaine could see were old wires.

"The wires were old and the insulation surrounding them created an excess of heat. When they sparked, the insulation caught on fire. The rest is history." The chief dropped the stack of photos back into the folder and closed it.

"They overheated? Just like that?"

"Well, not exactly like that. We also discovered a small gas leak coming from the stove. Bottom line is, Mrs. Atherton needs a lot of updates on her property."

Elaine nodded slowly, trying to let the pieces fall into place. "Is it possible the fire was caused by something else?"

The chief's thick brows drew downward. "Like what?"

"Like a person?" Elaine kept her tone light.

He straightened in his seat. "Why? Are you suspicious of someone?"

Elaine shook her head. "No, not exactly. I'm just wondering how you rule that out."

Gillespie studied her for an uncomfortable moment. "You sure do have a lot of questions, Mrs. Cook."

"I know. Macy is my friend, and I suppose I'm just hoping to help give her some closure if I can."

He held her gaze for a number of uncomfortable seconds before finally leaning back in his chair. "It's highly unlikely."

"I see."

"You want to know how I know it's unlikely, don't you?"

She smiled. "I do."

"We found no trace of accelerant anywhere in the cottage. Other than a few sheets of paper which we determined were present in every cottage, we found no physical evidence implicating individual involvement."

Elaine glanced back down at the photos. "I guess I'm confused about something." She turned the photo toward him, pointing to the outlet and supposed cause of the fire. "The outlet is here, above the stove."

"That's right."

"And you said there was a small gas leak coming from the stove?" Elaine asked. "Could the natural gas have been left on intentionally? Almost like an accelerant?"

"Sure, it's possible," the chief said. "But again, it's highly unlikely. If someone was going to start a fire, they wouldn't wait for the possibility of bad wiring to do the job."

That was true, and yet the chief didn't know about the missing vase or the likelihood that the fire had been started to conceal the theft. What was Elaine missing?

"It must get boring in Lancaster," Chief Gillespie said.

Elaine frowned. "What do you mean?"

He shifted in his seat. "I think you're looking for a crime that's not really there."

"You're probably right, Chief Gillespie. I hope I didn't take up too much of your time today."

"No harm in curiosity," he said. "I can appreciate someone wanting to learn about how fire works. It is a fascinating topic, after all."

"It really is." She stood, sliding her purse straps over her shoulder. "You enjoy the rest of those muffins."

"Will do, Mrs. Cook." He saw her out. "Thank your cousin for me. Maybe me and the guys will have to take a trip to your tearoom one of these days. Think you can handle a bunch of old brutes slurping down your Earl Grey?"

"Well, we certainly could," she laughed. "And I would love to see it."

On her drive back to Lancaster, Elaine replayed her conversation with the chief over and over again, trying to figure out what they'd missed. The chief was right—the case seemed cut-and-dried. The wires seemed to have overheated, sparked the insulation, and started the fire. Whether or not natural gas had been involved didn't change the fact that an arsonist would've likely used gasoline or lighter fluid to make sure their target was destroyed.

So if the authorities were certain this fire had been an accident, why didn't Elaine feel the same way? What had she missed? To her, the missing vase and the fire seemed too linked to be a coincidence.

CHAPTER NINE

Throughout the day, Jan's attention was divided between her duties at the tearoom, the books she'd picked up at the library that morning, and a separate stack of books Elaine had brought home from the Bookworm.

Just after lunchtime, both Jan and Elaine sat at the counter in the kitchen while Rose appeared, then disappeared, waiting on the few customers who'd come in during the afternoon lull.

Jan swallowed the bite of turkey sandwich in her mouth. "Rose, you can sit down and take a break for a few moments if you'd like."

Rose gave her a weary but genuine smile. "I'm perfectly fine, Jan, but thank you. There's still a little bit of cleanup from the earlier rush, and I'd prefer the two of you have a little break."

Jan gave her a thankful nod. "She certainly is a wonderful addition to this place."

Elaine glanced up. "She is quite special."

Jan closed her laptop and set it aside. Her eyes landed on one of the paperback books on local history Elaine had picked up at the Bookworm. It looked interesting, not just for gleaning information about the Wood family, but also because she loved exploring the rich history of this region.

She should probably just let Elaine take a look at the book tomorrow, but...well, she could look through it briefly before moving on to her next task at the tearoom.

"Do you mind if I look at the book you bought?" Jan asked.

"No, that's fine."

Jan opened the cover and turned to the table of contents. The early chapters covered the Native Americans who had roamed this land hundreds of years before any European settlers arrived. The earliest of these were mostly British or from northern Europe, though an influx of French-speakers had come down from Quebec in the early part of the twentieth century to work in the many mills and factories that had once been the lifeblood of this area.

Jan started reading the history from a bit before the house was built. She turned to a chapter entitled "Industry Reigns," and skimmed the first page. The writing, she discovered, was actually quite engaging. She skimmed a little bit more, reading about a woolen mill that had once stood on the shore of Chickadee Lake. It was strange to imagine a mill here, belching out smoke and wastewater, where there were now only charming homes and businesses, where people swam and boated in the crystal-clear waters all summer long.

But just as she was about to put the book down, she saw something. Wait a minute, was she reading this right?

Jan flipped back and started over at the beginning of the chapter, and when she got to the section that caught her attention, she read it over carefully again. Yes, it did seem like this was talking about the Wood family, probably the same one that...

"Is everything okay over there? You're turning pages furiously," Elaine said with a smile.

"Actually, yes," Jan said. She felt her heart race, as it did when she was on the right track in a mystery. "I think I found something."

Elaine set down her sandwich and gave Jan her full attention. "Well, don't keep me waiting." She grinned. "You know how impatient I am."

As she skimmed the page again, Jan filled Elaine in on what she found there. "One of the earliest mills in the area was owned by the Wood family," Jan said. "It was a woolen mill, and it was right here on the shore of Chickadee Lake, situated about halfway between Penzance and Lancaster."

"Well, that's interesting." Elaine sat up straight in her chair. "Woolens, huh?"

"Yeah. Apparently that was quite an industry around here back then. I remember reading that years ago, when I was teaching the kids Maine history, but I'd long forgotten it. But in any case, the mill was started in the late 1880s and it quickly grew to be one of the largest in the region, turning out thousands of yards of fabric every month. The mill was started by Jameson Wood, whose grandfather had come over from England in 1787. Jameson grew up in Massachusetts..."

"Back when Maine was still part of Massachusetts," Elaine added.

"Well, right. So Jameson grew up on a farm out in the woods, where he was responsible for, among other things, caring for the sheep. He gained expertise in carding, cleaning, and spinning wool, and eventually started making his own. Then, shortly after Maine became its own state"—she nodded at Elaine—"Jameson moved up here, with a small inheritance he'd received when his wife's father, Arthur Milton, died, and he started the mill. At first, it was just Jameson and a few low-paid employees, but apparently the fine quality of the wool was quickly recognized, and the mill grew."

"That's fascinating," Elaine said. "There's just one problem."

"Right. Knowing the Wood family owned a woolens mill doesn't exactly explain how the ring came to be in our wall."

"Exactly."

"That was all I could find in the book you got at the bookstore, but I'm going to keep looking. I can head back to the library, for starters. There might be some more information there."

"Let's hope."

They continued working throughout the day and Jan did her best to stay focused, but found her mind drifting. As much as she loved their customers, she was thankful when it came time to close for the day so she could steal away to the computer with her book and the notebook of research she'd begun to assemble close at hand. She studied everything she could on antiques: most specifically, what makes them valuable, something she'd only peripherally understood herself.

What made some works of art priceless when others were worth nothing? If the vase truly was valuable and Macy simply hadn't known, Jan wanted to find out.

She'd been nestled in the sitting room for over two hours, her laptop on one side and her stack of books on the other.

Elaine had been doing some bookkeeping in her office after her visit with the fire chief and a full day in the tearoom. Seeing for herself that the fire really did appear to be an accident had only raised more questions for Elaine, and Jan hoped that somehow her research would turn up something worthwhile.

Elaine plopped down on the sofa and let out a weary sigh.

"It's been a long day," Jan said, sympathizing with her cousin.

"But your lemon cake had the customers talking." Elaine smiled in spite of her obvious exhaustion.

Jan couldn't help but smile back. "I saw you sneak a piece."

"Just one?" Elaine giggled. "You missed a few. But they were small."

For a moment, Jan felt like a little girl again. More than once she and Elaine had spent the night with their grandmother, and while they always thought they were sneaking treats from grandma's cookie jar, they found out later she'd known all along.

"It's a grandmother's job to spoil her grandkids, then send them back home to their parents filled up with love," she'd said. "And in my world, love often shows up in the form of cookies." She would wink at Jan, and Jan had known she and

Elaine had only been sneaking what their grandmother had intended for them all along.

Jan loved the thought that she was carrying on the tradition now, not only with her granddaughters, Avery and Kelly, but with so many people here in Lancaster—serving baked goods that were filled with love.

She flipped another page in her book and squinted for a better look at the vases pictured, comparing them to the photo Macy had given them.

"Have you made any progress?" Elaine asked.

"I know what makes an antique valuable," Jan said.

"Well, that's something." Elaine sat up a little straighter. "What did you find out?"

Jan looked down at her notebook where she'd jotted down some of the things that gave an item value, according to multiple Web sites. "The first thing is rarity. I know this is obvious, but if there were only a few of something made or if there are only a few of something left, it's going to be more valuable."

Elaine nodded. "That makes sense. So maybe the vase was especially rare." Elaine's brow knit together as she considered the possibility.

"Or maybe it was made by somebody who went on to become really famous." She showed Elaine Macy's note about the maker's mark on the bottom of the vase. "This must be a clue as to where this vase came from in the first place."

Elaine read over the description. "A triangle with the letter *E* in the middle." She glanced up. "Did you look that up?"

Jan nodded, opening her laptop and clicking around until she found the tab with a catalog of various marks found on ceramics, pottery, sculptures, and other artwork. Jan explained that this mark, a signature of sorts, could reveal exactly where the vase came from. "But a search of the database turned up nothing. There are letters and there are triangles, but I haven't found anything that puts the two together."

"Maybe Macy knows something about it. We hadn't discussed that with her before. We can ask tomorrow."

They'd decided to start talking to Macy's staff first thing in the morning, but Jan wondered if she'd get any sleep at all that night. Her body was tired, but her mind was full of energy.

She'd learned that in addition to an item's rarity, there were other factors that made something valuable—was it authentic to a certain time period? Was it made with valuable materials? Was it the work of a well-known artist?

But as Jan closed the last of her books, she wondered how to determine any of that with nothing but a photograph.

She opened her computer and started searching "valuable antique vases." The images that popped up bore no resemblance to Macy's vase. She clicked around, studying each example, sometimes opening a Web site that looked promising. Macy's vase didn't appear to be from China, India, or Egypt. It was different from most of what she found.

Elaine disappeared only to reappear a few minutes later in her pajamas. "How about I make us some chamomile tea?"

Jan nodded mindlessly and continued searching. She picked up the photo of Macy's vase and looked more closely. The first thing she'd noticed in the close-up shot was those two birds on branches protruding from the side.

She typed in "two birds in crystal vase."

She didn't know if the vase was crystal, but when an image popped up of a vase that looked remarkably familiar, Jan gasped. The one in the image was taller and thinner, but if vases had relatives, this one would certainly be a sibling to Macy's vase.

Elaine's footsteps in the hallway pulled Jan's attention from her screen. "Elaine, I found something!"

Seconds later, Elaine was at her side, reading over Jan's shoulder about something called "lost wax glass casting," a technique dating back to the early Egyptians but also used by modern artists.

"It says the technique was made popular early in the twentieth century, so maybe Macy's vase is from around that time," Jan said, skimming the words on her computer screen. She read the description of the process, which sounded very involved, with a number of steps that needed to be rigidly followed. It involved creating a wax mold, melting the glass into it, then bringing the temperature down very slowly so the glass could properly form. After that, there were still a number of sanding and cleaning steps before the piece was finished.

"My goodness," Elaine said. "Think of all the time it took to create Macy's vase. Was that one of the criteria for determining value—how much work went into making it?"

"I don't think so," Jan said. "But it feels like it should've been." She studied the photo a little closer, reading the caption underneath.

One of a trio of crystal vases stolen from prominent Jewish families during Hilter's occupation of Poland in WWII.

Jan reread the caption out loud, then turned toward Elaine.

"Surely Macy's vase isn't part of this collection," Elaine said.

Jan wrote down the name of the Web site, which was nothing more than a seemingly obscure blog by a woman named Jenna whose contact page said she was a researcher at the United States Holocaust Memorial Museum in Washington, DC.

Jan clicked over to her e-mail and typed in Jenna's address.

Dear Jenna,

I stumbled upon your blog tonight and am looking for a little more information on the vase featured in your blog post last year on May 4. Can you tell me where the trio of vases is now or any other details about it, including its value? I'm doing a little research of my own.

Thank you.

Sincerely,
Jan Blake

She hit Send. It was the first time she had any hope of finding out anything about Macy's vase since they first learned it was missing, but even as she closed her laptop, her mind swirled with thoughts of where that vase may have originated. She'd read stories of the Nazis' plunder, and if her memory served, there were still many pieces unaccounted for. Artwork and jewelry and yes, she supposed even items like crystal vases, had been taken from homes and museums only to be stowed away by Hitler and his men.

Was it possible Macy's vase had been one of those items? She thought of the sweet, romantic story Macy had attached to the vase. Perhaps it was all true and her grandfather had sent the vase, filled with daisies, ahead to his wife.

But maybe the vase hadn't come from a florist at all. Maybe it had been stolen and given to Macy's grandfather, or—worse—maybe he'd stolen it himself.

Jan's heart sank at the thought, one she quickly pushed out of her mind.

"I can see you're trying to fit everything together," Elaine said. "But this is only one piece of the puzzle. It's a wonderful find, Jan, but let's wait and see if this Jenna replies before we jump to any conclusions."

Elaine was right. They didn't have enough information yet to say anything for sure, but at least now they knew a little bit more about the vase and where it had come from.

That night, Jan stared at the ceiling, unable to fall asleep. Her thoughts bounced around her mind like a host of Ping-Pong balls, each one pulling her in a different direction.

Moonlight filtered in through her windows, casting a blue hue on her runaway thoughts.

Sleep was a lost cause. She was wide awake and now there were too many unknowns floating around in her mind. She couldn't seem to land on anything that made sense. The mystery nagged at her until finally she threw back the covers, tiptoed down the hall, and knocked lightly on Elaine's bedroom door.

When no answer came, she pushed the door open.

"Elaine?" she whispered into the darkness.

Still no answer.

"Elaine?"

Her cousin stirred, but only slightly. Jan reached down, shook her shoulder, and said her name one more time.

Elaine shot straight up with a gasp. "What's wrong?"

"Nothing, nothing," Jan said, trying to calm her down.

Elaine looked at the clock. "It's after midnight. Are you okay?"

"I can't sleep."

Elaine reached over and clicked on the lamp on her nightstand. "What is it?"

"It's the vase," Jan sat on the edge of the bed. "I keep thinking of all the possibilities. Nazi plunder? I certainly hadn't expected that."

Elaine pulled the covers up as she pushed herself to a sitting position. "It is troubling, isn't it?"

"If we do recover the vase, is Macy the rightful owner?" Jan's conflicting feelings rose to the top.

Elaine covered Jan's hand with her own. "It's not up to us what happens to the vase. Our only job is to track it down. What happens from there is up to Macy."

"Should we tell her what we found?"

"I'm not sure," Elaine said. "But I don't think so. Not until we have something a little more concrete. After all, we have no proof the vase is one of those that was stolen during the war."

Jan let out a soft sigh. "I suppose you're right. I hope Macy's staff can shed a little light on this whole thing."

Elaine lay back down. "I remember when you used to wake me up because you were in the kitchen baking something you'd dreamed about."

Jan laughed. "I seem to get my best ideas at night. I'm sorry I woke you."

"It's fine." Her cousin pulled the covers up. "But we better get some sleep or neither one of us is going to be worth anything tomorrow."

"You're right," Jan moved toward the door.

"Good night." Elaine reached across her nightstand and turned off the lamp, leaving Jan standing in the doorway wishing she could turn off her thoughts so easily.

CHAPTER TEN

The following day, an unrested Jan sat in the kitchen with a cup of espresso. "The hard stuff," as Elaine called it, was the only thing that would do after a night of so little sleep. After Jan had left Elaine's room, she'd still struggled to fall back to sleep, various theories bouncing around in her mind like little silver balls in a pinball machine.

The more they learned about this vase, the more she wanted to locate it—but the further away it felt.

Elaine walked in, also looking a little weary.

She inhaled a deep breath, then stopped. "Is that...?"

"I had a feeling we could both use a cup today," Jan said.

"'Desperate times,' as they say." Elaine smiled.

Jan poured the fragrant coffee into a mug. "I'm sorry again for waking you last night. I suppose I shouldn't stay up so late reading." She handed Elaine the steaming drink.

"Oh, it's okay. I can hardly wait to get out to Green Glade now. I have more questions than ever. Besides, the espresso will have us wide awake in no time."

They finished their drinks and about a half an hour later they were on their way back to Green Glade, both properly caffeinated and feeling a bit more awake.

When they arrived, Elaine parked her car near one of the cottages. They'd been in touch with Macy regarding Sarah's schedule for the day, so they knew where to find her when they arrived. She would be cleaning "Peace" and "Tranquility" that morning, though Macy wasn't sure which one she'd be starting in.

They exited the car and Jan inhaled the crisp autumn air. A chill had swept through Lancaster as October took hold, and soon the trees, now full of the vibrant shades of red, orange, and yellow, would be bare. Jan loved autumn in Maine best of all. It had always been her favorite season. Somehow it seemed like the scenery had been created just for her, the way it spoke to the deepest part of her spirit.

She reveled in that stunning shade of reddish orange that the maple tree in their front yard wore. The first autumn in their new home promised all kinds of pleasures.

As they walked, sticks cracked beneath their feet and Jan thought it was nice the cottages had a good amount of space between each. It would be easy to feel secluded out here at Green Glade, something everyone could use from time to time.

As they approached one of the cottages, Jan read the sign near the front door. "That's Tranquility. Should we knock?"

Elaine nodded and led the way. When they knocked, the door opened slightly, an invitation for them to come in. Elaine pushed the door open and called out, "Hello?" There was no answer, so she called out again.

Still no answer.

"Maybe she's in a different cottage?" Jan suggested, but as she did, they heard movement coming from the upstairs.

"Hello?" Elaine was a little louder this time. When there was still no answer, she moved toward the stairs and started up just as someone appeared at the top.

When the young woman saw them, she gasped, pulling earbuds out of her ears. "Oh, hi!"

"So sorry to frighten you," Elaine said.

"It's okay. I probably shouldn't listen to music while I work," Sarah said.

Elaine waved her off. "Oh, why not?" she asked with a smile. "If it makes the work go faster, seems like a good idea to me. What are you listening to?"

"You'll laugh at me, but I'm listening to Jars of Clay's very first album. Old school!"

"I love that album. 'Faith Like a Child' is one of my favorite songs."

"It's my son's favorite song too. He's actually part of the reason I've started listening to this again."

"That's as good a reason as any," Elaine said.

"So are you guests, or...?" Sarah looked confused as to why they were in the cabin in the first place.

"No, actually, we're unofficially helping Macy learn more about what happened with the fire," Jan said, "and we were hoping to chat with you about the Escape cabin, since you've spent so much time in it. Your insight might help us better understand the layout of the space."

It was technically true, Jan decided. Sarah didn't need to know they had suspicions about Macy's staff, herself included.

Until those suspicions were founded, they'd consider Sarah a source.

"Do you have a few minutes to show us the cabin?" Elaine asked as they followed Sarah into the living room. Tranquility was nearly identical to Escape, minus the fire damage. Jan remembered checking this cottage after they found out the vase had gone missing. Macy's trinket for Tranquility was a set of small teacups and saucers, which was on a shelf above the chest in the entryway. Jan glanced at it, mostly content to learn it was still there but also wondering if Macy might be hiding another treasure in plain sight.

Sarah smiled. "Of course. I'm happy to help if I can. Follow me."

As they walked, Jan studied her. Brownish hair, pulled back in a ponytail. Thin frame covered by a uniform that reminded Jan of a fancier pair of hospital scrubs.

"What was the cabin like when you cleaned it that day?" Elaine asked.

They walked by the one cabin between Tranquility and Escape, which was just as pristinely landscaped and painted as the others. Jan looked at the door, which held a plaque that said Serenity, and wondered if Macy had simply used a thesaurus to title her cabins.

"Was there anything out of the ordinary?" Jan asked.

"Everything seemed completely normal right until the moment I punched out and left," Sarah answered.

"What time did you punch out?" Jan asked when they had entered the Escape cottage. Sarah looked confused at the question.

"It will help us put together a time line for the day," Jan clarified.

"I see. That makes sense. Um..." Sarah seemed to check her mental calendar, and for a little longer than seemed reasonable, Jan thought. It was only a couple days ago. How hard could it be to remember? Sarah put her finger up. "I remember. It was around two thirty. I pick up Dylan—that's my son— from school every day at three."

If she picks him up every day at three, why would she have such a hard time remembering what time she had left? Perhaps something else had distracted her, Jan thought. But then she saw Elaine jot something down in the small notebook she'd pulled from her purse and wondered if she had thought the same thing.

"So you're sure nothing seemed unusual that day?" Elaine repeated Jan's earlier question.

"Not at all," Sarah said confidently, her memory fully intact again. "I follow Mrs. Atherton's system, ensuring that every square inch of every cottage is polished, dusted, and spotless by the time we're done. The staff has been trained to be very meticulous. When I left, nothing was missing and everything was sparkling."

Jan could see the pride in Sarah's face at the work she did, and she could certainly understand that.

Elaine pulled the photo of the vase from her purse and handed it to Sarah. "Sarah, what can you tell us about this vase?"

Sarah glanced at it. "Well, that's the vase that was here, on the mantel. I know Mrs. Atherton is very proud of it and I'm so sorry that it's gone missing." She seemed genuine, Jan noted.

"Whenever she's inspected my cleaning, she's always paid special attention to it. And I've overheard her telling more than one guest the story of how this vase came into her family in the first place."

"Oh yes, Macy told us about it too," Elaine confirmed.

"Would you be willing to walk us through your cleaning process?" Jan asked. "You mentioned that Macy has a specific system she wants you to follow. Could you describe it to us?"

"Of course," Sarah said. "I always start upstairs." She looked at Jan. "And actually, that day, I did notice that the cottage hardly looked like it had been used. The guests were very clean."

Jan took a sheet of folded paper from her purse, scanning it with her eyes. "The guest's last name was Rollins, correct?"

Sarah shrugged. "I don't know, actually. I really don't interact with them unless they need me for something."

Jan nodded and tucked the list of past guests Macy had given them back in her purse.

"Then I vacuum and dust the living room and then sweep the entryway. I run the rag over the chest here," she said, moving toward the entryway where the chest sat. "Then I straighten the dining room chairs and sweep underneath the table. Then I move to the kitchen."

Jan paid special attention to Sarah as she followed her into the kitchen, which was where the fire started.

"I always wash any dishes in the sink, but there weren't any that day," Sarah said. "I spray the counters and wipe them down, clean out the sink, and then spray the stovetop and the front of the oven and…" Sarah stopped talking.

Jan waited. Sarah stared at the charred oven with a frown for a brief moment, then continued. It was only a split second, but something had stopped her in her tracks.

Sarah stood straight again and continued. "I wipe the oven down, then sweep the floor, then take out the trash. Mrs. Atherton requires me to work in that order, because otherwise there's a trail of crumbs if I sweep before I dust the oven. She's meticulous, but there's a reason behind every rule. As a detail-oriented person, I appreciate that about her."

Jan met Elaine's eyes. Her cousin's expression made her wonder if perhaps she'd also noticed the glitch in Sarah's story, the way she'd seemed to hit a mental speed bump at the exact moment her memory landed on cleaning the stove that day.

"The routine seems fairly reasonable to me," Elaine said, her tone encouraging. "Just one last question."

"Anything," Sarah said, her eyes wide and willing to help.

"Did you see anyone else here that day?"

Sarah crossed her arms over her chest. "Now that you mention it, I did. When I first walked up, the guest was leaving the cottage. I remember thinking it was a little late for checkout, but it happens sometimes and I know Mrs. Atherton tries to be accommodating. I took a quick break in the clubhouse for about ten minutes and when I came back, it was all clear."

"What time was that?"

Sarah hesitated, as if working it out in her mind. "I suppose around one? Maybe a little after. Do you think the guest stole it?"

"Oh, it's hard to say," Jan told the young housekeeper, not wanting to point fingers at anyone. "The cottage has had many guests over the last six months alone. We just want to be thorough."

Sarah nodded and followed the cousins out on to the porch.

"Thank you for your time today, Sarah," Jan said.

"I don't feel like I was very helpful." Sarah's face fell. "I wish there was something more I could do."

"You've been very helpful," Elaine said. "It sounds like you're very thorough in your work."

"Yep," Sarah said. "I made sure everything was in its place when I left at two fifteen to pick up Dylan."

Elaine and Jan looked at each other. Earlier, the "detail-oriented" Sarah had said she'd left at two thirty.

CHAPTER ELEVEN

Elaine plodded up the hill toward the Green Glade club-house, where guests checked in for their stay, Jan close on her heels. They hadn't spoken to any other employees yet, but she wondered if any of them could give them a little insight on Sarah Clayton.

"She seemed like a nice young woman," Jan said, once they were out of earshot of the cabin where they'd left Sarah on the porch.

Elaine nodded. "She did, but I felt like she's hiding something."

"Did you notice the way she paused when she talked about the stove?"

Elaine shook her head. It wasn't unusual for Jan to pick up on the small details Elaine missed. It was part of what made them such a great team, especially since Jan found asking pointed questions difficult. Somehow that was Elaine's favorite part.

"When she was going over her cleaning routine," Jan said. "It was barely noticeable, but she definitely seemed rattled for a second."

"Maybe one of her coworkers can fill in some of the gaps in her story," Elaine said as they approached the clubhouse. It wasn't extravagant by any means, but it was lovely, with all the amenities any hotel would have. Behind the clubhouse was a fenced-in outdoor pool, now closed for the season, which Macy sometimes opened to local kids in the summer, depending on how busy Green Glade was.

White trim encased the doors and windows of the large cream-colored building, and the landscaping had been perfectly manicured. The bright summer marigolds and petunias had been replaced with yellow and orange mums in large brown pots surrounding the entrance. A lovely touch, Elaine thought. It reminded her that she wanted a few pots of mums for the front porch of the tearoom. Perhaps Murphy's General Store had a nice selection. She made a mental note to check the next time she walked by.

Elaine pulled open the door and they walked into the clubhouse with its buttery-yellow walls and high ceilings. On the other side of the room, an impressive stone fireplace invited guests to sit and stay a while. Two sand-colored club chairs flanked either side of the fireplace with a coffee table between. A loveseat had been positioned with its back to the first two chairs, and three more club chairs had been positioned to form another sitting area, inviting the kind of long, lingering conversation vacationers would relish.

Once again, Elaine had to hand it to Macy. She'd done an impressive job of creating a space that would draw people in. Even she wished she could curl up with a good book next to the fireplace.

In the foreground, off to the left, stood a long check-in counter, and behind it, a young man dressed in a suit.

When Elaine and Jan approached him, he looked up and gave them a smile. "Welcome to Green Glade, ladies," he said. "Do you have a reservation?"

Elaine glanced down at his name tag, which read Brett. "No, I'm afraid we don't."

"That's no problem," Brett said. "I can check our availability."

"Actually, I'm Elaine Cook and this is my cousin Jan Blake, and we're friends of Macy's. We were wondering if we could trouble you for a little bit of information."

Brett frowned. "What kind of information?"

Jan took the folded sheet of paper Macy had given them out of her purse. "We were wondering if you could tell us anything about this guest with the last name Rollins." She slid the paper over the counter.

"Mrs. Atherton gave you this list?"

"Yep. She's asked us to look around, and try to figure out what happened the day of the fire out here at Green Glade."

He looked dubious. "I thought the fire was an accident."

"It appears to have been an accident," Elaine said. "But what do you think? Do you know anything that might make you think otherwise?"

Brett looked confused. "No, ma'am. It was just another normal day here until the fire trucks rolled up. I didn't even notice the smoke before it happened. They said another guest called the fire department."

"Do you remember the guests that were staying in that cottage that day?" Jan asked. "Macy's list only gives a last name. She said you could give us the rest of the contact information."

"It was a woman who checked in," Brett said. "Nice lady. Said she had a deadline and that's why she was there. Didn't see much of her."

"A deadline?" Jan asked.

"Some kind of writer," Brett said with a shrug. "She didn't seem like an arsonist though."

Elaine almost laughed. She wondered how many arsonists Brett knew, but chose not to ask.

"Do you know the other employees here very well?" Jan asked.

"Sure," Brett said. "There aren't many of us. We all hang out sometimes after work."

"Can you tell us anything about the housekeeper who was working that day—the one who cleaned Escape?"

Brett leaned against the counter. "Would've been Ruby or Sarah—not sure which one was assigned to that cottage on that day. But they're both cool."

"Cool?" Elaine wondered what that meant exactly, at least in this context.

Brett nodded. "You know—neither one of them would ever set fire to a cottage. They're good people, honest and trustworthy."

He seemed awfully confident, but Elaine couldn't shake Sarah's confusion over when she punched out.

The back door of the clubhouse opened and a young woman with striking red hair wearing the same uniform Sarah had worn walked in. She glanced at them and smiled.

"Hey, Brett!"

"Hey, Ruby!" Brett looked at Elaine, then at Jan. "That's Ruby."

"I gathered," Elaine said. "Ruby, do you have a moment to chat?"

The girl faced them, a confused look on her face. "Me?"

"They're friends of Mrs. Atherton's," Brett told her. "They've got some questions about the fire."

"Well, about the day of the fire," Elaine said. They asked Ruby about the guests, but she, like Brett, hadn't seen or interacted with them during their stay. Apparently, whoever was in Escape that week was quiet and meticulous. By all accounts, the perfect guest.

"How do you like working here?" Jan asked. "Have you made good friends with the staff?"

Ruby shrugged. "I've only been here a few months." She looked back at Elaine with a smile that looked forced. "But I hope one day I'll feel that way."

"Are you kidding, Rubes?" Brett gave her a playful nudge. "You and Sarah are tight. I'm the third wheel around here."

Ruby clenched her jaw, but didn't look at Brett. "I've got to go. Lots of work to do today." Without another word, Ruby walked away.

Elaine glanced at Jan, then back at Brett. "Brett, could we trouble you for the contact information for this guest—Rollins?" Jan asked. "Macy said you could get it for us. Phone, address, whatever you have. And if it's not too much trouble, perhaps the information for the rest of the names on this list?"

Brett nodded, then started clicking around on the computer.

While he worked, Elaine wandered away from the front desk, giving her cousin a knowing nod that she hoped said "keep him busy."

As she heard Jan ask Brett about what school he went to and whether he played sports, she moved around to the other side of the front desk area where there was an Employees Only door. She tried the handle and was delighted to discover it was unlocked. After she passed through it, she found herself standing in a small lounge with a refrigerator, microwave, and a row of lockers. A table and chairs stood in the center of the room with various magazines and a few books strewn across it. Through the door, she could hear Brett talking about football.

Next to the door, she found what she was looking for—the time cards. She pulled out Sarah's, scanning it quickly with her finger until she landed on October 3, the day of the fire.

Huh. According to the card, Sarah punched out at two forty-five. That wasn't either time Sarah had said she left that day. She stuck the card back in the holder and returned to the lobby just as Brett handed over the printouts of the additional contact information for the list of the guests who had stayed in Escape over the last six months.

"Here you go," he said.

"Thank you, Brett," Elaine said. "You've been a great help."

"Tell that to Mrs. Atherton," he said. "I could use a raise."

After they left the clubhouse, Elaine and Jan headed back to the tearoom for a full day. Around lunchtime, they sat around the island in the kitchen for a quick sandwich and most likely a cream puff or two.

Elaine took out the paper Brett had given them and determined that "Rollins" was, in fact, Elizabeth Rollins, and she lived only an hour away, in a small town just beyond Penzance, on the other side of Chickadee Lake.

"Should we call her?" Jan asked between bites of her turkey on rye.

"I think so. She's just an hour away. I'll ask Rose to clean up so we can go visit her this afternoon." Elaine finished the first half of her sandwich, then took out her phone.

She called Elizabeth, who was very polite, and they set up a time to meet later that afternoon.

"She didn't mind the intrusion?" Jan asked.

"She seemed happy to help." Elaine hadn't told Elizabeth much, only that they had a few questions about her recent stay at Green Glade and it would be better if they could talk in person.

A few hours later, after their last customer had gone and the sun was beginning to set, they were driving through a pristine neighborhood with two rows of newer homes on either side of the road. The houses resembled one another, but each had its own charming details. Each home had thick white trim around the doors and windows, painted shutters, and wide pillars on each front porch.

Elaine slowed down, looking for number 3621. They neared the end of the block where the street widened into a cul-de-sac and at the very back of the circle stood a two-story white house with black shutters and a red door. "This is it." She pulled into the driveway and parked the car.

"Doesn't it seem strange that this couple drove only an hour up the road for a mini vacation?" Jan asked as Elaine turned off the engine.

"Brett mentioned the woman had a deadline," Elaine said. "Maybe she was working while her husband was fishing in the lake. Macy did say their guests come to Green Glade for all different reasons."

"True. Just because I want to sit on the porch of one of those cottages with the latest issue of *Code Busters* drinking in the fresh air and sunshine doesn't mean that someone else couldn't spend their time at Green Glade in a more productive manner." Jan smiled.

They made their way up the long sidewalk to the front door. "It's a beautiful home." Elaine rang the doorbell. "Perhaps Elizabeth Rollins is a successful author."

The door opened and a plump woman with cropped white hair appeared on the other side. "Hello!" A wide smile spread across her face.

"Elizabeth Rollins?" Elaine smiled her friendliest smile.

"Yes, come in!" She opened the outer door. "I didn't realize when we spoke on the phone that it was you two who were coming to visit me. You're from Lancaster, right?"

Elaine and Jan exchanged a quick, confused look. "That's right. I'm Elaine Cook and this is my cousin Jan Blake."

"I almost didn't recognize you without your Victorian gowns." Elizabeth had affected a faux British accent as she said the words.

Elaine studied the woman for a few seconds, trying to place her.

"You were at Tea for Two last weekend." Jan put it together before she did.

"That's right," Elizabeth said. "Your high tea. It was wonderful, I might add."

Apparently Elizabeth Rollins had been to the Lancaster Community Church high tea.

"I'm so glad you called and I get to tell you how much I loved those delicious mini maple croissants you made." Elizabeth closed the door behind them as Jan and Elaine stepped in the entryway of her home.

"That's so sweet of you to say," Jan said. "It was my mother's recipe. And thank you so much for agreeing to talk with us today."

"Of course. Would you like anything to eat or drink? I don't have anything as wonderful as your mini chocolate croissants, but I think I have some sugar cookies."

"I'm so glad you enjoyed the croissants." Jan followed Elizabeth into a sitting room just off the entryway.

"They were the best part of my weekend," Elizabeth said with a smile.

"We had a late lunch, but it is so kind of you to offer." Elaine glanced around the room, which was lent charm by a cheerful fire crackling in the grate.

"Please sit down." Elizabeth motioned to the two olive-green armchairs opposite the matching sofa. "What brings you here?" She sat on the couch across from them.

"We have a few questions about your recent stay at Green Glade," Elaine started.

"Oh, Green Glade." There was a soft sigh in Elizabeth's voice. "I hadn't been there in years, but I'm so glad I went. I was so shocked when the fire broke out. It's just terrible, isn't it?"

"Thankfully no one was injured and the fire was contained," Jan said.

"Definitely. It could've been so much worse." Elizabeth tucked a strand of hair behind her ear.

"Did you go to Green Glade alone?" Elaine asked.

"Yes, I did." A black cat crept into the room and wound itself around Elizabeth's foot, then hopped up on the sofa next to her. "Just me, I'm afraid."

The cat jumped onto Jan's lap.

"Oh, I'm sorry. She's such a cuddler," Elizabeth laughed.

Jan smiled and ran a hand over the cat's head. She was wonderfully soft, but Jan still couldn't help preferring their own Earl Grey. Especially when the cat jumped down and wandered out of the room.

Elaine scooted back in her chair, perusing the coffee and side tables. A few large coffee-table books were stacked neatly on the table to her left. A home decorating book, another one about coins and stamps, and a third, on the bottom of the stack, about the lost art of World War II.

"Did you have a nice visit at Green Glade?" Jan pulled Elaine's attention back to the conversation.

"Well, it was more of a working vacation," Elizabeth said. "I'm a novelist and my deadline is right around the corner."

"This home seems like the perfect place to write a book," Elaine said lightly.

Elizabeth smiled. "My husband was away for the weekend, and it should've been the perfect time to work, but I needed a change of scenery—sometimes staring at the same old walls can stifle my creativity. Don't get me wrong! I enjoyed the quiet in my own home. My husband is retired." She tipped her head and raised a brow, as if to communicate something unspoken.

"Ah." Elaine nodded. "Having trouble keeping himself occupied?"

Elizabeth groaned. "He is so bored. He doesn't seem to understand what it means to relax, and he certainly doesn't understand how distracting it is to be midsentence and have the entire bookshelf in the next room come tumbling down. I love that man, but he needs a part-time job. Or a hobby. Or a dog. Maybe I'll get him a dog."

Elaine laughed, her thoughts turning to Ben. He'd been newly retired when he passed away. Would he have driven her crazy with his boredom? She liked to think they would've spent those days just cherishing each other's company. Seeing movies. Visiting museums. Taking impromptu trips to see the grandkids.

"What kind of books do you write?" Elaine asked, shaking off the thought.

Elizabeth started to say something, then seemed to change her mind. "What kind of books do you read?"

"Oh, Elaine reads everything. She has shelves and shelves of novels. She's always been a reader."

"Mostly crime novels," Elaine added.

Elizabeth nodded with a smile. "You probably haven't read anything I've written. I don't have a knack for mysteries."

Elaine was about to tell her mysteries weren't the only kind of novels she read, but a crash in the other room stopped her.

"That would be the cat." Elizabeth hurried out of the room, giving Elaine a chance to take a peek around. Two other coffee table books about WWII had been stacked on the other side table, and on the bookshelves behind where Elaine had been sitting were a series of photographs that could have been from that era.

Elaine picked up a framed photo of a man in uniform standing next to a young woman wearing a very simple white dress.

"My grandparents." Elizabeth's voice behind her startled Elaine, but she managed not to show it. She set the frame back on the shelf.

"Was he a soldier?" Jan glanced at the photo over Elaine's shoulder.

"Yes, in World War II."

"You seem to have a lot of books on World War II," Elaine said. "It was a fascinating time, wasn't it?"

"Next to the Civil War, it's my favorite period of history," Elizabeth said. "Several of my novels are set in that era." As soon as she said those words, Elizabeth turned away.

"Do you by chance remember seeing a vase on the mantel in your cottage at Green Glade?" Elaine asked.

Elizabeth frowned. "I don't recall seeing one, but like I said, I was working most of the time I was there."

"It's a shame," Elaine said. "It's such a beautiful spot—I'm sure it would be a wonderful place to go to relax too."

"That's something I hope to do very soon." Elizabeth folded her hands in her lap and a lull hung above the three of them.

Elaine pulled the photo of the vase from her purse and held it out toward Elizabeth. "Here's the vase I'm talking about. Does it look familiar?"

Elizabeth took the photo and looked at it. "I suppose it could've been there, sure. I don't have the best memory."

"Macy likes to talk about the different pieces she's placed in the cottages." Jan leaned forward. "Because they're special to her family. It's her way of sharing a bit of the Atherton family with her guests—making them feel like Green Glade is more than just another place to stay."

Elizabeth nodded, a slight smile playing at the corners of her mouth. "That is a very nice touch. I'm afraid I didn't see Macy at all while I was there. I didn't hear the story, but I am sure it's really a lovely one."

Elaine tucked the photo back in her purse. "While you were at Green Glade, did you notice anything suspicious?"

Elizabeth shook her head. "Not at all. It was a perfectly wonderful couple of days. Quiet. Peaceful. I finished my manuscript just before I checked out at eleven thirty." Elaine made a mental note. Checkout was at noon. But didn't Sarah Clayton say the guest was there late? She'd said they tried to accommodate those who stayed past checkout time and that she'd seen the guest not too long before she left at two thirty...or whatever time she actually left.

Elaine cleared her throat. "Are you sure it was eleven thirty?"

Elizabeth looked away for a moment, as if she were running through the day in her mind. "Oh, I can show you." She stood and walked to the desk, sifted around, then pulled out a red folder. She turned and handed it to Elaine.

"A copy of my itinerary."

Elaine flipped the folder open. Inside was a stack of notes, the kind a novelist might have as she was piecing her story together. She pulled out the paper on top. When she did, she found a familiar paper underneath. It was the sheet of paper included in Macy's welcome packet—the one that detailed the story of the vase—and it was covered in handwritten notes, as if someone had been very interested in that story and that vase.

"Oh, I'm sorry." Elizabeth pulled the folder out of Elaine's hands. "I think those are just my notes. I take so many notes and I always try to keep them together." She walked back to the desk and pulled out another folder. "This is the one with my itinerary in it."

Elaine forced a smile as she opened the second folder, catching a quick glimpse of Jan as she did. Judging by the confused expression on her cousin's face, she was thinking the same thing as Elaine. Elizabeth had said she didn't remember seeing the vase.

"It's so hard for creative people to stay organized," Elizabeth laughed. "Why don't I get us some tea?"

But even Elizabeth's calm demeanor and polite expression couldn't erase the questions floating around in the back of Elaine's mind.

CHAPTER TWELVE

On Thursday morning, Jan and Elaine opened their doors to a wonderful rush of early customers. Jan thought she might have to pinch herself. This wasn't a dream, and folks really did love their little tearoom! Every time their tables filled with new or familiar faces, she said a silent prayer of thanks to the One who made it all possible.

A little later, Jan meandered through the west parlor, noticing Archie was busy charming their customers the way only he could. Their guests loved to hear him talk with his British accent and vast knowledge of teas, and Jan understood why. He had a kind way about him.

Archie or Rose must have turned on the music in the parlor—Vivaldi this time. Something bright that matched her mood.

Elaine met her near the door to the dining room. "I think the oven timer only has a minute left."

Ever since the banana bread incident, Elaine had shied away from helping her with the pastries. Jan thought it was amusing, because her cousin was a perfectly fine cook in her own right. She knew Elaine would come to her senses again soon, but for now she was oven-shy.

"I was headed there now," Jan said. "Care to give me a hand?"

They glanced at the parlor, content that everything was in order and in good hands, then made their way to the kitchen. As they pushed open the door, they discovered Macy standing at the counter, holding a purse and doing nothing to hide the fact that she'd just sampled one of the treats Jan had already plated.

"Hi, Macy," Jan said. "How are you?"

"I'm here for an update." Macy swallowed a bite. When she went in for another one, Jan swatted her hand away as if she were a mischievous toddler.

"Sorry," Jan said when she saw the wounded expression on Macy's face. "That must've been an instinct."

Elaine laughed. "But those treats *are* for our customers."

"But I'm your client. Don't I come first?"

Jan sliced another small piece of cake and placed it on the tray to fill the gaping hole Macy's sweet tooth had left, but she didn't answer the question.

"How can we help you today?" Elaine asked.

Macy spun around to face her. "I told you. I'm here for an update on my case."

"It's not the best time, I'm afraid," Elaine said. "We really do need to get back to our customers."

"Fine. Call me when you can fit your *client* into your busy schedule." Macy grabbed her purse off the table and headed toward the front door in a huff.

Elaine shot Jan a look, then headed for the door. Jan followed with a tray of sliced cake.

Elaine stopped short just inside the parlor, causing a near collision with her cousin.

"What's wrong?" Jan asked.

Jan followed Elaine's eyes just in time to see Macy sitting down at one of the tables near the back of the room.

"What is she doing?" Jan whispered.

They moved toward Macy.

"Now I'm also a paying customer." Macy made more than enough room for herself at the table, spreading her place setting out so much so that it invaded her neighbors' personal space.

Jan set the tray she carried in the center of the table, wondering if she should apologize to the others who were already seated.

"Are you going to get me my tea?" Macy held her empty cup midair.

"Of course," Elaine said, a question in her voice.

"Why do I feel like this is not going to end well?" Jan asked as they moved away from the table. "To be honest, I don't know what we can tell her anyway."

"We could tell her what we know so far—that Sarah said she checked out at two thirty, then two fifteen, then two thirty again," Elaine said. "But her time card says two forty-five."

"I suppose so," Jan said. "But Macy isn't going to like it, and besides, it's hardly conclusive."

"We could fill her in on our visit to Elizabeth Rollins," Elaine offered. "I still can't figure out why she'd say she knew nothing about the vase when she had Macy's printout."

"It is confusing," Jan agreed.

A disturbance at the back of the parlor drew their attention—and the attention of everyone else in the room.

"Have you seen it?" Macy was asking the other women at her table, doing nothing to keep her voice low.

Jan moved toward the table, careful to keep the smile plastered on her face. "Is everything all right back here?"

The unfamiliar woman sitting next to Macy glared at Jan. "This woman practically accused all of us of stealing an antique vase from a cottage we've never visited."

"We're from Waterville," one of the other women said. "We don't make a habit of vacationing ten minutes down the road."

Macy stared at the woman through squinted eyes. "I just asked if they had seen a vase like this." She held up a photograph of the missing vase.

"That's not all you asked." The woman's face said it all.

"Ladies, I apologize," Jan said. "I'm going to have Rose bring over a few special treats—on the house. And Macy, would you come with me?" The last thing they needed was for a fight to break out at the tearoom. Oh, just imagine the town gossip.

Jan waited beside the table as Macy made a production of getting up, tossing her cloth napkin on to the plate, and giving each of the women at the table one final stare-down.

Jan wrapped an arm around Macy's shoulder and pulled her away from the table, leading her all the way into the kitchen.

"That was quite a scene," Elaine said once they'd all escaped the parlor. "Do you really think those women had anything to do with your missing vase?"

Macy lifted her chin, indignant and unapologetic. "I'm investigating. Something you've obviously forgotten how to do."

Elaine rubbed the space between her eyebrows, willing away an impending headache. "Accusing our guests of stealing your vase is *not* investigating."

Macy scoffed. "I didn't accuse anyone of anything. I only asked where they were the day of the fire."

"Macy." Jan kept her voice calm, the way she used to when her children threw tantrums.

"And if any of them had a criminal background."

Elaine opened her mouth as if to speak, then closed it again. She took a deep breath and closed her eyes for a fleeting moment. Jan suspected she was sending up a quick but heartfelt prayer for wisdom and perhaps patience.

When she opened her eyes again, Elaine told Macy what they knew so far—the fire really did seem to be an accident, Sarah hadn't been honest about when she left that day, and Elizabeth Rollins appeared to be hiding whatever it was she knew about the vase.

"You could've told me that," Macy said when Elaine finished.

"I am sorry, Macy," Elaine said. "We aren't sure yet where any of this will lead. They feel like random pieces of information, and we're trying to connect the dots. I know it's hard to be patient, but these things take time, and they work best if you don't interfere."

Macy harrumphed.

Jan stepped in. "Macy, there is one more thing. Did your mother know anything more about where your grandfather purchased the vase?"

Macy shook her head. "All I know is that it was shipped very carefully home to a local florist, who added the flowers and delivered them to my grandmother. And that it was from a little shop in Warsaw. Why?"

"Have you ever had it appraised?" Elaine asked.

Again Macy shook her head. "No, I never saw the need. What's with all the questions?"

Elaine glanced at Jan, who began to explain what she'd uncovered about the vase and its possible ties to World War II. Macy listened wide-eyed, a look of disbelief on her face.

"We can't be certain of anything yet," Jan said. "I've e-mailed a researcher for the Holocaust museum, and I'm hoping she can give us some answers."

Twice Elaine checked on their guests in the parlor, and each time she returned, Jan felt confident Archie and Rose had everything under control.

After she caught Macy up on all they knew, Jan and Elaine both watched the other woman, surprised to discover her eyes had the sheen of fresh tears.

"I don't believe that's true." She stood and moved away from the island, perhaps trying to compose herself. "That would mean my grandfather stole it, and I just don't think any-one in my family is capable of such a thing."

"We don't know that for sure," Jan said. "It could've been given to him, or maybe he found it somewhere and just thought it was pretty."

"If the vase is what you say it is, then there's no way my grandfather knew where it had come from. He purchased it in a little flower shop in Warsaw—end of story."

"I'm sure that's true." There was sympathy in Elaine's voice, even if she didn't entirely mean what she said. "There are a lot of unanswered questions, but at the very least, it does seem likely that the vase is valuable. Somebody must've known that and decided to take it for themselves."

"If I'd known any of this, I never would've put that vase in one of the cottages. I would've kept it under lock and key." Macy turned away with a sigh. "So what now?"

"We'd like to go back out to Green Glade and talk with Sarah again," Elaine said. "Her time card and her story don't line up."

Macy hugged her purse. "Well, you won't find her there today. She called in sick."

Elaine looked over at Jan with raised eyebrows.

"Does she do that often?" Elaine asked.

Macy shook her head. "This is the first time she's called in sick since I hired her three years ago."

LATER THAT AFTERNOON, Elaine and Jan stood on the porch of a very small house on the other side of Lancaster.

With peeling white paint and a small, ramshackle porch, the old house needed a lot of work. Beside the door, there was a small black mailbox affixed to the side of the house with metal numbers over it, two of them crooked. Elaine didn't know much about Sarah, but standing here at the address Macy had given them, she had to wonder if the girl was on her own.

Elaine reached up and knocked, but there was no answer—no sound at all for several seconds.

She knocked again, and finally they heard movement inside.

The front door opened and a disheveled Sarah stood on the other side, wearing pajamas under a fluffy pink robe, tied at her waist.

At the sight of them, she smoothed her messy hair and pulled the belt of her robe tighter. "Mrs. Cook, Mrs. Blake, what are you doing here?"

One thing was certain—Sarah Clayton didn't seem to be faking this illness.

"We're sorry to drop in on you like this, Sarah," Jan said. "Macy told us you weren't feeling well, so we brought you some of our homemade tea blend. Now I wonder if I should've whipped you up some homemade chicken soup too."

Sarah waved her off. "I'll be fine. But you're very kind."

Elaine wasn't so sure.

"Why don't we come in and I'll make you a cup?" Jan suggested. "It's very soothing."

Sarah didn't appear to have the strength to protest. Instead, she walked away, leaving the door wide open.

Elaine and Jan followed her inside, closing the door behind them. The house was as run-down inside as it was outside, and Elaine wished she were wealthy and could fix it up for the poor girl.

Of course, being short on cash could be an excellent motive for stealing a valuable vase.

"Do you have a kettle?" Jan made her way into the tiny kitchen, which consisted of only the essentials and very little else.

"Under the sink." Sarah plopped down on the sofa in the living room, which was small. "I can't seem to shake this headache."

"How long have you been sick?" Elaine asked as Jan filled up the kettle.

"I've had a headache for a few days, but today is the worst. And I'm just so tired." She closed her eyes. "I'm sorry to be such a terrible hostess."

"Don't give it a second thought." Elaine moved into the kitchen and found a small rag on the counter. It looked clean, so she ran it under cold water and wrung it out, then took it over to Sarah and set it on her forehead. "My kids always loved a wet washcloth on their forehead when they were sick."

Sarah didn't open her eyes, but nodded ever so slightly. "Thank you."

The kettle whistled and Jan prepared Sarah a cup of tea, setting it down on the table beside the sofa.

"If you can drink some of this, you should," Jan said. "Maybe it will help."

Sarah seemed to force herself to a somewhat sitting position and took a sip of the tea. "That's good." She let her head fall back on to the sofa. "Why are you being so nice to me?"

Elaine laughed. "We try to be nice people."

"Well, you are. Thank you."

They sat in silence for a few seconds and then Jan picked up a framed photo from the table. "Is this your son?"

Sarah opened her eyes. "Dylan."

"He's adorable," Elaine said.

"He's the best." Sarah reached for the frame, smiling at the little boy as if he could see her through the photograph. "He's at school right now."

"Sarah, I know this is terrible timing, but we've been talking about the fire at Green Glade and wondered if we could ask you a few more questions," Elaine said. "About the guest you saw leaving the cottage before you cleaned."

Sarah set the frame back on the table. "I've already told you everything I remember, but if I think of anything else, I'll be sure to let you know."

"Thank you, Sarah," Elaine said. "We just wanted to find out what time it was when you saw Mrs. Rollins leaving the cottage that day."

Sarah covered her face with her hands, rubbing her forehead and most likely wishing away the pain of her headache. Jan glanced over at Elaine with a look that seemed to say *Take it easy on her.* Elaine nodded, and Jan smiled and retreated to the kitchen. Maybe they should have waited to interview her. She hadn't counted on Sarah actually being sick.

The girl propped herself up and took another sip of her tea. "I guess it must've been around one thirty? About an hour before I left."

"Because you left around two thirty," Elaine confirmed.

"That's right. I forgot to punch out that day, so I had to call and ask one of the other housekeepers to do it for me."

"Oh?" Elaine frowned. Sarah hadn't mentioned that before.

Jan moved around in the kitchen—was she cleaning?

"Yes. I had to adjust it with the bookkeeper," Sarah said. "I'm forgetful sometimes."

"Do you have anyone to help you with your son?" Jan asked from behind the kitchen counter.

Sarah shook her head. "Just me."

Jan returned to the room. "That must be difficult."

"He's worth it," Sarah said. She gave Elaine a wan smile.

Elaine knew that feeling. She would do anything for her kids.

"I hope he doesn't catch whatever it is you have. It's always so hard when little ones don't feel well. My son, Brian, was always the worst patient. I think he's even worse as a grown-up." Jan laughed.

Sarah shifted, setting the cup of tea down again as if she couldn't get comfortable. "Actually, I think he gave it to me—whatever it is. He went on an antibiotic so he's doing better. That's why he's at school right now."

Jan only responded with a quiet nod, then went back into the kitchen. Leave it to her cousin to whip that place into shape in the few minutes they were there.

"So Mrs. Rollins left around one thirty," Elaine repeated, trying to lasso the conversation back to the reason they'd come.

"I'm assuming she was there too." Sarah pulled an afghan up to her chin.

Elaine looked at Jan, who'd stopped scrubbing the counter long enough to give Sarah her attention. "What do you mean?"

"I didn't see her." Sarah's eyes fluttered open. "I only saw her husband."

Jan came back into the living room, wiping her hands on a kitchen towel. "Her husband?" Why would Elizabeth lie about her husband being there at the cottage with her?

Sarah shrugged. "I mean, I assume that's who it was. I saw a man leaving the cottage about an hour before I left. I didn't see a woman."

"That's curious," Elaine said. "What did this man look like?"

"He was tall and thin," Sarah said. "Kind of scrawny, actually, but I saw him from a distance, so I didn't get a great look at him. I'm probably not much help, am I?"

Elaine took out a notebook and jotted down Sarah's description. "Actually, you are. Do you remember anything else about him? What was he wearing?"

"A black jacket that came down to about his midthigh, dark sunglasses. He had black hair."

"Could you tell how old he was?" Jan sat on the edge of the sofa. "If you had to guess, I mean."

"I'm bad at guessing ages," Sarah said. "But I think he looked older than I am. Maybe in his thirties? But that's a guess."

Elaine glanced at her notebook. "So a tall, thin, dark-haired man wearing a long black coat left the cottage around one thirty. Do you remember if the vase was there when you went in and cleaned?"

"The truth is, I was kind of in a hurry that day. And I've been doing my job long enough that I pretty much go on auto-pilot, you know? Cleaning toilets isn't mentally difficult work, so my mind wanders. I honestly don't remember."

"Totally understandable. And anyway, we should let you rest," Elaine said. "But I can freshen up your tea before we go."

Sarah moved slowly, but she picked up her cup and handed it to Elaine. "Thank you both. You've both been so nice. I'll have to come visit your tearoom when I feel better."

Elaine moved into the kitchen while Jan told Sarah the tearoom's hours. She didn't know how her cousin had done it, but she'd managed to spruce up the place quite nicely. The kettle sat on the stove, and as she retrieved the milk, her eyes fell to a small dry-erase calendar stuck to the front of the refrigerator.

She quickly scanned it and discovered the typical activities a mom with a young son would write on a calendar—class field trip, soccer practice, their weekend with the class pet.

She glanced at October 3, the day of the fire.

Dylan—Dr. McInnis, 2:00 p.m.

Elaine read it again. Sarah's handwriting was impeccable. There was no denying she'd written 2:00 p.m. on October 3.

But if Sarah had taken Dylan to the doctor at 2:00 p.m., there was no way she left at 2:30...or 2:15 or 2:45 either, for that matter. And if she had lied about what time she'd left work, then Elaine had to wonder—had she seen a man leaving the cottage at all?

CHAPTER THIRTEEN

That afternoon, while Jan settled down with a copy of the new crossword puzzle and a cup of tea, Elaine put on her coat and scarf and headed for the Lancaster Public Library to try to find out more about the Wood family. The desire to know how that ring had ended up in their wall was a constant nagging desire, and it felt appropriate to take a break from the mystery of the vase so she could spend some time working on their other mystery.

Elaine waved hello to Priscilla Gates, the librarian, and headed to the local history section, a section she noted she'd frequented more than usual lately on her search for information about the sapphire ring.

Elaine knew that *The Penzance Courier* hadn't digitized its old files, so for really old editions you could either search through the hard copies in the dusty, dry basement of the library or squint at the strange blue-lit type on the microfiche machine screen. Neither was particularly romantic, but she decided to roll up her sleeves and do the dirty work regardless.

She headed down the stairs and into a small, low-ceilinged room. There was one small transom window, but otherwise the only light came from overhead fluorescents. Filing cabinets with long drawers filled three sides of the room, and one microfiche reader was along the fourth wall.

Elaine consulted the notes she'd taken. *Hmm.* It looked like the factory was started in the late 1880s, so she'd start with 1886 and see what she could come up with.

This was daunting. Sometimes these sorts of tasks delighted her, but right now, thinking of all she had to do, she felt overwhelmed and not particularly energized by the thought of spending her whole day digging. She did want to find out as much as she could about this family, she just

She had an idea. She went back up the stairs and stood at the counter where Priscilla, looking autumnal in a pumpkin turtleneck with a leaf-shaped pin that read, "Fall in love with books," was typing on her computer.

"Need some help, Elaine?" Priscilla looked up cheerily.

"I do. I have the daunting task of potentially searching through half a century of newspaper reports. Any chance you have any ideas for how to streamline the process?"

"So you don't relish the prospect of spending your day buried underground searching through tiny newsprint on a difficult-to-read-screen? I'm shocked." Priscilla joked.

Elaine laughed. "Exactly. As tempting as it sounds." She lifted the shoulder strap of her purse, which had started to slip down her shoulder. "Basically, I'm trying to find information on the Wood family, who I believe owned a wool mill here in the late 1880s."

Priscilla thought for a moment. "How about this? You leave me the names of the people you're interested in and the name of their company, and I'll see what I can dig up for you."

"You would do that?" Elaine felt a load lifting off her shoulders.

"I know searching through the basement isn't everyone's cup of tea, but it's definitely mine," Priscilla said, smiling. "It may take me a few days, since I'll have to work on it around my other duties, but if there's anything in these files, I'll find them."

"You're the best, Priscilla."

"I try," Priscilla winked. "It's my pleasure." And by the smile on her face, Elaine could see that she really meant it.

Elaine stepped out of the library feeling lighter. The sky seemed brighter, even though it remained dark and overcast. She would need to do something nice to thank Priscilla. For now, she was freed up to head back to the tearoom.

LATE FRIDAY AFTERNOON, Jan prepared for her dinner with Bob. She'd decided to invite him over for a home-cooked meal; he'd seemed very excited about the idea and said "It's a date" happily as they hung up the phone.

It still seemed strange to Jan to think of "dating," though she'd never articulated any of her thoughts on the subject out loud.

Jan savored the quiet of the tearoom when both their customers and Rose and Archie had gone home for the day.

She pulled the pork chops from the refrigerator and plunked them into the marinade she'd just prepared. These pork chops had always been a favorite of everyone in her family, and it brightened her mood to think of sharing them with someone new.

To complement the pork chops, she'd decided on roasted red potatoes, green beans, rolls, and for dessert, a homemade apple pie with fresh whipped cream.

"It smells wonderful in here." Elaine inhaled as she entered the room.

"It's the pie." Jan glanced at the timer on the oven. Just a few more minutes and it should be perfect.

"Apple?" Elaine drew in another deep breath.

Jan nodded. "Bob's favorite. He mentioned it once at the farmers' market. There's a baker there—did you know that?"

Elaine sat on the opposite side of the island. "I didn't. You could sell pies at the farmers' market! I bet they'd fly right off your table."

Jan felt heat rush to her cheeks. She always struggled to take a compliment, but she appreciated Elaine's kindness. "Who has the time?"

"Well, Bob is a very lucky man to have a feast like this," Elaine said. "And a companion as wonderful as you."

Jan glanced up from the potatoes on the cutting board. Her cousin was a strong woman and not prone to wearing her heart on her sleeve, but they hadn't talked about Ben lately, and Jan wondered if it was difficult for Elaine to see her spending time with a man. After all, sometimes it was even difficult for Jan, and her Peter had been gone for ten years.

"You're sweet to say so. Hey, I have an idea. You should have dinner with us!"

"Me?" Elaine shook her head. "I don't want to intrude. Besides, I've already planned a date for myself with a new novel I've been wanting to read."

"It will be so much fun. Bob is a wonderful conversationalist, and I would love for us all to spend an evening together."

Elaine smiled warmly. "You don't have to do that, Jan. I truly am fine. And I want you to know how very happy I am that you've found such a wonderful man to spend time with."

Jan wiped her hands off on a dish towel. "It's still hard sometimes—having feelings for someone else."

Elaine covered Jan's hands with her own. "Peter would want you to be happy."

Jan's eyes filled with fresh tears. "You really think so?"

"I know so, Jan. Ben and Peter are gone, but we are still here. We can't close ourselves off from new friendships or the possibility of love. They wouldn't want that."

Jan pressed her lips together and looked away as a soft tear trickled down her cheek. "Thank you for saying that." She didn't realize she needed to hear it, but her sudden emotion told her she did.

Elaine squeezed Jan's hands. "I should've said it weeks ago, from the looks of it. I'm sorry I didn't."

Jan shook her head. "No, the timing is perfect." She met Elaine's eyes. "I really like him, Elaine." Sometimes she liked him so much it scared her a little. It was almost as if Elaine had known that even though Jan hadn't said a word.

JAN'S INSISTENCE THAT Elaine join her and Bob for dinner had eventually won Elaine over, though she wondered if she'd feel like a third wheel with the two of them. Of course she meant the things she'd said to her cousin. Peter would want her to be happy, but Ben's death was still too new to consider such a thing for herself. Part of her felt like a hypocrite giving that advice when she doubted she'd ever take it. She couldn't imagine ever feeling differently—she still ached for Ben every single day.

Thankfully, she and Jan and Bob had all been classmates many moons ago, so she hoped that would give them fodder for their dinner conversation.

With dinner in the oven and the house smelling heavenly, Jan had disappeared upstairs to change clothes and freshen up, giving Elaine a few solitary minutes in the office. She glanced over her calendar, making a note to pay the electric bill on Monday, then clicked open the Tea for Two e-mail account.

She was scanning through the new messages, deleting the spam e-mails, when her eyes settled on one with the subject line "Valuable Vase."

Elaine remembered Jan had e-mailed someone online hoping for insight into the value of Macy's vase—she must've sent it from their work e-mail. While she fleetingly considered waiting for Jan to open it, her curiosity got the better of her.

Dear Ms. Blake,

Thank you for writing to me about your vase. Of course, it's diffi-cult to tell anything from a photograph, but if your vase is what I think it is, I'm very intrigued.

Her reading was interrupted by the sound of the doorbell.

Bob was right on time. *Oh, Bob, why are you so punctual?* She sent the e-mail to the printer and walked out of the office.

"I'll get it," Elaine hollered up the stairs, knowing Jan was probably still getting ready.

She welcomed Bob, hung his coat on the hook by the door, and ushered him into the dining room.

"Thank you for coming to dinner tonight," Elaine said. "And for allowing me to join you."

At Elaine's request, Jan had called Bob to be sure he wouldn't mind her joining them. Somehow, now that he'd arrived, she didn't feel awkward about it at all. It was almost like three old friends were about to spend an evening together and not like she was crashing a date. She supposed Bob's friendli-ness had something to do with that.

He smiled. "My pleasure. I never pass up a home-cooked meal with two beautiful ladies."

Now Elaine might be the one blushing. "Well, we appreci-ate it. I'm going to go check on Jan. Can I bring you a drink? We have lemonade."

"Sounds perfect."

Not too many minutes later, Jan appeared in the kitchen and Elaine helped her bring the food out to the table.

"Something smells wonderful." Bob stood as they walked in. "Can I help?"

"Of course not. You're our guest." Jan flashed him a smile.

He sat as Elaine set his drink above his plate. Once everything had been assembled, they all took their seats, said grace, and began eating.

"This is wonderful, Jan," Bob said.

Elaine liked that he complimented Jan, and while Jan would never say so, and it likely embarrassed her, she imagined her cousin liked it too. That kind of attention was always welcome, especially from a handsome suitor.

As they ate, Bob caught them up on his latest news. He was in the middle of a particularly tedious case. As a lawyer, he had several of those, but he seemed to take it all in stride. He had a nonchalance about him that suited him so well. "Enough about my week," he said. "What have the two of you been up to?"

Together, Jan and Elaine explained their thoughts on what had happened at Macy's while Bob listened intently. Jan told him about their visit to Elizabeth Rollins and how they'd seen the story about Macy's vase with notes all over it, despite the fact that she'd told them she didn't know much about it. Elaine explained the discrepancies in Sarah's story, specifically that she'd claimed to have left at two thirty that day, but her calendar told a different story.

"Then there's the question of the man Sarah says she saw outside the cottage," Jan said, just before taking a sip of her lemonade. "We have so many questions right now that I'm afraid we may never discover what really happened to that vase."

"I have faith in you two. Did those books turn up any more information?"

"Oh!" Elaine gasped. How had she forgotten the e-mail? She rushed into the office and pulled the sheet of paper from the printer. "I got so caught up in dinner I forgot about this," she said when she returned to the dining room. "We got an e-mail from that researcher you wrote to. The one we hoped might know something about the vase."

Jan glanced at Bob. "We found a photo in one of the books—it was of a vase that looked a lot like the one we're looking for. The caption said something about its being one of a trio but that the others were missing." She leaned closer to Elaine so they could read the e-mail together.

"'Dear Ms. Blake,'" Elaine read out loud. "'Thank you for writing to me about your vase. Of course, it's difficult to tell anything from a photograph, but if your vase is what I think it is, I'm very intrigued. It appears to me that this vase might be the missing piece from a very important collection, one of three that were stolen during World War II.'"

Jan gasped, her eyes wide. "It's as we suspected."

Elaine continued. "'Without having the actual vase, I can't be certain, of course, but there were three of these pieces made in the early twentieth century and given to prominent Jewish families before the war. During the war, however, all three went missing.'"

Jan covered her mouth with her hand, shaking her head slowly. "This is unbelievable."

Elaine scanned the next paragraph. "She says the other two vases have already been recovered and are in a museum in

Washington, DC." She glanced up, aware she had both Jan and Bob's full attention, then continued reading. "As you can imagine, these vases are very valuable on their own, but to complete the trio would increase the value not only of your vase, but of all three. To many, they are priceless."

"Priceless?" Jan breathed the word in a whisper.

"You don't think she actually means they're *priceless*?" Elaine asked.

"She does say 'to many' they are priceless. Perhaps they are extremely valuable, but their origin and the fact that they're missing World War II artifacts makes them more so?" Bob finished his last bite. "Does she say anything else?"

Elaine's eyes fell back to the paper in her hands. "'I would love the opportunity to see your vase for myself to authenticate it and possibly discuss adding it to the collection at the museum. I'm sure we could come to some sort of agreement that was mutually beneficial. Please let me know if this is possible at your earliest convenience. Sincerely, Jenna Kushman.'"

Elaine met Jan's wide eyes. "Do you really think it's possible that Macy's vase was stolen Nazi plunder?"

Jan frowned. "If it is…" She stopped, as if she was unsure she should admit her feelings out loud.

"Jan?"

"If we do track down the thief and recover the vase, how do we give it back to Macy?" She glanced up, an embarrassed expression on her face. "Not that I would keep it from her, of course, but if this is true, and the vase was stolen from a prominent Jewish family during the war, it didn't rightfully belong to her either."

"True," Bob said. "But maybe you should cross that bridge after you've recovered the vase?"

"I agree," Elaine said. "No sense borrowing trouble."

With a priceless antique missing and at least two women who weren't being entirely truthful, Elaine and Jan certainly had more than enough trouble already.

CHAPTER FOURTEEN

After church on Sunday morning, Elaine and Jan decided to spend some time in the yard. Leaves littered their front lawn and Elaine had wanted to add splashes of color with pots of mums on the front porch. Jan's friend's son Reggie had done some landscaping for them when they'd first bought the house, but they had decided to maintain it themselves to the best of their ability.

They came home and changed out of their church clothes and Jan whipped up a quick lunch of BLTs and chips just for the two of them. Elaine reminded her of the times their grandma had made them BLTs followed by root beer floats and suddenly they each found themselves craving one.

How long had it been since Jan had had a root beer float?

"Why don't we get some ice cream and root beer when we pick up the mums?" Jan suggested, her mouth watering.

Elaine grinned widely. "I can't think of a better way to spend a Sunday afternoon."

Once they'd finished eating, they donned their jackets and walked outside to find several of their neighbors in their yards too. Faith Lanier was positioning a homemade scarecrow on the porch of A Little Something, and off in the other direction, Mark Payson was pressure-washing the front of the Bookworm while his wife, Bristol, cleaned out the flower boxes.

Jan and Elaine waved to each of their neighbors as they walked over to Murphy's General Store, thankful there was a place so close by where they could purchase both ice cream and potted flowers. While they were there, Jo insisted on giving them two hay bales and a few cornstalks "to beautify their gorgeous front porch."

Of course, both of the cousins protested, but Jo let them in on the secret that they made her sneeze and she really needed them out of the store.

In that case, Jan decided they could oblige and Jo promised to have them delivered straightaway.

Once they'd made their purchases, they happily walked back home, content to drink in what could very likely be the last of the year's warmth. They both knew this unseasonable sunshine should not be wasted.

"Should we indulge in our floats right away or reward ourselves after an afternoon of yard work?" Jan asked as they walked into their kitchen.

"Practically speaking, we should probably wait." Elaine stuck the root beer in the refrigerator and the ice cream in the freezer. "Maybe it'll make the work go more quickly."

Jan nodded, but as she did, she realized that while she loved the promise of ice cream as much as the next person, she also loved working in the yard. It felt good to own this home with her cousin, and making it beautiful had become more than a pastime. It had become a joy and a privilege.

Outside, they scooped up leaves and bagged them in yard waste sacks, stacking them neatly at the curb. They cleared out their flower beds and swept the front porch. Once the hay bales and cornstalks arrived, they spent a good deal of time getting them in just the right spot on the front porch to make their house and tearoom look inviting and full of autumn cheer.

By the time they finished, the sun had dipped down on the horizon and Jan's stomach was growling. Jan felt a wonderful sense of accomplishment as she stood back and admired all that she and Elaine had done that afternoon.

"I think we've certainly earned our root beer floats." Jan glanced at her cousin, who was still staring at the house. She sometimes admired the large Victorian herself—the space, the porch, the tower. It was a beautiful home. But something in Elaine's eyes told Jan it wasn't admiration she was feeling.

"Are you okay?" Jan asked quietly.

Elaine sniffed, then dabbed at the corner of her eyes. "I don't know what came over me. I'm just happy, I suppose."

Jan watched her for a long moment. Elaine was a strong, independent type—something Jan often admired about her cousin. But finding herself alone had surely been a shock. It warmed her heart to think that their partnership was exactly what they both needed.

"Sometimes I have to pinch myself," Elaine said. "I still can't believe we've really done this."

Jan wrapped an arm around Elaine's shoulder. "Not only have we done it, but people actually love it."

Elaine swiped away an unwanted tear. "You're right. They do!"

"Now, let's go get ourselves a well-deserved treat and spend the evening on the screened-in porch." Jan led the way inside the house. As she scooped the vanilla ice cream into two large glasses, she said a silent prayer of thanks that God had seen fit to bring her and Elaine back together in this season of their lives.

JAN AND ELAINE were up early Monday morning. According to Macy, Brett and the rest of the staff at Green Glade started their morning shift at seven o'clock, which was perfect because they could get out there and confirm a few lingering details before Tea for Two opened for the day.

"I got the invitation for Tara's jewelry event at A Little Something." Elaine backed her car out of the garage. "That's sweet of Faith to showcase her like that."

"Faith said Tara's jewelry is just flying out of the shop." Jan beamed at the thought of it. She'd never dreamed that Tara would settle down in Lancaster, just a few minutes away from her, but she was certainly happy she had. Of course there was always the possibility of her running off to the big city, but Jan had decided to enjoy every moment with her daughter, and this Meet the Artist event Faith had put together seemed like the perfect way to do that.

"I'm not surprised. I love the little silver hoop earrings she made me for Christmas last year." Elaine waved to the Paysons, who were just arriving at the Bookworm.

"She does have quite a talent." Jan glanced to her wrist. The gold bracelet she wore had been one of Tara's early pieces—and she'd given it to Jan.

They reached Green Glade just as a Jeep Wrangler pulled into the parking lot beside the clubhouse. The music was especially loud and seemed out of place with the quiet morning and peaceful setting. Elaine turned off the engine of her own car and they watched as the driver moved his head along to the music, as if he needed to enjoy just a few extra seconds of the song before he could turn it off.

Finally, the driver emerged from the Jeep and Jan wasn't surprised to see Brett, looking a bit disheveled. She got the impression he wasn't a morning person, but there was something wonderfully innocent about him. She suspected the young man had a knack for tardiness, given that according to her watch, he was ten minutes late for his shift.

They hung back for a few seconds, watching him enter through a back door—most likely an employee's entrance. Once he disappeared inside, Jan and Elaine made their way to the clubhouse.

As they entered, they were greeted by the faint smell of coffee, which, according to the Green Glade literature, was brewed fresh every hour. Guests were welcome to help themselves throughout the day. Personally, Jan would've preferred a cup of tea, but thankfully Macy sent her guests their way for that.

With the exception of a couple reading over by the fireplace, the clubhouse was empty. They approached the empty counter.

"You were late again, Brett," an unseen female voice called out.

"Did you cover for me?" Brett's voice responded.

"Lucky for you I did," the girl said.

Jan and Elaine exchanged a look and Jan imagined they were both wondering the same thing. How often did Macy's employees "cover" for each other? And more importantly—had one of them covered for Sarah on October the third?

"You're the best, Rubes." Brett appeared in the doorway off to the side, his expression changing as soon as he saw Jan and Elaine.

"I already know that." Ruby, the other housekeeper gave him a little push. "You owe me..." Her voice trailed off as she followed Brett's gaze to the two of them.

"Mrs. Blake, Mrs. Cook," Brett said, pretending like nothing had happened. "What brings you two lovely ladies out here?"

Oh, this boy was charming, Jan thought. He was a little too handsome for his own good, and if she was reading the situation correctly, Ruby had noticed. Jan found the two of them adorable, despite their poor choices when it came to their employment. She would play along.

"Good morning, Brett," Elaine said. "We're sorry to intrude so early today."

"Not a problem."

"It smells wonderful in here," Jan said. "Like a really good cup of coffee."

"Oh, the coffee's the best," Brett said. "Mrs. Atherton's son, Shane, found this awesome local place where they roast the beans fresh every week. Ruined me for the store-bought kind, that's for sure. You want me to get you a cup?"

"That would be nice." Jan drank coffee only on rare occasions, but she figured it might be smart to make an exception.

"I'll get it," Ruby said.

"What about you, Mrs. Cook?" Brett asked. "Fancy a cup of joe?" His grin was lopsided and reminded Jan of Brian when he was about eight years old.

Elaine returned the smile but politely refused the coffee.

"How can I help you ladies today?" Brett leaned against the counter.

"We were hoping you could confirm something for us," Elaine said. "The guest who was staying in Escape the day of the fire—do you have a record of when she checked out?"

"Do I ever!" Brett cracked his knuckles dramatically, then started clicking around on the computer. "What was the name again?"

"Elizabeth Rollins," Jan said. Ruby returned with her coffee and Jan smiled in thanks.

"Here she is," Brett said. "Says here she checked out at 11:27."

So Elizabeth was telling the truth about that.

"Was she alone when she was here?" Elaine asked.

"According to this she was," Brett said, consulting his computer screen. "Unless she had friends over or something."

Ruby shrugged. "I didn't see anyone visiting her, but like I told you before, I didn't see the guest either."

Then who was the man Sarah saw? And given the holes in this timeline—what time did she actually see him?

"Do you remember seeing her that day?" Elaine asked.

"Sarah was assigned to clean that cottage that day." Ruby looked away.

"Sarah said she forgot to clock out that day. It was nice of you to do that for her."

Brett glanced at Ruby. "She took the extra time off her time card the next day. She made it right." Ruby looked uncomfortable.

"Just tell them," Brett whispered to Ruby, who shot him a look most likely intended to shut him up.

Brett didn't take the hint. "Sarah left early that day." They'd suspected as much, but having proof was certainly welcome.

Ruby smacked his arm. "Brett!"

"She didn't do anything wrong." Brett's eyes were on Ruby, then he turned to Jan and Elaine. "She didn't do anything wrong," he repeated.

"We were just watching out for each other," Ruby said. "Her son was really sick, so I took some of Sarah's workload that day."

"Escape?" Jan frowned.

"No, that was Sarah's last cottage before she left for a doctor's appointment. I think she was running late, though, and I'm pretty sure she rushed through it."

"What makes you say that?" Jan asked.

"She left the linens on the porch," Ruby said, as if there was an obvious implication in that statement. "We always have to take them to the laundry, but she forgot. Our job is kind of monotonous. We have a routine, and Sarah was so frazzled that she forgot one of the basics. It wasn't like her. I didn't want her to lose the day's pay, so I helped. She's got enough problems and...it was the least I could do."

Poor girl. Single mother with a sick kid trying to juggle a job that she desperately needed and a mound of medical bills she couldn't afford. Jan felt sorry for her, even if the financial trouble did give Sarah a motive to steal the vase.

"I think Sarah was so worked up that day because she felt like she was being dishonest," Ruby said. Jan understood the reasoning, but it didn't change the fact that Sarah *was* being dishonest, not only the day of the fire, but every time she said she left at two thirty.

"Yeah, if you knew her, you'd know she could never steal from Mrs. Atherton, or from anybody," Brett said. "And she definitely couldn't start a fire. Not her style."

Sadly, Brett's word wasn't proof of anything. Desperate people did crazy things. Was Sarah desperate enough to commit a crime?

"What time did she actually leave Green Glade that day?" Elaine asked.

Ruby looked away. Jan understood her hesitation— she didn't want to rat on her friend. "We just want to get to the bottom of this. We aren't trying to get anyone in trouble."

Ruby met her eyes. "She left around one thirty."

"And you punched her out around two forty-five?"

"Yes, I completely forgot to do it, and it took me a little longer than I thought it would to get my work and Sarah's finished." Ruby stilled. "I'm really sorry I didn't tell you all this in the first place."

"Hey." Something on Brett's screen pulled his attention. "Don't know if this matters, but that Rollins woman has stayed in Escape before."

Elaine shot Jan a look. Elizabeth hadn't mentioned that. "When?"

"In April. Same exact cottage. She must've requested it."

So Elizabeth Rollins would've received Macy's story about the vase all the way back in April, and she hadn't said a word about it when they were at her house.

The only question was...Why?

Before they left Green Glade, Jan asked Ruby to allow her and Elaine to walk through Escape one more time. Ruby led them out to the charred cottage and opened the door.

"I don't think you're going to find anything else." She stood back, allowing them to pass through.

"Maybe not, but I just want to walk through it one more time."

The cottage hadn't changed, though Jan hadn't expected it to. The place still smelled like smoke, and while the floor and walls were no longer damp, they were certainly still charred.

Jan walked toward the kitchen, trying to see things differently than she had initially. What had they missed? Was it really faulty wiring that had caused that fire? Or had there been some sort of foul play made to look like faulty wiring?

She leaned across the stove and checked the electrical outlets, then knelt down to look inside the stove. As she ran her hand across the oven, she noticed one of the knobs was considerably looser than the others.

"That's odd," Jan said.

"What is it?" Elaine asked, joining her in the kitchen.

"This knob is very loose," Jan said as her cousin inspected the stove for herself.

"Do you think someone loosened it?"

"Seems like there would be easier ways to start a fire, don't you think?" Elaine knelt down and examined the loose knob for herself.

"Maybe it was an accident," Jan said.

"What are you thinking?" Elaine stood upright.

"Sarah was in a hurry that day," Jan said. "What if she wasn't careful around the loose knob and accidentally left the natural gas on?"

Elaine shrugged. "I suppose it's possible, and it seems more likely than Sarah purposely starting the fire. It's just a hunch, but she doesn't seem capable of committing a crime like this."

"Then I suppose we need to keep digging until we find out who is."

CHAPTER FIFTEEN

It's almost time to go," Jan called down the hall toward Elaine's room. They'd had a wonderful day at the tearoom with a whole group of brand-new customers who'd come over from Waterville. Apparently the women Macy had intruded upon weren't completely run off, as they were the ones who'd sent a group of friends the tearoom's way with very high praise.

Tonight, though, was not about tea or customers or even about baking. Tonight was about Tara.

Jan had spoken to her daughter earlier in the day, and she could hear the buzz of excitement in her voice. She'd stopped in for a cup of tea and a pastry, and Jan had been able to steal away for a few minutes to chat.

"I hope people show up," Tara had said when Jan sat down across from her.

"Oh, they will," Jan said. "I've seen three women in here just today wearing jewelry I'm sure you designed. Faith said she's having trouble keeping it in the store."

Tara's cheeks turned a warm rose color the way they always had when she was a little embarrassed. But this wasn't something to be embarrassed by—it was cause for pride. Jan couldn't be sure, but she might have enough of that for the two of them.

"It's going to be a wonderful evening," Jan said. "Are you sure you don't need me to bring anything?"

Tara swallowed her bite of cream puff and smiled. "I'm sure, Mom. I don't want you to lift a finger."

"Will Amy and her family be there? And Brian and Paula and the girls?"

"I think so. At least Brian and Paula and the girls will be. Avery and Kelly made me promise to save them each a bangle bracelet," Tara said.

Jan's heart swelled at the thought of her family together celebrating just one of the many things they had to celebrate.

Now, though, she couldn't find the necklace she wanted to wear and she was panicking a little over the fact that they needed to leave in a matter of minutes.

Elaine appeared in the hallway wearing a flowy flowered skirt and an adorable sweater set. She held her hands up behind her ears, drawing Jan's attention straight to the little silver hoops Tara had given her.

"They're just perfect, aren't they?" Elaine waggled her eyebrows in a way that reminded Jan of when they were younger. "Are you all ready?"

Jan took one last look at herself in the mirror. "I was looking for my gold necklace, the one with the cross on it."

Her dressy black pants and tunic top seemed to need a little something special.

"Why don't you just plan on finding a new one when we're there?" Elaine suggested. "Surely we want to do something to support our girl."

Jan loved the idea, and she loved Elaine for suggesting it. "That sounds perfect to me."

They turned off the lights downstairs, grabbed their jackets, and walked over to Faith's store. Outside she'd hung white lights and the store was lit from the inside, casting a soft orange glow on the lawn out front. Even from a distance, Jan could tell the event was going to be beautiful.

Already there were several cars parked around A Little Something, and they watched as a few different groups of people made their way inside.

"You must be very excited for Tara," Elaine said. "It sure seems like Lancaster is excited to support her."

"I am," Jan agreed. "Faith did a wonderful job of publicizing this celebration. I'm not sure she's ever done something like this for a local artist, but I think it's a wonderful idea."

Faith had hung posters around town and sent out beautiful postcards inviting all the local business owners to stop in and meet "talented local jewelry designer Tara Blake." Oh, Jan had been thrilled to see those words in print. Brian was a bit more skeptical, wishing his sister would choose a "more sensible" career, but Tara was so happy—what more could a mother want?

"The write-up in the newspaper was a nice touch," Elaine said. "A meet and greet with the artist is just so exciting."

Jan pulled open the door to A Little Something and she and Elaine walked inside. The shop was by no means upscale, but tonight it certainly seemed to have taken a step in that direction. There were white lights dangling from the ceiling and sprigs of fresh autumn flowers neatly positioned around the store. Faith had cleared out a section near the back, just off to the side of the sales counter, for a full display of Tara's most recent jewelry.

"There she is." Jan stifled the urge to giggle. "She looks so elegant."

Tara was dressed in a beautiful, simple black dress with black heels and just a touch of embellishment. The silver necklace around her neck dangled happily, a perfect match to the earrings that sparkled in her ears.

The store buzzed with activity, and there seemed to be no particular age or demographic attending. There were teenage girls slipping on bracelets and women older than Jan and Elaine looking in the mirror while holding earrings up to their ears. Everyone seemed to love Tara's work.

As they walked through the crowd toward the back of the store, Jan overheard words like "rare talent" and "elegantly simple." She made mental notes so she could share with Tara just as soon as her daughter got a free moment.

"Grandma!"

Jan recognized Avery's voice and turned in her direction. The girl was wearing a cute dress Jan had only seen her wear to church on Sundays, and she wiggled her fingers at Jan, as if to draw her attention to her hand.

Jan glanced down and saw a silver ring, handcrafted in the perfect size for Avery's little finger.

"Aunt Tara made it special just for me," Avery said.

"It's almost as beautiful as you are. Where are your mom and dad?"

"Over there with Aunt Amy. Uncle Van is home with the boys." Avery pointed, and Jan followed her gaze to a table with punch, sparkling cider, and trays of finger foods on it.

"Ah, your dad found the food, I see." Jan laughed and ushered the girl back to where Brian and his wife, Paula, were chatting quietly with Amy and a tall man and a woman Jan assumed was his wife.

"Hey, Mom," Brian said as Amy hugged her mother.

The older couple turned and faced them and only then did Jan recognize the woman: Elizabeth Rollins. The other woman's face lit with recognition. "Jan! Elaine! So good to see you both again."

Brian's brow furrowed. "You know each other?"

Jan nodded, feeling suddenly awkward. "We met recently. How've you been, Elizabeth?"

Elizabeth linked an arm through her husband's. "Good, now that my book is turned in and I've got Walter back."

Jan gave the man a discreet once-over. Sarah had described the man she saw as "tall and thin," but Elizabeth's husband was only one of those. The man was stocky with an ample belly hanging over his dress pants. He had silvery hair and a very distinguished appearance.

"Walter, this is Jan Blake and Elaine Cook. They own that adorable tearoom I told you about." Elizabeth looked elegant in a sparkly black top with a simple pair of black dress pants.

Walter turned toward Jan and Elaine. "I've heard all about your tearoom. Sounds like my Bess had her share of maple something-or-other while she was there. Maybe I can get a sample of those the next time we're in town."

"I'd be happy to share them anytime," Jan said.

"Walter, Elizabeth tells us you've just been away on a little trip. Somewhere warm, I hope." Elaine's casual change of topic was the perfect escape for Brian, who was likely counting the minutes until he could go home. He turned back toward the refreshment table and started filling his appetizer plate.

"I do a golf trip twice a year down in Florida," Walter said. He took out his phone and swiped it to life. Seconds later, he was showing them both a photo of four men—one of them Walter—posed on what appeared to be a beautiful golf course.

Jan noticed the man did seem a bit tanner than most people in Lancaster this time of year. They had no reason to doubt Elizabeth's husband had been exactly where she said he was the day of the Green Glade fire, but there was still the lingering question of that paper Elizabeth had accidentally shown them. What possible reason did she have to lie about having been to Green Glade before and having taken a special interest in Macy's vase?

"What brings you two here tonight?" Elaine's question halted Jan's wandering imagination.

Elizabeth glanced up at Walter. "We're on a date." She smiled as if she'd just told them a secret. "And Faith is a good friend of mine. She carries my books in her store."

At that moment, Faith Lanier entered the room looking absolutely dazzling. Jan thought perhaps the folks of Lancaster should dress up more often—they certainly did it well.

Faith whisked her way through the room, stopping to talk with various people along the way, but when she spotted them, she made a beeline in their direction. When she reached them, she greeted them all with a hug, taking a special moment with Jan to tell her how proud she was of Tara.

"Thank you again for doing all of this," Jan said. "It's just such a fun evening for all of us to celebrate."

"And it gets people in the store. Your Tara is quite the draw."

Jan looked around. She had to agree.

"I can't take all the credit though. I got the idea from one of Elizabeth's book signings." Faith pulled Elizabeth into a quick hug. "So glad you made it tonight."

"You have book signings here?" Elaine asked. Surely the reader in her was excited to hear it.

Elizabeth nodded. "We've been doing it for years."

Walter wrapped a beefy arm around his wife. "She brings in a big crowd too."

Faith held up a finger as if she'd just remembered something. "Be right back." She vanished for mere seconds, and when she returned, she handed all of them a postcard. On it was a photo of Elizabeth and a book titled *The Secret Within*.

"I thought you didn't write mysteries," Elaine said.

Elizabeth shrugged. "Oh, it's not a mystery. It's a romance." She waggled her eyebrows.

Jan's eyes scanned the text underneath the details for Elizabeth's upcoming book signing, which was still several months away. *The Secret Within* was about a modern-day woman who uncovered the true story behind a vase of flowers her grandfather, a soldier in World War II, had sent to his young wife. The last line on the postcard read *Present day collides with the past as one woman sets out to uncover why the flowers made it home, but the soldier did not.*

"Doesn't it sound gripping?" Faith asked. "I'm going to read it with tissues. I'm going to need tissues, aren't I?"

Elizabeth's eyes glimmered. "If I did my job right you are."

A cell phone buzzed and Walter excused himself. "Maybe it's the airline with an update about my luggage."

"I should go mingle. And see if Tara needs anything." Faith walked off.

Tara, yes. This was her night. Jan should concentrate on Tara. And yet the coincidence she'd just discovered had stolen her attention.

When they were alone, Elizabeth seemed to avoid their eyes. Elaine and Jan exchanged a confused expression, but neither seemed to know what to say.

Finally, Elizabeth spoke. "I wasn't entirely forthcoming with you before. I have been under a lot of stress to get this book finished, but none of my ideas were working." Elizabeth motioned for Jan and Elaine to step off to the side, away from the rest of the people. "I stayed at Green Glade once before. I was determined to get that book finished, but when I was there, I read the story of Macy's vase, and I started to let my imagination run wild. I have a tendency to do that."

"Seems like a good trait for an author to have." Elaine picked up one of the glasses of punch from the refreshment table and took a drink.

"I didn't know how Macy would feel about my using her story as inspiration for my book," Elizabeth said. "And last week, I was just about to finish up my final edits and thought it would be wonderfully poetic to do that right there in the cottage that inspired it in the first place. Walter was out of town and I had nothing else to do, so I went."

"Did you have any visitors while you were at Green Glade? Or see anyone hanging around?" Elaine asked.

Elizabeth shook her head. "Not that I saw. I'm afraid when I get in my writing zone, I'm not very observant."

Jan nodded, still trying to put it all together.

"I'm distraught about this vase," Elizabeth said. "It obviously means a great deal to Macy—and, in a way, to me. It's a shame someone would steal it. I wish I could be more help, but when I left that morning, the vase was still on the mantel." Elizabeth took out her phone and pulled up a photo.

Jan and Elaine leaned in and saw the image of Macy's vase, exactly in the spot where it should've been.

"I was planning to tell the story of Green Glade and how I was inspired by my visit there once the book came out," Elizabeth explained. "I took this photo because I thought it would make a nice visual. And look..." She clicked a few buttons on the phone until she revealed a time stamp. October 3 at eleven in the morning. "Of course, now I am afraid I'll look guilty of stealing it. But I didn't. I swear I didn't."

CHAPTER SIXTEEN

The following day, Elaine sat in her office rereading Jenna Kushman's e-mail. While she couldn't be certain, it seemed like this Jenna had done extensive research about this trio of vases, and given that she'd e-mailed two more times to attempt to set up a video chat to talk more about it, she seemed very interested in the vase's whereabouts.

How would they tell her they didn't actually have it in their possession?

Elaine clicked out of her e-mail and went through the motions of the bookkeeping duties, wishing she knew the truth about that vase. They had no proof it was stolen Nazi plunder that belonged with the other two pieces—only suspicion. In fact, did they know for certain it was from the World War II era at all?

As she stewed about it for several long seconds, she thought perhaps it was time to ask an expert about this vase—and she happened to know the perfect one.

Elaine glanced up at the clock. They would open in less than an hour, and judging by the delicious aroma wafting in from the kitchen, Jan was ready. She closed her books and found her cousin standing over the sink, washing up the last of the dishes she'd dirtied. They had a state-of-the-art dishwasher, but Jan still washed over half of their dishes by hand. She said it relaxed her.

"Tara's event last night was just lovely." Elaine poured herself a cup of tea. "Such a great turnout, and from what I understand, Faith had to place another order."

Jan's face brightened. "Isn't it wonderful?" She turned off the water and dried her hands on a dish towel.

Elaine sipped her tea. "What do you think about handling things around here this morning without me?"

Jan met her eyes. "Is everything okay?"

"Oh yes. I was just thinking I might drive over to Waterville and talk to Nathan about our vase. Jenna sent another e-mail, and I would feel better having another opinion before we respond." She filled her in on the contents of the latest message, hoping her cousin would agree that a trip to see Nathan Culver could be beneficial.

"Nathan! What a wonderful idea! Yes, go. Rose and Archie and I can handle everything here."

Elaine thanked her, then grabbed her purse and jacket and gloves as she headed out the door. During the drive to Nathan's, her mind wandered. She started off thinking about all the unknowns surrounding the fire and the missing vase. Perhaps the fire was an accident after all and not the distraction they originally thought—though that would be some coincidence, wouldn't it?

As hard as it was to believe, Sarah still looked guilty. She had the opportunity to steal the vase, she lied to them more than once, and she had a financial need that could potentially lead to surprising behavior. However, Sarah hardly seemed like the criminal type.

But then, people did crazy things all the time, especially when it came to the care of a child, and Sarah was all alone on that front.

She hoped Nathan would be able to help her at least determine if the vase really was what Jenna Kushman seemed to think it was. She parked in the vast parking lot in front of Nathan's auction house and turned off the engine. Culver Auctions was famous around these parts and had been for years. Elaine could still remember spending days as a girl racing through the swarms of people who turned up every time the doors were open. There was such excitement in the air at an auction. Some folks were serious bidders and others came just for fun, but either way, Nathan's family welcomed them in.

As an auctioneer, Nathan had more experience with antiques and heirlooms than most people, so Elaine was hopeful he might be able to shed some light on the value or origin of this vase. Though their research had been thorough, she supposed she was looking for confirmation. If anyone could point her in the right direction, Nathan could.

She exited her car and walked up the sidewalk toward the auction hall—a one-story building that bore a striking resemblance to a barn.

Inside, the spacious room stretched out in front of her, and for a fleeting moment, she heard the echo of voices in the back of her mind. She could recall the energy and excitement, the buzz of activity, so easily it was almost as if the auction hall wasn't empty.

She made her way through the sales hall and toward Nathan's office, off to the left, past the registration booth where a person would go to get a bidding card on the day of an auction. While she'd never expected Nathan to go into the family business, it certainly suited him. Her friend had done well for himself—and she wasn't surprised. He was one of the smartest people she knew.

Nathan had been one of her oldest friends thanks to the friendship of their fathers, but she'd assumed he'd remain in the past like so many other old friends. It made her quite happy that wasn't the case. When she moved back to Lancaster, they had picked up where they left off, and she was grateful for his unique friendship.

She found the door to his office open and the desk empty. She should've called first. What if Nathan was out for the day? She hadn't noticed his car in the lot, though if she remembered correctly, he parked around on the other side of the building.

"Hello?" she called out.

She heard movement in the back of the sales hall and then Nathan appeared in a doorway. "Well, my, my. To what do I owe this honor?"

Elaine flashed a smile that matched his. "I was in the neighborhood."

He gave her a playful frown. "I'm not buying it. Just admit you missed me and you had to rush on over here to get your fix."

Elaine rolled her eyes playfully. "You think I'm here on a social call?"

He walked toward her. "Why else?"

She scrunched her nose. She needed a favor and she hated to ask, even though she was quite certain he'd be more than willing to help.

"Out with it, Cook. What is it this time?"

"I wondered if you could help me with something."

He held up a hand, as if to stop her. "Only if you'll tell me about it over coffee. There's a great little shop down the street that just opened. I like to support local business—especially if they're making a good cup of joe."

Elaine nodded. "Sounds perfect to me, though you know I'll be having tea."

He slipped his jacket on. "Come on, live a little. The hard stuff won't hurt you."

She laughed. "I'm not quite desperate enough for the hard stuff. At least not yet." A strong cup of tea would do her well.

They walked outside and Elaine drew in a deep, crisp breath, once again smitten with this New England autumn. Of all the places she'd lived, nowhere had gotten into her bones quite like Maine. The seasons were among her favorite things about her home state. The seasons, the sea, the color, the people— she loved it all. Funny to think of it now when it hadn't been too many months ago she'd been in deep mourning for the loss of her husband.

For a while, she wondered if she'd ever be happy again.

And in that very moment, she realized she had begun to have more happy moments than unhappy ones. She whispered a silent prayer of thanks. God's hand had been on her all along, even in the midst of her heartache.

As they walked down the sidewalk, Elaine caught him up on the party they'd attended for Tara and he recounted a particularly excellent golf game he'd had over the weekend—one of the last, he feared, before winter took hold.

Conversation with Nathan came easily to her, perhaps because of their long history. It was good to have a friend, and she couldn't ask for a kinder one.

They arrived at The Java Hut, a small coffee shop on the corner of two sleepy streets in downtown Waterville. Outlined by two full walls of windows, the space was full of natural light, though it still managed a cozy feel with its rustic wooden accents and richly colored seating. Behind the counter, the menu had been handwritten on chalkboards divided into four panels, and overhead, vintage silver lights that looked like they belonged in a barn somewhere cast a soft, warm glow.

While the space didn't exactly suit her taste, Elaine found it charming.

After they ordered their drinks—Nathan a large black coffee and Elaine an herbal tea with a splash of milk—they sat at a table near the back of the small shop.

"This coffee shop is lovely. You're lucky to have it so close to work."

Nathan agreed. "The owner has outfitted much of it with pieces he's gotten from my auctions."

"Ah," Elaine said, sipping her warm drink, "so you feel a personal connection."

"I'd like to see them succeed."

Elaine knew their time for small talk was rapidly coming to a close, and while she didn't want Nathan to feel she was taking advantage of his knowledge, she did feel the pressure of finding out all she could about the vase. Their own research had certainly proven helpful, but so many pieces still remained.

"You have that look on your face." Nathan's face warmed to a kind smile. "What is it?"

Elaine imagined a pink blush on her cheeks. Of course he would know she needed his help—he seemed able to read her like a book. "Is it that obvious?"

"To me it is." Nathan took a drink, then set the cup down on the table, leaning back as if she had a grand story to tell. And she supposed she did.

She gave him the quick version of what had happened, filling him in on their dead ends and rabbit trails, explaining how they'd determined Macy and Elizabeth Rollins couldn't be responsible for the missing vase or the fire.

"Seems like the maid did it," he said. "You said yourself she's lied and it seems obvious she started the fire."

"It's *possible* she started the fire."

"Accidentally?" he asked.

Elaine took another drink, working the ideas together like turns on a Rubik's Cube. "Funny you should say that. It's reasonable to assume it was purely an accident."

Nathan frowned. "And had nothing to do with the missing vase?"

"The fire marshal said the fire was not set intentionally. After all, they found no lighter fluid or gasoline—nothing an arsonist would use to purposely light a house on fire."

Nathan said nothing, giving her space to sort it out.

"The stove in the cottage has a loose knob on it. Sarah was in a terrible hurry that day—trying to get out of there to get her son to the doctor. If she wasn't careful, she might've accidentally turned the knob, releasing the natural gas into the air so when the wire sparked—*Boom!*"

"Boom?" His incredulous look told her he wasn't on board with this theory.

"You haven't met this girl, Nathan. She's kind and sweet."

"But she lied."

"She did lie, but, I think, out of desperation."

"Couldn't she have stolen out of desperation too?" He took another drink.

Elaine wasn't sure. Sarah seemed like a loving single mom who was worried about her son, and she seemed to have no connection to the vase at all. "Let's assume we're on to something, and Sarah started the fire by accident. Before she went in to clean, she saw a man leaving the cottage. She did mention that."

"She did?" Nathan asked.

"Yes. She gave us a description." Elaine stirred a small spoonful of honey into her tea. "This is very good."

"Glad you like it." Nathan folded his hands on the table and met Elaine's eyes. "I'm guessing there's a way for me to help with all this?"

"You know me too well." Elaine smiled. "I need more information on this vase." She fished a photo of it from her purse and pushed it across the table. She explained everything they'd discovered about the vase so far, including the story Macy had been told as well as what Jan's research had uncovered. By the look on his face, their thorough research impressed him once again.

"You see all kinds of things come through your auction house. I thought maybe you'd be able to help us determine if this vase really could be what the researcher thinks it is."

Nathan studied the photo for a few long seconds. "I could do a bit of digging with my sources, but if this vase is from the World War II era, I know someone you could talk to today."

"You do?" Elaine hadn't expected to get any answers for days. The prospect was exciting.

"His name is Harrison Ellerby," Nathan said. "I've dealt with him a few times. He's a prickly fellow, but he does know his antiques."

"Is he local?"

"Owns a little antique shop across town," Nathan said. "I can take you over if you like."

"That would be wonderful." Elaine breathed a sigh of relief. "Can you spare the time now? Since I'm in Waterville already?"

"Of course." Nathan finished off his coffee and stood. "Anything for you, Elaine." He looked into her eyes intently, then pulled his keys out of his pocket. "Let's go get my car."

On the walk back to the office, Elaine was quiet, consumed by her own thoughts.

"I hate to point this out," Nathan said as they reached his office, "since you sound like you have a soft spot for Sarah, but what if she stole the vase and sold it already?" His eyes met hers.

Elaine shook her head and looked away. "It's possible. But I just don't see it. She doesn't seem to be the criminal mastermind type."

"Many criminal masterminds aren't the 'criminal mastermind type,'" Nathan said.

"Is that right?" Her tone teased. "Have you known many criminal masterminds?"

He smiled at Elaine, amusement lighting his eyes. "I watch a lot of mysteries."

"Well, I hate to think that way," Elaine said as they both got into his shiny black Cadillac, resuming the effortless conversation that seemed less like small talk and more like playful banter between old friends.

They drove through Waterville, a town almost as charming as Lancaster. Main Street boasted a number of adorable little stores—an old-fashioned ice-cream shop and candy store, an art gallery, a toy store.

"You should have Jan's daughter come over here." Nathan pointed to a building out the passenger side window. "That jewelry store might be willing to carry some of her jewelry. It's an old family-owned business, and last I heard they were looking for ways to update and attract younger customers."

Elaine made a mental note to tell Jan about the little store in Waterville. They continued through town and Elaine spotted a sign that read "We Restore."

"There's Heather Wells's place." She pointed down College Avenue, drawing Nathan's attention to the sign. She and

Jan had taken a teapot there for cleaning and restoration shortly after opening Tea for Two, and it had turned out to be something far more interesting than they ever could have guessed.

"Yes, Heather's great, but let's try Ellerby's first. He's something of an expert on the World War II era—it's his specialty. If he can't help us, we'll go talk to Heather."

Elaine nodded. Two possible experts. Obviously talking to Nathan had been a wise decision.

"Here we are." Nathan parked his car across the street from a small shop in the middle of the city block, labeled only with large gold letters spelling the word *Antiques* above the door. Somehow it reminded Elaine of a European shop rather than a little storefront in Waterville, Maine.

"It doesn't look like much." Nathan turned off the engine. "But this guy knows his stuff."

Elaine studied the building, which was nondescript. Something about it made her imagine it must be one of the oldest in town. Dark-brown wood encased large display windows on either side of the door, and while it looked like plenty of light filtered in, the store still managed to look dark, even foreboding.

Or perhaps Elaine had watched one too many mysteries herself.

They exited the car and walked toward the little shop, but before he pulled the door open, Nathan stopped. "I should warn you, Harrison Ellerby is a...unique personality."

Elaine felt her eyes widen. "What do you mean?"

"You'll see." That amused look returned to Nathan's eyes.

With that, he opened the door and they entered what could only be described as a treasure trove of rare items Elaine hadn't seen in any other shop or flea market around Lancaster.

The dim overhead lighting did nothing to dull the interesting, if cluttered, antique store—a rare gem, Elaine thought, for Waterville. How had she not been here before?

She turned to her left, marveling at the sheer number of items Harrison Ellerby had on display. If they weren't so beautiful and elegantly displayed, she might fancy him a hoarder of some sort. A tall chest of drawers stood angled against the wall with three vintage suitcases stacked on top of it. Next to it, a small, intricately carved table boasted an old lamp with a frilly shade. Her eyes wandered across large, hand-carved containers and displays locked up in glass cases until they landed on a shelf of antique teacups. They were nesting on what appeared to be hand-painted saucers, situated around a perfectly preserved teapot.

"Oh my goodness." Elaine let out a breathy sigh. "This is beautiful."

"It's English made." The voice came from behind her.

Elaine spun around to find a tall, thin man with dark hair slicked back and combed over to one side. He wore a pair of round glasses and black clothing from head to toe. If Elaine were casting a villain in a movie, she might consider this man, if only on looks alone. And was it a coincidence or did his physique match Sarah's description of the man who'd left Escape exactly?

"It's quite lovely." She chose to ignore the fact that Mr. Tall and Lanky had materialized out of thin air like a ghost. She turned her attention back to the tea set. Each cream-colored piece was rimmed in gold, boasting the perfect combination of pink and red roses.

"It's Royal Sutherland fine bone china." The man stepped closer to Elaine and seemed to admire the set as much as she did. His voice was nasally and he spoke with an accent not quite British, but certainly highbrow. "Old English Summer Rose pattern. It's nearly a complete set and in mint condition. It's stunning, really—one of my favorite items in the shop right now. I would hate to part with it, actually, unless of course it was going to a very appreciative buyer."

Elaine wished she could buy it right there and take it back to the tearoom to show Jan. Surely her cousin would love it as much as she did. Their collection continued to grow, but this seemed a rare find—nothing like those they picked up at flea markets around town. Still, she felt as though she would have to lobby for permission to purchase the set, given the way Harrison Ellerby was eyeing her.

The man peered at her over the top of his glasses. "Should I wrap it up for you?"

She smiled at him, then turned her attention back to the collection. "Not just yet. Let me think it over. I never make a large purchase without sleeping on it first."

He drew in a deep breath, letting it out slowly. "I can't promise it will still be here if you wait."

"Of course," Elaine said. "I understand."

He looked at Nathan, as if noticing him for the first time since they'd arrived. "Mr. Culver. I haven't seen you in a couple of weeks. How are things?"

"I can't complain." Nathan's cheerfulness stood out like a neon sign next to the bleakness of Harrison Ellerby. Nathan took a step forward. "Mr. Ellerby, this is my dear friend, Elaine Cook. We're actually not here to shop."

Harrison Ellerby did nothing to hide his annoyance at this admission. "Then why are you here?"

Elaine noted the slow cadence of his voice. How had Nathan described this man? Unique and prickly? He'd been spot-on.

"I'm told you're quite the expert when it comes to World War II antiquities." Elaine figured flattery would go a long way with this man.

"That's not exactly a secret," he said, proving her theory wrong.

"I was hoping to get your expert opinion on something," Elaine said. "A vase went missing from a cottage in Lancaster." She rummaged through her purse to find the photo.

"Macy Atherton's vase?"

Elaine stopped and met his eyes. "How did you know that?"

"An educated guess." He walked away.

Elaine glanced at Nathan, who shrugged slightly, then followed Ellerby to the back of the store where a large glass counter separated it into two sections.

So few people knew the vase was missing, Elaine thought. How had Ellerby known about it?

He reached up onto a shelf and pulled down a set of silver candlesticks. He laid the pair on a soft cloth and began buffing one with another soft cloth, staying silent the entire time.

"Those are quite beautiful." Elaine focused on the candlesticks.

"Indeed." He seemed to have no interest in small talk.

She glanced at Nathan helplessly.

"We didn't realize you knew about Macy's vase when we came in," Nathan said. "Even better. Maybe you could tell us what you know about it."

He studied the candlestick. "Why would I do that?"

Elaine realized there was no reasoning with this man. He was intent on making them work for any shred of information he was going to give

"The vase is very beautiful," Elaine pulled a photo from her purse. She set it on the counter next to the candle-sticks. "And from what we understand, rare. It's from World War I."

"It's from World War II," Harrison corrected her, doing nothing to hide his irritation at her "error."

Nathan's eyes darted to hers briefly as if to commend her for her keen thinking. A man like Harrison Ellerby loved to show off his intellect. If Elaine had to pretend to know less than she did to find out what he knew, so be it.

"Is that right?" Elaine's eyes fell to the photo. "But it is rare, I'm told. Only about a hundred ever made."

"Where do you get your information?" Harrison prac-tically spat the words. "This vase is one of three that were made during World War II. They were stolen from some very important Jewish leaders and were thought to be gone forever. That is, until someone found the other two."

Elaine feigned ignorance. "How can you be sure this is the third vase?"

"This one has a maker's mark on the bottom," Harrison said. "A triangle with the letter *E* inside."

"Is that significant?" Elaine asked, still pretending she knew nothing about the vase at all.

"The man who made it, Josef Eisner, was a well-known artist in Poland. You can look him up." Harrison looked down his nose down at her. "If you know how to do that."

Elaine felt her feathers ruffle, and she quickly reminded herself not to give in to his goading. After all, her know-nothing ruse seemed to be working.

"This mark was special though. Different than Eisner's usual mark, which was a triangle with the letter *J* in the middle. He used his other initial because he said these three were special to him. Priceless."

Elaine studied the photo. There was no way to see any mark on the bottom of the vase in the picture, though Macy's documentation did say it was there.

"Are you sure this vase has the mark?" Elaine stared at the picture, determined not to give him *too* much attention.

"I've seen it with my own eyes," he said.

She glanced up, meeting his gaze. He'd intended to puff himself up a little, but what he'd done was implicate himself. And judging by the expression on his face, he seemed to have just realized it.

He set one of the candlesticks down and picked up the other. "I've cleaned and restored a number of items for Mrs. Atherton. I don't know of another vase valuable enough to be worth stealing, at least not in Lancaster."

He said *Lancaster* as if the word was an unpleasant taste in his mouth.

Mr. Ellerby moved out from behind the counter, carrying the candlesticks, and setting them on a display near a wall at the back of the store.

"Macy didn't mention you'd restored the vase." Elaine followed him, but left a wide gap between them.

Harrison waved his hand in the air dismissively. "She didn't even mean to bring it over here. She said it got 'mixed up' with her valuables. She had no idea what she had in that box."

Elaine wondered how Harrison Ellerby and Macy Atherton got along. She couldn't imagine it was very well, both such strong personalities.

"Did you tell Macy how valuable it was?"

He turned and looked at Elaine for the first time since discovering she wasn't there to shop. "I did not." He walked back to his spot behind the counter. "If Macy Atherton doesn't have the good sense to determine the worth of her possessions, who am I to set her straight?"

His smile reminded Elaine of a child who'd just pulled one over on his unsuspecting teacher. "And anyway, I don't see how any of this is my concern. I take no responsibility for what Mrs. Atherton did or didn't know about her own possessions.

She paid me to restore it, not to appraise it. Besides, she was not very pleasant. I'm not in the business of doing favors for people who have no appreciation for the finer things."

Well, there it was—the answer to her unspoken question about how Harrison and Macy had gotten along.

"If you knew how valuable the vase was," Nathan said, eyebrow raised, "did you try to take it off Macy's hands?"

Mr. Ellerby pressed his lips together and narrowed his gaze at Nathan. "I might have made her an offer to buy it."

Elaine straightened. *Good question, Nathan!* She was impressed. Her friend's eyes didn't leave Ellerby's.

"Was it a fair offer?" Nathan asked. "Considering Macy wasn't aware of its value and all."

Mr. Ellerby took another deep breath and blew it out in a huff. "I don't like what you're implying." He pressed his thin lips together, eyes darting from Nathan to Elaine, to the front door, then back to Nathan. "If you must know, it is *possible* my offer was less than generous. However, I am a businessman, and it's in my best interest to turn a profit."

"But that vase was priceless." Elaine was a bit horrified by his take on the whole thing. "Taking it off her hands for hardly anything is its own kind of theft."

He shrugged. "If you want to look at it that way. I certainly don't. It's not my fault if the common folk in Lancaster aren't as educated as I am, and Macy Atherton is certainly not as educated as I am no matter how she makes herself sound."

He turned his back to them, busying himself with items on a shelf behind the counter, mumbling under his breath.

"Why else would she put the vase on display in one of her cottages?"

When he turned back around, he met Elaine's eyes and what must've been an expression of surprise. She hadn't told Harrison Ellerby that Macy's vase had been on display in that cottage. How had he known? Perhaps Macy had told him. Or...

"It seems to me that Macy Atherton deserved to have the vase stolen." Mr. Ellerby seemed unaware of his accidental admission. "If you can't take care of your antiques, perhaps they're better off with someone who can."

Before Elaine could respond, another man appeared in the shop, behind Harrison Ellerby.

"Oh, George," he said, "did you finish polishing that brass I gave you?"

The other man—George—looked caught. "Almost, Mr. Ellerby."

"Come meet Nathan Culver and his friend Elaine Cook." Mr. Ellerby put a little too much emphasis on Elaine's last name, giving the *k* a hard edge. "They're not here to shop. They're asking questions about a theft." His tone mocked them. Elaine glanced at Nathan, whose eyes seem to apologize to her, though he said nothing.

The younger man stared at them, wide-eyed. "A theft? From here?"

"No, George," Ellerby said with spite. Then he looked back at Elaine. "If we hear anything more about the missing vase, we'll be sure to get in touch." He dismissed Elaine and Nathan with a quick flick of his wrist.

He disappeared into the back, leaving his employee, George, to face them alone. The man seemed glued to his spot on the floor, though Elaine imagined with a boss like Harrison Ellerby, she would likely be terrified to make a wrong move too. Her thoughts turned to Archie and Rose. She wanted the tearoom to feel more like a family than a business. It didn't seem Harrison Ellerby shared the sentiment.

"Have you been working here long, George?"

The man moved toward a workbench on the opposite side of the counter from where Nathan and Elaine stood.

"About a year." George didn't look at them.

"Are you from Waterville?" Nathan's boisterous baritone filled the otherwise quiet store.

"Not originally," George said. "I moved here for the job. Mr. Ellerby is an expert in World War II artifacts and antiquities. He's taught me a lot already." George shuffled some papers around on the workbench, still avoiding their eyes.

"Does Mr. Ellerby ever leave the store during the day?" Elaine busied herself with a porcelain cat on a glass shelf to the right of the counter.

George frowned. "I don't feel right sharing personal details about Mr. Ellerby."

"Fair enough."

George glanced over his shoulder, then back at Elaine, but before he could say anything more, Harrison Ellerby returned.

"You're still here," he said.

"We were just leaving," Nathan said.

Elaine held George's gaze for several long seconds, then finally turned around to go. Before they exited the store, however, she took out her phone and snapped a photo of the tea set, not that she'd be purchasing anything from the likes of Harrison Ellerby.

While she had her phone set to its camera mode, she glanced at Mr. Ellerby, waiting for a moment when he wasn't looking her way. When the opportunity presented itself, she quickly turned her phone toward him and clicked a series of photos, feeling like a real private investigator.

Hmm. A tall, thin man who knew how valuable Macy's vase was. Perhaps the next time she visited Ellerby's antiques, it would be with the deputy and an arrest warrant.

CHAPTER SEVENTEEN

J an had just finished mixing the glaze for her lemon Bundt
cake when Elaine rushed through the back door. Her eyes
were wide, as though she had a secret to tell, but before she
could say anything, the kitchen door swung open and Rose
appeared, the look on her face matching her cousin's.

"My, my," Jan said. "It's been quiet in here for hours and
now you both practically exploded into the room at the exact
same time. What are the odds?"

"Macy's here," Rose said. "I saw her parking her car out
front. I thought I should warn you. You know, for the sake of
our customers."

Jan realized they did have a few details to tell Macy. After
all, they'd learned the truth about Elizabeth Rollins, though
Jan wasn't sure she wanted to be the one to tell Macy the
author had used her grandparents' love story as fodder for a
romance novel.

"Maybe she'll be flattered," Elaine had said when the subject
came up the day before. *"I would be flattered if someone thought my
history was worth writing about."*

Jan didn't remind Elaine this was Macy they were talking about. What if she hated the idea and was angry with Elizabeth? She decided maybe it wasn't her place to say anything on the subject.

"I asked Macy to come." Elaine took off her jacket and hung it over her purse on the hooks by the back door just as Macy entered the kitchen.

Jan stopped her glaze mid-drizzle. "Did you find something?"

"I certainly hope so," Macy said. "I didn't drive all the way over here for tea and biscuits. Though if you've got tea and biscuits, I'd happily partake." Macy plopped down on the stool on the opposite side of the counter.

"Do we have time to chat now?" Elaine glanced at Jan. "How does it look in the parlors?"

"We were very busy earlier, but we had a nice break, so I thought I'd get a jump start on this cake before tomorrow." Jan wiped her hands on her apron. "What's going on? Did Nathan have news on the vase?"

Macy looked confused. "Nathan who?"

"Nathan Culver. As you know, he's an auctioneer, so he knows a lot about antiques. And it turns out he was a great help."

Macy reached across the island and slipped a small raspberry tart from a tray next to Jan. Jan raised a brow at the other woman, who pretended not to notice.

Elaine turned toward Macy. "Remember when we asked you who all knew about your vase?"

Macy nodded.

"Is it possible you left anyone out?"

"I don't think so," Macy said. "Why?"

"Because Nathan took me to a little antique shop in Waterville today." Elaine paused, as if waiting for the lightbulb to go off over Macy's head.

When it did, it was unmistakable. Her eyes widened and she leaned forward in her chair. "Harrison Ellerby, that little weasel."

"He knew all about you and your vase. He said he tried to buy it from you."

Jan gasped.

Macy shook her head. "It was years ago. I didn't mean to bring the vase at all. It was in the box with some things Shane packed up. I'd forgotten all about it."

Jan spent the next few minutes listening to Elaine's details about the antique store, Harrison Ellerby, and the uncanny possibility that he could be the tall, thin man Sarah saw the day of the fire.

"I hate to say it, but he doesn't sound very nice," Jan said.

"He's a weasel," Macy repeated. She popped another tart in her mouth and swallowed it without chewing. Jan resisted the urge to tell her the tarts were better when you actually tasted them.

"He was difficult to like, I agree," Elaine said with a sigh. "The worst part is, he has an English-made tea set I would love to purchase."

"You can't purchase anything from him." Macy held up a finger. "Not if he's the one who stole my vase."

"We don't know anything yet," Jan said. "It's only suspicion, and we've all been wrong before."

"Jan's right," Elaine said. "He almost seemed to enjoy the notion that I might think he was guilty. There's a very good chance he's simply leading us astray for his own amusement."

"That's a horrible thought," Jan said. "Who would do that?"

"Harrison Ellerby." Macy eyed the tray of tarts, but before she could take one, Jan casually moved it to another counter.

"Macy, he is innocent until proven guilty." Elaine's brow furrowed, as if she was working out something in her own head.

"Then let's do that!" Macy smacked a hand on the counter. "Let's prove him guilty!"

Elaine pulled her phone from her pocket, then scrolled through her photos, a frown bringing out a deep crease in her forehead

"What's wrong?" Macy asked.

Elaine turned the phone around and set it on the table. "I must've been moving when I snapped the photo. It's too blurry to see anything. I was hoping to show it to Sarah. I thought maybe she could tell us if this was the man she saw that day."

"Now what are we going to do?" Jan asked.

Elaine's frown persisted. "I suppose we'll have to take Sarah to the store."

"I want to come along," Macy said.

"I don't know..." Elaine tucked her phone back into her pocket. "He will know we're up to something if you come with her."

"I'll stay in the car. I am the victim here." Macy pouted.

Elaine stared at Macy, as if making up her mind. "Fair enough, as long as you don't come into the store," she said. "It might be better to send Jan in with Sarah. Mr. Ellerby and I weren't exactly fast friends."

Jan's pulse raced at the thought. What if she slipped and mentioned something about the vase or Macy or her cousin?

"I can see by the look on your face you're already worrying about this," Elaine said. "You'll be fine. You're just two ladies out shopping."

Jan met Elaine's eyes. "Of course." Two ladies out shopping in hopes of catching a thief.

The next day, Elaine parked her Malibu across the street from Ellerby's Antiques. Sarah and Macy occupied the backseat while Jan clung to her purse in the front. Sarah had been more than happy to offer any kind of help she could. Jan gathered she wanted the criminal caught as much as she and Elaine did. She must be aware she'd raised everyone's suspicions.

"Aren't you supposed to be better at this by now?" Macy asked. "You act like a big scaredy-cat."

Jan waved her off. "I get nervous in these situations."

"Well, I'm not nervous. Give me five minutes with that weasel and I'll tell you if he's guilty." Macy crossed her arms.

"Somehow I don't think your opinion will hold up in a court of law," Elaine said. "We need proof."

"Let's get this over with," Sarah said as she opened the back door and got out.

"Just locate Mr. Ellerby and see if he looks like the man you saw leaving the cottage," Elaine instructed. "Then come back to the car."

Jan nodded and joined Sarah on the pavement. "Here goes nothing."

They walked toward the shop.

"I hope you can find whoever did this," Sarah said as they crossed the street. "The sooner this mess is behind me, the better."

Jan didn't respond.

"I'm sorry I lied about what time I left. I need this job to support Dylan, but I know it was wrong not to be honest from the beginning."

Jan met her eyes, confused about how she knew they had found out she'd lied.

"Ruby told me she talked to you both," Sarah clarified. "I'm going to tell Mrs. Atherton the truth about what happened that day. So you don't have to."

Elaine had shared with Jan her suspicions that Sarah may have accidentally started the fire. Jan wondered if Sarah thought so too.

"What will you say?" Jan asked quietly.

"I'll tell her I punched out early and I did a poor job that day." She met Jan's eyes, stopping her just outside the door to the antique shop. "And there's another thing...but I'm terrified to say it."

Jan touched her arm. "It's about the fire, isn't it?"

"Yes," Sarah's eyes looked almost frightened. "Mrs. Blake, I think I may have started that fire. But I give you my word that in no way did I intend to."

A wind kicked up, blowing leaves down the sidewalk and on to a sewer grate.

Jan nodded. "I agree it's possible, and I believe you that it wasn't intentional. But Elaine and I have been wondering the same thing. We can't be sure yet." Jan patted her arm again.

Sarah looked away. "I'm a hard worker, Mrs. Blake. I always have been." Her eyes clouded with tears. "I'm just so preoccupied with Dylan these days. I'm worried about him. They're sending us to a specialist. His doctor has no idea why his fever isn't going away."

Suddenly Jan thought it was a mistake bringing Sarah here today when she was so upset. This was the last thing the poor woman needed when she had so many more important things to think of.

"You just concentrate on that little boy of yours," Jan said. "And we can ask Macy for grace when it comes to your job. We all need a little grace every now and then."

Sarah's smile seemed forced. "Thank you for that."

"Let's get this over with," Jan said, squeezing her hands.

Sarah nodded and they entered the shop. Jan's eyes were instantly drawn to the tea set Elaine had described to her. It was just as Elaine said—exquisite—and it would make a lovely addition to their collection.

They moved through the cluttered store, which smelled of old books. Behind the counter, a thin man Jan assumed was Ellerby worked quietly, though Jan couldn't tell exactly what he was doing. He did not, however, appear eager to offer them any help. From the look of him, he didn't even realize they'd entered the store.

Not the greatest customer service, she thought. At the tearoom, they made a point to welcome each of their guests with a big smile and open arms. It seemed this man couldn't be bothered.

Jan drew Sarah's attention toward the back of the store. "What do you think?" she whispered.

Sarah studied the man behind the counter, then turned to Jan. "It's so hard to say. It could be him. The man I saw wore a long black coat and a hat and sunglasses. He kept his head down. I know how important this is to you, but I'd hate to point fingers if that isn't him."

"May I help you?"

Jan gasped as she turned and found the man standing next to her. How'd he do that? It was like one second he was across the store and the next, he was at her side. Judging by Elaine's description, this was definitely Harrison Ellerby.

"Did I frighten you?" He turned up his nose at them.

Jan shot Sarah a look as if to prod her to study the man now that she had this rare up-close view of him, but Sarah's mind seemed to be elsewhere.

"You did startle me," Jan said. "We are visiting town and thought we'd stop in." It wasn't a lie. She wasn't from Waterville, so technically she was a visitor.

"Are you looking for anything in particular?" He peered at her over the rim of his black glasses.

It unnerved her.

"No, nothing in particular." Jan's eyes wandered to a small cookie jar in the shape of a squirrel. "This is nice."

"It's kitschy," Mr. Ellerby said. "But people like you seem to like it."

Jan spun around, but before she could ask him to elaborate on what he meant by "people like you," he was gone.

"Let me know if you need anything," his voice rang out from somewhere in the middle of the clutter.

"It's a wonder anyone shops here," Jan whispered.

"Let's go." Sarah led the way to the door. "I'm sorry I wasn't more help."

"Well, you didn't rule him out," Jan said as they walked back to the car. "And that's something."

Outside, on the way to Elaine's car, Sarah stopped abruptly. "I just remembered something else."

Jan turned to her, hopeful she had some bit of information that might lead them to the proof they needed.

"The man I saw was wearing running shoes. Bright-blue ones."

Jan frowned. That didn't sound like Harrison Ellerby. "Are you sure?"

"Yes. It's strange, now that I think about it. Almost like the shoes didn't match the rest of what he wore."

"That *is* strange," Jan said.

They returned the car and explained that Sarah hadn't made a positive ID but she'd remembered something interesting about the man's shoes. Both Macy and Elaine were disappointed.

"Well, I'm not giving up," Elaine said. "If Harrison Ellerby is our thief, we will find proof. Blue running shoes or not."

Macy snorted. "He had motive. He knew that vase was worth a lot more than he offered to pay me." She muttered something under her breath.

"That doesn't explain why he would wait years to steal it," Jan said reluctantly. "Or set fire to the cabin."

"Maybe his little store is in trouble?" Macy's tone suggested she wanted it to be true. "Money is a great motive."

"That's true," Jan said. "I hate to say it, but I think it's time to call the police and let them in on everything that's happened."

"I agree." Elaine started the car and pulled away from the curb.

"And you'll need their help if you're going to look into Ellerby's financials," Macy put in. As if they'd get access, Jan thought. "Though I doubt you'll find anything. A man like that probably hides his money in off-shore accounts. I'm telling you—he's our man." Macy seemed so sure.

Jan chose not to indulge the fantasy. Though they had motive and opportunity, they had no actual proof, and she knew that was the one thing they needed to solve this mystery once and for all.

CHAPTER EIGHTEEN

J an rummaged through her jewelry, searching for the match for her amethyst earring. She finally found it, hiding underneath a silver bracelet.

She put on the earrings and studied herself in the mirror. They were a lovely complement to the lavender blouse she'd chosen for her evening out with Bob.

He'd called her that morning and invited her out for an impromptu date at the Community Opera House in Waterville. According to Bob, a local community group was presenting one of his favorite musicals, *The Music Man*. Jan hadn't been to the opera house in years, and she thought she'd enjoy it. Besides, it would be nice to get out of the house for the evening.

They closed the tearoom and cleaned up from a rather slow afternoon. In the beginning, Jan panicked a little on days like today, but she'd learned to accept the ebbs and flows of owning a business. She'd also learned that God always provided everything she and Elaine needed—a truth she reminded herself of daily.

Once she was satisfied with her attire, she applied a light sheen to her lips, pressed them together, and headed downstairs.

Elaine was in the west parlor, setting up a Scrabble board.

Had she forgotten that Jan was going out for the evening?

She glanced up as Jan entered the room and her eyes glimmered her approval. "You look stunning. That Robert Claybrook is one lucky fellow."

Jan waved dismissively. "You are too kind."

"I hope you don't mind if I borrow your Scrabble board for the evening," Elaine said, returning to the table. She pulled the tiles from the box, then stowed it away in a cabinet nearby.

"Not at all. Do you have a Scrabble date?"

"Nathan Culver has challenged me to a game."

Jan laughed. "I hope he isn't expecting to win."

Elaine tossed Jan a look. "He doesn't know I've been practicing."

The doorbell cut their conversation short. Jan opened the door and found a dapper-looking Nathan standing on the porch. Seconds later, Bob's car pulled up out front.

How fun that both she and Elaine had social plans for the evening. Her heart would rest well knowing Nathan was keeping Elaine company, even if he was going to lose horribly at Scrabble.

Before she and Bob left, she set out a tray of macaroons for Nathan and Elaine—"just in case they got hungry"—and they were on their way.

She followed Bob out to the car and stood back while he opened the passenger side door for her.

"You look lovely tonight," he said.

She thanked him and got in the car, inhaling the woodsy scent of him as she did. How was it that at her age this man's nearness could make her heart race the way it did?

She supposed the excitement of something new would never get old—and she was glad of that.

The Community Opera House in downtown Waterville was one of the oldest buildings in town, and it had gone under an extensive renovation just a few years ago. Bob had been one of the leaders who'd made that renovation happen and Jan thought there was a part of him that felt very proud at all they'd accomplished. She couldn't wait to see it for herself.

They arrived about a half an hour early, which gave them time to admire all the work that had gone into bringing the old building back to its original glory.

Bob led her through the front door into the lobby, where a young girl dressed all in black was waiting for their tickets.

"Good evening, Mr. Claybrook." She took the tickets from Bob and directed them down the hall and to the left. "You want the center door. But I guess you already knew that." She flashed him a smile.

"Thank you, Maddie." He led Jan through another set of doors and into an ornately decorated lobby

"She and her mom were both on the volunteer team I ran," Bob said.

"This place is beautiful." Jan's eyes wandered up the gold walls to the ceiling overhead. It reminded her of something you might see in an art museum with its elaborate carvings and ornamental decorations.

They walked to the center aisle where another woman, also dressed in black, was waiting to take them to their seats. She handed them two programs, glanced at their tickets, and led them down the aisle to the fourth row.

They were right on the aisle, which Jan appreciated.

"This place is beautiful." They took their seats. In front of them was a wide stage with a thick red velvet curtain and above that, more of the same ornamental decor she'd seen in the lobby. She looked up at the ceiling and saw what could only be described as a work of art.

"It's come a long way. It would've been such a shame to see this place torn down."

"Is that what they were going to do?" Jan couldn't imagine it. The theater must be a historical landmark.

"That's what they were talking about," Bob said. "Until we got together and decided to save it."

Jan glanced up at him, half-listening as he told her a story about how their efforts had been nearly thwarted by pigeons who had made their home in the rafters. As he spoke, it occurred to her how much she admired his philanthropic work. He truly wanted to make the area a better place to live, and it showed. So many people talked about doing something good, but Bob actually did it. And look at the stunning results.

The lights flickered, indicating the start of the show, and Jan settled in. She hadn't seen a live stage production in years.

"I know the guy playing Harold Hill," Bob whispered as the lights dimmed. "He's a lawyer here in Waterville, but he was once in a Broadway show. He was just in the chorus, but that's still pretty impressive." He reached over and picked up her hand. "I hope you like it."

"I'm sure I will."

As the lights went down, she glanced down at his hand wrapped around hers and she realized he had no intention of letting it go.

The music from the live orchestra started and as the show began, Jan found herself thoroughly enjoying it. At one point she leaned over and whispered, "Are you sure these are all local actors?"

Bob nodded, flashing a smile.

At intermission, the audience applauded until the curtain hit the floor and the lights came up. A voice came over the sound system announcing that there would now be a twenty-minute intermission.

"Should we get up and stretch our legs a little?"

Jan nodded and they made their way out to the lobby with the rest of the crowd.

"Would you like a drink?" Bob stopped in front of a refreshment counter.

"I'm just fine, thank you." Jan was impressed by how many had come out to show their support for the Waterville Players, as the program called them.

"I'm going to grab a water," Bob said. "I'll be right back."

Jan moved off to the side to wait for him.

"Mrs. Blake?"

She turned and found Deputy Sheffield at her side, accompanied by a woman Jan presumed to be his wife.

"Deputy Sheffield." Jan instantly felt guilty that they owed him a phone call and an update about Macy's vase. She reminded herself that he didn't know about any of that and smiled warmly.

"It's just Arnie tonight," he said with a smile.

"Okay. Deputy"—she stopped when she saw he was raising a brow at her—"Arnie, Elaine and I were planning to call you tomorrow."

"To invite me over for some of those fabulous cream puffs everyone is always raving about?" His grin reminded her of a schoolboy.

"People are raving about my cream puffs?" The thought excited her. "That's very kind."

"They've been the topic of more than one conversation down at the station."

"But I don't remember serving any officers at the tearoom." She supposed she simply hadn't realized...

"Their wives bring them home," he said. "No offense, but a tearoom isn't exactly the kind of place most guys are going to go."

She narrowed her gaze. "Is that right?"

He shrugged. "It's not really a masculine kind of place."

She laughed. "Well, I was planning to invite you over tomorrow so we could share a few things we've learned about the fire out at Green Glade, but perhaps you'd be more comfortable meeting elsewhere?"

Arnie glanced at his wife, who wore a look of amusement, then back to Jan. "Will there be cream puffs?"

"Oh yes, Arnie. Perfectly masculine cream puffs."

"I suppose I could make it. After you close up for the day."

"Perfect. See you tomorrow at four." The lights flickered.

As they walked away, Bob appeared at her side with two bottles of water. "Just in case you get thirsty."

She took one and followed him back to their seats, thinking it was awfully nice to have someone taking care of her like that.

CHAPTER NINETEEN

The following day, Elaine and Jan ushered their last customer out just as the squad car pulled up in front of Tea for Two.

They exchanged a quick glance as if to say "here goes nothing."

Jan had returned from her date last night bursting with energy, not only about how well done the show had been, but also about her run-in with the deputy.

"It seems my cream puffs have quite the reputation," she'd said with a smile.

Nathan had just lost his third game of Scrabble, but his spirits were still high. "Of course they do," he said cheerily. "You're a superb baker."

Of course Jan had blushed at the compliment, but before she went to bed she whipped up a fresh batch of cream puffs specifically for Deputy Sheffield.

DEPUTY SHEFFIELD ambled up the walk and met Elaine at the top of the front steps. "Good afternoon, Mrs. Cook."

"Good afternoon, Deputy Sheffield." She stood out of the way so he could pass through the front door and into the entryway. "We'll be in the east parlor, just this way." She led him into the parlor where Macy was waiting for them at a table that had already been set. At the center, Jan had arranged not only cream puffs, but maple croissants, raspberry tarts, and cinnamon streusel muffins.

Jan stood at Macy's side and smiled widely when they entered the parlor.

"Won't you sit down?" Elaine waited until the deputy sat in an empty chair across from Macy and then she and Jan took their seats.

"It's awfully good of you to do all this," Deputy Sheffield said. "It looks really nice in here."

Jan smiled a thank you.

"Help yourself, Deputy," Elaine said. "I'm sure you're wondering why we've asked you here today."

He reached out and filled his plate with one of each of the pastries. "The thought did cross my mind, yes."

"Someone stole my vase," Macy said.

Elaine put a hand on her arm, noticing the deputy's eyebrows had lifted like a question mark.

Deputy Sheffield raised a brow. "Is that right?"

"It was the day of the fire out at Green Glade," Elaine explained.

"That fire was ruled an accident." He bit into the cream puff, then sat back in his chair while he chewed. "This is really good."

Jan smiled. "You can have as many as you like."

"She made them especially for you." Macy took a cream puff and popped it into her mouth, ignoring the reprimanding look Jan was giving her.

"When we discovered Macy's vase had gone missing, we thought perhaps someone was trying to conceal the theft by starting the fire."

"But we're starting to believe that it was just a very strange coincidence," Jan said.

"The fire was an accident," Macy said. "There's a loose knob on the stove and—oh, it doesn't matter. It was just an accident."

"So we're not looking for an arsonist."

"Just a weasel," Macy groaned.

The deputy bit into the croissant. "So you're saying there was a vase stolen the same day as the fire?"

"Yes," Elaine said. "And it turns out, it was a very valuable vase. Invaluable, probably."

"So I'm guessing, knowing you two, that you've got suspects at this point. Am I right?" He took a drink of water while his tea went untouched. They should've guessed he wasn't going to drink tea out of a floral teacup.

Elaine's mind instantly turned to Harrison Ellerby, but she didn't want to share everything with Deputy Sheffield— not just yet. Instead, she presented the list of everyone they'd considered, including Sarah and Elizabeth Rollins, though she was quick to point out that both were innocent.

"I see." Deputy Sheffield leveled her gaze. "And the one you're not telling me about?"

Elaine studied the young deputy. She was impressed. He was very good at his job.

"Harrison Ellerby," Macy offered with no hesitation. "He's cleaned and restored several pieces for me over the years. He offered to buy that very same vase from me. For much less than it's worth, I might add."

"You think he did it?" Deputy Sheffield turned his attention back to Elaine, and for a moment, it almost seemed like he was asking her as a colleague. Had she and Jan somehow won his respect? And if so, didn't she owe him the same in return?

"He seems to be hiding something," Elaine admitted. "And he had motive and opportunity—we think. But we have no proof. Mr. Ellerby is smart and well-connected. If he did take it, he may have already sold the vase."

Macy helped herself to a scone. "If it wasn't my vase that had gone missing, I might find this all terribly exciting."

"Unless he already had a buyer lined up for that vase, odds are he's still trying to sell it," Deputy Sheffield said. "We should look into his financial situation. I can see if he's made any large deposits."

Elaine smiled.

The deputy paused. "What is it?"

"You said 'we.'"

He took the cloth napkin off his lap and laid it on his empty plate. "I guess it was good I ran into you last night, Mrs. Blake."

"So we're not in trouble?" Jan asked with wide eyes.

"I can't say I'm happy you waited this long to tell me about this. But if you can assure me you've told me everything you know, *and* you agree to come to me sooner next time you discover a crime has been committed, I will let it slide."

"Oh, thank you," Jan said.

He stood, and the others followed suit.

"Will we still be able to help you solve this mystery?" Elaine asked, hopeful. She knew herself—and she wouldn't be able to rest until she'd figured this out.

"The way I see it, you ladies have done most of the legwork on this one, so I see no reason to shut you out now."

Elaine wanted to hug him, but she refrained.

"But I'm going to be involved from here on out."

"Of course," Elaine said.

"It was the cream puffs, wasn't it?" Jan teased.

He grinned. "Might've been the cream puffs."

"Thank you, Deputy Sheffield," Elaine led him toward the front door. "We won't let you down."

"See that you don't." He opened the door and tossed one more glance over his shoulder. "I'll be in touch."

CHAPTER TWENTY

When Bob had called and invited Jan over to his house for dinner, she instantly agreed, though she'd confirmed whether he was sure he wanted to see her so soon after they'd gone out.

He made a joke about how he'd like to see her every day, which made her blush, then told her what time to arrive at his house.

As she stood on the porch waiting for him to answer the door, she wondered if she should've offered to bring a dish. Or a dessert. Or an entire meal. She wasn't used to letting someone else be in the driver's seat. Peter had passed away so long ago—she'd gotten used to her independence. But that didn't mean she minded all this doting...

Still, she did like the idea of taking a little time away from what seemed like the unsolvable puzzle of the stolen vase. Now that the deputy was involved, they had more of a chance of finding some sort of evidence Harrison Ellerby had stolen it— whether it be a large deposit in his bank account or even proof that the man was in financial trouble. Jan hoped he could turn up something, and in the meantime, she'd give herself the night off.

Dinner with Bob would take her mind off all of that.

He opened the door and smiled at her. He wore a black cashmere sweater with a blue button-down underneath. A pair of dark jeans and black shoes. He looked awfully handsome, but then, he always looked handsome.

Jan's eyes fell to the loose blouse she'd layered over a pair of dark jeans Tara had forced her to buy. She hoped she didn't seem underdressed. She'd never been a fashion plate, but she wanted to look nice for Bob.

Judging by the way he was looking at her now, she'd done okay.

She met his eyes with a smile.

"I've been looking forward to seeing you all day."

Jan could feel the blood rush to her cheeks and she wished her own body wasn't such a tattletale.

He moved out of the way to allow her to enter his beautiful— if masculine—home.

She shrugged off her coat, which he quickly took from her, hanging it on the coat tree beside the door.

"You look beautiful," Bob said.

"You do too." Jan laughed at her own reply. "Handsome, I mean."

"I hope you like duck." Bob led her into the dining room.

"I do, in fact." Jan followed him, inhaling the aroma. "I didn't realize you were such a chef."

He pulled her chair out, then scooted it under her as she sat. "I have a few tricks up my sleeve." He disappeared into the other room and returned a few moments later, carrying a tray that looked like something out of *Bon Appetit*.

"This is wonderful." Jan noted the growl of her empty stomach.

"I thought it was about time someone cooked for you. Though I don't know if it will meet your standards."

"Don't be silly. I'm sure I will love it." Her fingers itched to reach over and serve them both, a motion they'd grown very accustomed to over the course of a lifetime of meal preparation. When was the last time someone had waited on her like this?

While Bob carved and served the duck, Jan took a moment to look around the room. White linens covered a large, somewhat ornate dining table, which had been neatly decorated with a festive autumn centerpiece. Two orange taper candles flickered in the center of the table, surrounded by an elegant dish of green beans and another of mashed potatoes. A basket of bread finished off the feast.

Jan stilled, taking a moment to study the man who spooned a heaping serving of potatoes on to his plate. He'd done all this for her. It seemed Bob was always willing—happy, even—to do things for her.

Her heart warmed at the thought of it.

He turned to her, meeting her eyes with a half smile that faded when he looked at her. "Is everything okay?"

She took the dish he passed to her. "More than okay."

"Don't say that until you taste everything," he said with a grin.

"I know I'll love it all. It was so sweet of you to do this for me."

His eyes searched hers and she forced herself not to think about how plain she often felt as she held his gaze. "I'm crazy about you, Jan Blake."

She looked away. She couldn't let him see how poorly she accepted compliments, but as she did, he reached over and took her hand.

"And you don't have to tell me how crazy you are about me. I already know."

She looked up and found him wearing a teasing grin, one she couldn't help but match.

"Ah, I live for that," he said. "Making you smile is the high-light of my day."

"We should eat." Jan was eager to get change the topic of conversation. She'd never enjoyed being the center of atten-tion, though she seemed hopelessly attracted to a man who seemed to like to put her there.

"Yes, before it gets cold."

Their conversation caught them up on each other's lives, giving Jan a chance to recount the case of Macy's stolen vase and to settle it all in her own head. It helped to talk through the details with Bob, just in case they had missed anything, and as she did, her mind wandered off on its own.

"What are you thinking?" Bob's question pulled her back to the present.

Jan shook her head. "Just that it seems odd that Harrison Ellerby would've waited so long to steal that vase. If he really wanted it, it seems like he would've gotten it years ago."

"Unless he was waiting for a buyer." Bob buttered his warm slice of bread.

"I suppose," Jan said. "But then the odds of our finding it are much smaller, so I hope that's not the case."

Their conversation turned from Macy's vase to their night out at the opera house to Bob's friend who'd played Professor Harold Hill. It was a lively, easygoing conversation and it made Jan happy. They finished their meal and Bob grew quiet.

"Thank you for doing all of this for me," Jan said. "It was very thoughtful."

"Ah, but was it delicious?" He waited for her response with raised eyebrows.

"It *was* delicious."

He nodded, seeming to relish the victory. "Anything to help out my girl."

She stared at her empty plate and felt the smile that warmed her face. "You say the sweetest things." Her voice was quiet. She'd given up thinking she'd be anyone's "girl" ever again.

"I do, don't I?" His tone teased.

She looked up and found his eyes. "I hope you know I feel the same way about you."

Bob's gaze did the opposite of unnerve her. It calmed her somehow. She let him see who she was, even her vulnerabilities, and he wasn't looking away. Surely he knew she'd never planned on feeling this way about anyone ever again, but she did. And Elaine was right—Peter would want her to be happy. He would want her to be taken care of, even though she'd proven over the past ten years that she could do a pretty good job of that on her own.

As the thoughts tumbled around in her head, he leaned forward in his chair and brushed a strand of hair behind her ear. "I'm so glad to hear you say that." Bob's hand made its way to the back of her neck as his thumb brushed across her cheek.

If her heart wasn't racing at his gentle touch, she would've reminded herself to work up the courage to tell him her feelings more often. He deserved to know his affections were returned.

But she could hardly focus long enough to form a coherent thought, not with the warmth of his hand resting on the nape of her neck. Not with the steady look in his eyes. Not with the nerves dancing in her belly.

She forced herself not to look away, to hold his gaze. She didn't want to discourage him when everything inside her wanted him to lean over and kiss her.

As if he'd read her mind, Bob's eyes fell to her lips and his other hand found the other side of her face. He moved slowly, unable to be rushed, or perhaps wanting to treat her with the gentle respect she deserved.

He moved toward her, eyes dancing and a smile playing at the corners of his mouth. As their lips met, she closed her eyes and inhaled his woodsy scent. His kiss washed every doubt and worry out of her mind, filling her with an expectant hope.

After several blissful seconds, he pulled away, daring to search her eyes with that confidence she loved so much.

"We should do that more often," he said.

A rare boldness raced through her and she nodded in agreement. "We really should."

Bob kissed her one more time, then leaned back in his chair and studied the table. "I think it's time for dessert."

Jan gasped. "You made dessert too?"

He picked up their plates and walked them into the kitchen, returning with a gorgeous German chocolate cake. "This I picked up at the bakery." He grinned. "I know my limits."

It didn't have to be homemade to make her mouth water. The cake was the perfect ending to a perfect evening.

THE AIR WAS cold, but the quick walk warmed Elaine up, and a few minutes later she stepped inside the library. Aside from a few people using the computer terminals and a mother and toddler, the main space was pretty empty, but it was evening on a weekend, so that didn't surprise her. Priscilla was seated behind the main circulation desk, and she looked up and smiled when Elaine walked inside.

"I see you rushed down here after you got my message," Priscilla said with a smile.

Elaine didn't have the heart to tell her it was either this or billing, so she just nodded. "Did you find anything?"

"I sure did." She reached into her desk and pulled out a manila folder. "There were actually quite a few references to the Wood family and Jameson Wood. He was an interesting character." She gave Elaine a wink. "You're in for a treat. You're welcome to use the reading nook if you can't wait to dive in," Priscilla said, handing Elaine the folder. Elaine stifled a laugh. She was curious, but not that curious.

"I appreciate that, but I think I'll take this all home and look over it there," Elaine said. "But I can't thank you enough."

"It was my pleasure." Priscilla smile was genuine, so Elaine decided to believe her. She tucked the folder into her purse, waved, and stepped back out into the raw evening.

With Jan out on her date with Bob, Elaine had the house to herself, so she made herself a cup of Earl Grey and ventured upstairs with the folder tucked under her arm. She settled into the window seat, tucking an heirloom quilt around her for warmth against the cold air seeping in through the window, and opened the folder.

The first piece of paper was a printout from the front page of *The Chariot*, dated July 16, 1893. She hadn't heard of this newspaper, and assumed it must be long defunct. Judging by their graphic design, she could see why. There must be two dozen headlines on the front page, with about two inches of text beneath each. She squinted, reading each one carefully, until she found the one that had caught Priscilla's attention.

"Fire Destroys Woolens Mill," the headline read. She gasped and read the few lines beneath the headline. Apparently, what started as a small fire from the heating system quickly spread throughout the factory, leveling the wooden structure in mere hours. Elaine followed the story to the next page in her stack, where it picked up again. No one had been hurt, thank goodness, but the building was gone, and with it the Wood family business.

Well, that was a rather sour note after everything she'd read so far about the Wood family. She hoped they had rebuilt. She read on to find out.

The newspaper the next day had another column following up on the story, where it was reported that the ashes were still smoldering but Jameson Wood had vowed to rebuild.

The next page in the stack from Priscilla was another copy of *The Chariot,* dated January 23, 1894. "Former Mill Owner Arrested," the headline read.

Jameson Wood was taken into custody last night after an altercation outside Murphy's Tavern. According to witnesses, Wood and Henri Dumas had gotten into an argument inside the tavern. Other patrons didn't over-hear what the argument was about, but Dumas owns the Dumas Woolens Company, a former rival to the Wood Woolens, which was destroyed in a fire under myste-rious circumstances last summer. Once the fight esca-lated, bartender Pete Smith claims he heard Jameson accuse Dumas of destroying his business.

Well, that was an interesting twist, Elaine had to admit. Mysterious circumstances? What were the circumstances? When did those come out? She shuffled back through the papers Priscilla had given her, and there was nothing in it. Either those rumors never made it into print or the library was missing the issues of the paper where they were printed. Priscilla had said the collection was spotty this far back.

It also appeared, if this account was to be believed, that Wood had not rebuilt his mill yet. These things probably took a while, she reasoned. Maybe he was waiting until spring to begin construction. This far north, that made a lot of sense.

She kept reading. The next mention in the newspaper was from April 3, 1894. "Site of Former Woolens Mill Sold," the headline read. Elaine read that the land was being sold by the

Wood Woolens Company. The owner, Jameson Wood, had hoped to rebuild after a devastating fire, but the land was now being sold to pay off debt.

There were several more articles, each of which painted an increasingly bleak picture of the fortunes of Jameson Wood and his family. In 1895, the grand home he had built was sold off, again to cover debts. One of the articles hinted that these were not business debts; they were from gambling, though of course they didn't come out and say that.

What of his wife and children? What did they do through all of this? What did they think? How did they cope with their changing fortunes? Elaine was so curious—but of course, these things were not recorded in the sources she had. Such things were not news. Elaine would likely have to find personal documents, such as letters or journals, to get a glimpse into a woman's world at the time, and even if such things did exist, she had no idea where to find them. Besides, she realized, she had gotten what she needed, mostly. She now understood the basic trajectory of the Wood family's fortunes. After the fire destroyed the mill, Jameson Wood had lost most of the rest of what he owned through drinking and gambling. It was a sad tale, but a familiar one.

It put the ring into some context as well. Elaine guessed that the sapphire ring had been purchased during the family's prosperous days. But she still didn't understand how it had come to end up in the wall here, what the motto meant, or who it had belonged to.

Those questions, she thought, were not answered in these articles. She closed the folder and stretched her arms over her head.

She should go down and work on the billing she'd been putting off. The bit of tea left in her mug was cold, and her eyes were starting to go bleary from looking at the small type, but she was comfortable tucked up here in the window seat, and she thought through the possibilities for how the ring ended up in their wall. The articles and books hadn't said exactly where Jameson Wood had built his grand home—was there any chance this was it? But then Elaine knew that their house had been built by Harold and Beatrice Gardner in 1903, and then had stayed in the Gardner family until 1968, when it was sold to Maynard Binns. It was at no point owned by a member of the Wood family, as far as she knew. Unless...

Could Beatrice Gardner have been a Wood? Or perhaps her daughter-in-law, Rachel, who was married to Beatrice's son Paul, had been a Wood...? Was there any chance one of them had some other connection to the Wood family? Elaine thought it through, trying to decide how to work that out. Would the vital records department at the county office have records like this? She might check into that.

CHAPTER TWENTY-ONE

The phone call came late the following evening, much later than they were accustomed to getting phone calls. When Elaine picked up the receiver, there was a pause on the other line, long enough for her to say "Hello?" a second time.

Finally, a man's voice responded with a stutter, then a quick "Hi."

"Hello?" Elaine said again, not recognizing the voice.

"Is this Mrs. Cook?"

"It is."

"Mrs. Cook, this is George Newsome, from the antique store."

George's voice was very quiet and Elaine plugged her other ear to drown out the sound of the television. "Hello, Mr. Newsome. How are you this evening?"

"Can you come back to the antique store tomorrow morning? Mr. Ellerby will be out for about an hour around lunchtime and there's something I think you should see."

Oh my. The man's voice sounded somewhat ominous, and Elaine wondered if they might finally get the proof they needed to find Macy's vase. Archie and Rose would have to handle things at the tearoom if both she and Jan were going to be out and about—not something she wanted to make a habit of—but if they set everything up ahead of time, it should be fine.

"We'll be there around noon," she replied.

"Or about ten after," George said. "Just in case he's slow to leave tomorrow."

"Very good." Elaine hung up the phone and went to find Jan in the sitting room working on a crossword puzzle. They both agreed this was a very strange, very interesting turn of events, and one that had Elaine's imagination running wild until she finally drifted off to sleep much later than she wanted to.

After a full morning of tea service and a brief meeting with Archie and Rose, the cousins drove to Waterville, their heads full of questions and half thought-out theories about what George Newsome could possibly have to say.

"He was insistent that we come when Harrison was out of the store." Elaine parked her Malibu near the back of Ellerby's Antiques.

"It's certainly unexpected." Jan followed Elaine's gaze to the back door of the antique shop.

"We didn't get to look around much when we were here last time," Elaine said. "Maybe we'll find something that helps shed some light on this mystery. Waiting around for the deputy's report on Ellerby's financials is very difficult. I much prefer to be doing something."

They'd arrived a few minutes earlier than they intended to. Probably their own excitement had them moving more quickly than usual.

Around noon, Harrison emerged from the back of the building wearing a black, knee-length coat, a hat, scarf, and gloves.

Elaine snapped several quick photos. "From here, he fits the description Sarah gave."

Jan watched as the man got into his car. "He most certainly does, except for the shoes. Harrison Ellerby doesn't strike me as the gym shoe type. "

"Maybe he wore them for a quick getaway." Elaine clicked another photo.

"Make sure at least one of them isn't blurry."

Elaine glanced at her phone. She'd done a better job this time. Maybe now Sarah could identify their thief.

They waited until he pulled out of the back parking lot and disappeared around the corner before they exited the car. They crossed the street and headed toward the front door of the antique shop.

"I feel a little giddy," Jan said. "Like we're about to find out a very important secret."

"I hope that's exactly what's about to happen." Elaine pulled open the door and led them into the cluttered shop, inhaling that familiar, dusty smell.

Her eyes made their way back to the counter where Harrison's assistant worked diligently in his boss's absence. They moved over toward the English tea set Elaine had admired on her first visit. She did not want to give Harrison Ellerby a penny of her money, but she did want that tea set in their collection. The adorable teapot with its red and pink flowers would look so lovely in Jan's armoire among their others.

"Here goes nothing," Elaine whispered, moving toward the back of the shop.

"Excuse me?" Jan's voice cut through the silence. "Mr. Newsome?"

George Newsome looked up, then tossed a glance over his shoulder, as if making certain his boss really had gone.

"We saw Mr. Ellerby leave," Elaine said. "We waited until the coast was clear."

An interesting emotion washed over his face. If Elaine had to guess, she would've said it was guilt that he was about to tell them something unflattering about his boss. Surely there was a level of guilt that went along with that, even if it was the right thing to do. They would have to tread carefully.

"It doesn't look very busy this afternoon," Elaine said. "What are you working on?"

"I'm cleaning a series of antiques brought in by your friend, Nathan Culver, actually." George held up a small bronze trinket box that looked like nothing very special.

"This was found at an estate sale in Penzance. We're still tracing its origin, but I believe it's French and said to be very valuable. Mr. Culver should get a good amount for it."

"I'm sure he'll be happy to hear it," Elaine said. "Do you do all of the appraisals yourself?"

George turned his attention back to the bronze box. "Me? No. I just clean the pieces."

Silence hung between them and Elaine wasn't sure how much more small talk to make. She had the impression Mr. Newsome had something important to say, and there was no telling when Harrison would be back. Still, if he was getting cold feet about talking to them at all, she didn't want to spook him.

"It must be nice to be here alone every once in a while," she said. "It seems like a peaceful place to work."

"It is sometimes." George flicked a loose strand of hair out of his face. George had a boyish look about him—baby-faced with kind eyes and what was proving to be a rather shy nature. "It's not exactly peaceful when Mr. Ellerby is here."

Elaine felt Jan's eyes dart her way. "Is he gone often?"

George shrugged. "Seems like it lately. He's always rushing off, but never wants to say where he's going."

"Is that why you called us? To tell us he wasn't here on October third?" Jan's eyes were wide with curiosity.

"Not exactly. Follow me."

He motioned for them to follow him to a door off to the left, behind the counter. He pushed the door open and they followed him inside. The office was dark and masculine, the blinds on the windows facing the side street where she'd parked her car only slightly opened. He flicked the light on and it cast a warm, yellow glow across the large mahogany desk that sat in front of the windows. It was piled high with paperwork and books.

Books had been stacked and crammed into every square inch of free space on three built-in bookcases that stood off to the left. Two padded chairs faced the desk, though Elaine found it hard to believe Harrison Ellerby ever had company in this cramped office.

George moved over to the desk and started searching through the piles, but at this rate—and with this much stuff—it would take a year to comb through everything. She wondered what he was looking for.

Originally, she'd thought it likely that a man like Harrison Ellerby kept notes on his work, if for no other reason than he'd want to brag about it. With each piece he cleaned or restored, he had another story to tell, and ones as priceless as Macy's vase surely warranted such a tale. Perhaps she'd misjudged him, though, and keeping track of these items wasn't a priority. After all, there was nothing meticulous about the way he kept his office. It would seem their Mr. Ellerby was something of a hoarder.

George moved over to one of the built-in shelves. "I wanted to find this before you arrived, but he was in his office all morning." He continued searching.

"What is it we're looking for?" Jan asked. "May we help?"

George mumbled something, his finger sliding across the binding of a number of books. "Aha! Here it is. Mr. Ellerby calls it his memoir. He says the pieces speak for themselves." He pulled out a thin black hardcover book.

"His memoir?" Elaine resisted the urge to reach out for the book. She couldn't wait to see what was inside.

"It's a record of every notable piece he's ever worked on." George ran a hand across the front of it. "There's something I think you should see, but let's go back out to the front, just in case someone else comes into the store."

They followed him back out to the front, thankful there didn't seem to be much interest in antiques in Waterville at the moment. Both Jan and Elaine moved to the front side of the counter while George returned to his spot behind it.

George set the memoir on the counter and opened it. It seemed to be a sort of ledger, and while most people these days might use a computer for this sort of documentation, Harrison Ellerby seemed to prefer more traditional methods of record-keeping.

"Look at all the amazing pieces Mr. Ellerby has worked on over the years," Jan said with a sigh that almost sounded impressed.

"A large number," George agreed.

Too many pieces to count at a glance. Elaine wondered if any of the other objects mentioned in that book had gone missing, and if so, how they would ever be able to track such a thing.

"May I?" Elaine reached for the book.

"As long as you don't tell Mr. Ellerby I showed it to you." Worry passed over his brow.

She flipped through the book under George's watchful eye.

"There are so many." Elaine's eyes latched on to the image of Macy's vase, photographed in the very spot where they now stood. If the images had been placed in the book chronologically, Harrison had photographed it years before when he worked on the piece and not in the last few days.

"Yes, I thought you might find that page interesting," George said.

"Is this why you asked us to come?" Elaine was confused, as they already knew Harrison Ellerby had cleaned Macy's vase.

"Not exactly." George flipped to a page at the back of the book. "This is why I brought you here."

He set a finger on a list of names, then dragged it down the page. "This is a list of some of the men Mr. Ellerby has been known to associate with. They all specialize in finding the rarest pieces for collectors. Mr. Ellerby values their unique services immensely." He tapped the page three times, then pulled out a sheet of scratch paper.

"Are you saying we should talk to one of these men?" Jan asked, her eyes concerned underneath a furrowed brow.

George glanced at the back door again, then at the clock. "I'm saying you'll find it interesting to learn who some of Mr. Ellerby's most valued contacts are."

"Mr. Newsome, what aren't you telling us?" Elaine asked.

He pressed his lips together and Elaine willed him not to stay silent now. She hadn't sorted out the subtext of this visit, and she hoped he'd speak more clearly.

"I can't say for sure what happened to your friend's vase," George said. "But I can say that Mr. Ellerby's associates are worth looking into." He took out his phone and snapped a photo of the list, then took out a pen and notepad. "I'll just write down their contact information for you."

As he did, Elaine wondered exactly what kind of "unique skills" these men possessed. Why did Harrison Ellerby need someone with unique skills at all? He was an antique dealer.

"Mr. Newsome." Elaine tapped her fingers on the counter beside the book. "Would you mind if I took one more look through the book before we go?"

He held her gaze for several long seconds. "I suppose. Quickly though. Mr. Ellerby will be back soon."

"And while we're here, I was wondering if we could take another look at the English Rose tea set that's up front?" Elaine asked.

"Of course," George said. "I'll just go get it and we can look at it back here together."

He walked away, leaving them alone with the book for a few precious seconds. Elaine pulled out her phone and snapped a photo of the back page of the book where Ellerby had written down a list of names, just in case George's handwriting was illegible or he'd neglected to include everyone on the list.

"Is he coming back?" Elaine whispered.

Jan glanced toward the front of the store, then shook her head, giving Elaine a few quick seconds to photograph the last several pages of the book. Maybe they'd get lucky and something on one of those pages will have been reported stolen too. She wished she could tuck the entire book into her purse and head out the door, but that would never do.

She turned to the page with Macy's vase on it and snapped a quick photo, just as the back door opened and Harrison Ellerby appeared in the doorway. He looked at Elaine, then Jan, then back again, closing the door with a bit too much force.

As he walked toward them, George returned to the counter, closing the black book and setting the tea set down between it and Harrison.

"Mr. Ellerby, you're back," he said.

Harrison lifted his chin, his whole face falling into a glower. "What's going on here?"

"These ladies were interested in the English tea set." George's tone was a bit too chipper to be believable, especially since in the short time they'd known George, he'd been the exact opposite of chipper.

Elaine forced a smile.

"Why is this here?" He snatched the book off the counter and turned his attention to George. "This is private. As is my office."

"I'm sorry, sir," George said. "They had questions about the origins of the set. I wanted to be as thorough as possible."

"Questions," Ellerby said. "I'm sure they did."

"Mr. Newsome was very helpful." Elaine tried to ignore her racing heart. "Thank you, George, for helping us. Investing in real antiques is new for us. Most of our tea sets have come from flea markets, but we can see there is something quite special about this one. I'm sure this won't be the last you see of us." She flashed a smile at Harrison Ellerby, then lightly touched Jan's arm, although what she wanted to do was grab her and run. "Come on, Jan, we've got some big decisions to make."

They moved toward the front door, but before they went outside, Elaine tuned in to the conversation happening at the back of the store.

"Do you know who those two meddling women are?" Mr. Ellerby asked. George must've shaken his head because his boss proceeded to explain that Jan and Elaine were "nosy old biddies playing private investigator."

"Well, that is just unkind," Elaine said quietly to Jan, resisting the urge to turn around and tell him so. Jan grabbed her arm and pulled her toward the door, opening it quickly so she and Elaine could escape on to the pavement.

"Of all the nerve!" The mischievous twinkle in Jan's eye turned to laughter as they walked away. "'Nosy old biddies'!"

"Indeed!" Elaine felt her indignation give way and she joined her cousin in a good laugh. "Nosy, maybe, but definitely not old biddies."

They rounded the corner and walked back to Elaine's car. "So what do you think?" Jan asked.

"Well, I can't be sure. It seemed like George was just giving us bread crumbs, like a person who wanted to tell the truth without coming right out and telling the truth."

"My thoughts exactly. It certainly feels like Harrison Ellerby is our man."

Elaine nodded. "Now we just have to prove it."

CHAPTER TWENTY-TWO

J an had just escorted their last customer from the tearoom that afternoon when she saw a squad car pull up in front of the house. She stood on the porch of the large Victorian and the wind rustled her skirt, sending a cool autumn chill through her bones.

Business had picked up as the temperatures had cooled off. People must enjoy a warm cup of tea even more when the air outside was cold. For Jan, it didn't matter what it was like outside, tea was always welcome.

Deputy Sheffield stepped out of the squad car, carrying a manila file folder, which he waved in the air as he made eye contact with her. Did that folder mean he had news?

"Mrs. Blake," he said as he approached her.

"Deputy Sheffield. It's good to see you again."

He leaned against the railing and regarded her for a long moment. "That's some getup you've got on."

Jan's eyes fell to her Victorian gown. They'd had a special event in the east parlor that afternoon, a bridal tea. They'd barely made it back from Waterville in time to change and finish preparations, but Rose and Archie had everything under control.

"We like to create an atmosphere for our customers." She did feel a little silly sometimes, but mostly she enjoyed the play-acting of it all. A chance to pretend she lived in a different time—there was something wonderful about that.

"I'm sure your customers eat it up," Deputy Sheffield said. "Maybe you should audition for the next musical with the Waterville Players."

She laughed. "Oh, I don't think so! What a funny idea. I was just about to change."

"That might be a good idea considering what I've got here." Deputy Sheffield waved the folder in the air.

Jan turned back toward him. "What is it?"

"How about we make a trade?" Amusement stirred in his eyes.

"A trade?" Jan held his gaze.

"The information in this folder for a couple of those maple croissants everyone is always talking about."

"Oh? Have you moved on from the cream puffs?" she teased.

She didn't miss the glimmer in his eyes. "The guys at the station said the maple croissants are to die for. I felt left out since I'd never had one for myself."

"Well, we certainly wouldn't want that. I believe an agreement can be made, as long as it suits my cousin." She turned toward the door and motioned for the deputy to follow her inside. She led him into the parlor where Rose was clearing the last of the dishes. "Rose, would you ask Elaine to come out here for a minute?"

Rose straightened as her eyes latched on to Deputy Sheffield. Jan wondered if she should explain that they weren't in any kind of trouble, but Rose didn't give her time. Before she could say anything, the girl had already disappeared into the kitchen, leaving a stack of collected dishes on the table.

Jan found a freshly cleaned table and motioned for the deputy to take a seat. "Would you like some tea?"

"Do you have coffee?" he asked. "I'm actually more of a coffee guy."

"I suppose I can forgive you for that." Jan's eyes fell to that manila folder of secrets underneath his hand, the not knowing of it all weaseling its way under her skin. "Don't tell anyone else this," she said, sounding conspiratorial. "But Elaine enjoys a good espresso sometimes."

"I what?" Elaine walked into the parlor, still wearing her gown and drying her hands on a kitchen towel. "Rose said you wanted to see me?"

"That's right. Or rather, Deputy Sheffield. He seems to have information to share with us."

"Oh?" Elaine's eyes widened as she took a seat beside Jan.

"Information he will only share if we share something with him."

Elaine frowned.

"Don't put it that way," the deputy said. "I'm not blackmailing you for croissants or anything."

"Seems he's heard about our maple croissants and won't share his information without one." She looked at Deputy Sheffield with a smile. "Or two."

He wore a sheepish expression. "Like I said, the guys are always talking about them at the station."

"I'm not surprised. Jan is our secret weapon."

Jan warmed to the thought. "So it's a deal then?"

Elaine glanced at the deputy, narrowing her eyes as if making her decision, though Jan knew very well they would happily trade baked goods without a moment's hesitation for any news he might have about the vase. "It's not often we barter information for baked goods. Just let me tell Rose."

"With coffee?" Deputy Sheffield added.

"With coffee." Elaine's dress swished as she walked toward the kitchen, returning only a few seconds later with a nod that told them Rose was taking care of his treats. "Can you tell us what's in that folder? What did you find?"

"More than I expected to, actually," Deputy Sheffield said.

Rose emerged from the kitchen carrying a tray. She walked to their table and set a plate of petite croissants down in front of their guest, then poured him a cup of coffee and set the cream and sugar at the center of the table. "Do you need anything else?"

His eyes lit up like a child's on Christmas. "A couple more croissants?"

"You haven't even tried them yet. What if you hate them?" Never mind that Jan had yet to meet a person who hated them.

He picked one up and took a bite, closing his eyes as if to let the flavors fill his mouth. After he'd chewed and swallowed, he glanced at Rose. "Definitely going to need a couple more."

Rose nodded, then disappeared behind the kitchen door again.

Deputy Sheffield took another bite, then a sip, and for many moments, Jan wondered how long this game would go on. The curiosity was so strong she considered snatching the folder out from under his hand, though she had to admit, it was lovely to have a guest as appreciative of her baked goods as the deputy seemed to be.

"Turns out, snobby Mr. Ellerby has been known to associate with some pretty shady characters," he said between bites. Jan's thoughts turned to the list of names George Newsome had shown them. "Most notably, this man." He flipped open the folder and pushed it toward Elaine and Jan.

A mug shot of a bearded man with long, dark hair streaked with white was clipped to an arrest report. Elaine picked it up and pulled it closer, studying the image. "Who is he?"

Deputy Sheffield finished his last croissant just as Rose appeared with more. "His name is James Dawson. He's been arrested several times, most often for selling stolen goods. He's what we call a 'fence.' And he's been caught with some pretty expensive antiques before."

"You're kidding," Elaine said. "Where does he live?"

"Believe it or not, right here in Lancaster," Deputy Sheffield said.

"I didn't realize there was so much criminal activity here." Jan stared at the man's photo.

"Usually there isn't. Dawson grew up here. His mom still lives here, which is where we think he's hiding out."

"James Dawson," Jan said out loud. The man wasn't familiar, and yet his name... "Elaine, do you have that photo you took at Ellerby's earlier?"

Elaine shot her a look as the deputy stopped chewing.

"You went to Ellerby's?" he asked.

Jan's stomach dropped. Oops. "There's a tea set there..." She couldn't finish the half truth. It wasn't in her nature to tell a lie, and obviously a sheriff's deputy would see right through her.

"We did look at a tea set," Elaine said, her voice calm. "But we went at the request of Mr. Ellerby's assistant. He seemed to want us to know more about his boss. He showed us this." She searched through her phone, landed on what she was looking for and slid it across the table toward Deputy Sheffield.

Jan got her attention and mouthed a quick "So sorry," but Elaine waved her off, clearly not bothered by Jan's error. Apparently, her cousin had decided to trust the deputy. Jan was grateful for that—she liked the idea of aligning their investigation with his.

"Do you recognize anyone's name?" Jan asked, remembering why James Dawson sounded so familiar. She could still see Dawson's name scrawled on the back page of the ledger, like her mind had photographed that tiny detail for a reason.

"This appears to prove their association," Deputy Sheffield said. He glanced up from the photo on the phone. "But weren't you ladies going to keep me in the loop?"

"You're absolutely right, Deputy Sheffield. We should've called you before we drove over." Elaine's eyes fell. "Though I'm not sure George Newsome would've shown us anything if you'd been there with us."

"How'd you get this without Ellerby noticing?"

"He was out for lunch," Jan said.

"So it would seem that assistant knows more than he's letting on."

"It seemed like he wanted us to check into the names on this list," Elaine replied. "Maybe so we would find this connection to James Dawson."

"But he didn't come right out and say that?"

Jan shook her head. "He seemed very conflicted about the whole thing."

"So what next?" Elaine asked, surely suppressing the desire to race over to Dawson's mother's house straightaway and find out everything Dawson knew about Macy's stolen vase.

"I didn't find anything unusual in Ellerby's bank accounts, but I've flagged them so if he does make a large deposit, we'll know about it. After I talk to Dawson, if he seems suspicious, we can flag his accounts too."

Elaine stilled. "When are you going to talk to him?"

The deputy held up a croissant. "As soon as I'm done here."

"If you eat any more of those, you're likely to make yourself sick," Jan said, marveling at how easily he put them away.

"Not a chance, my stomach is like a steel trap." He patted his unfairly flat midsection with a grin, popping the last bite in his mouth.

"Deputy Sheffield," Elaine said, folding her hands on top of the table, "could we come with you to talk to James Dawson?"

Deputy Sheffield coughed. "No."

Elaine frowned. "I know it's not police protocol, but we are very invested in this case. *Please?*"

The deputy's eyes darted from Elaine to Jan and back again. "Fine," he said.

Jan gasped, surprised he'd agreed to such a thing.

"Since I'm just going to have a conversation with the man, I'll let you come along, but you have to promise to let me lead the charge."

Both Jan and Elaine nodded. "Of course," they said together.

"And one more thing." The deputy pushed his chair back from the table and stood. "There is no way you're going anywhere with me dressed like that."

After both of the cousins had changed into their regular clothes, they met the deputy outside and drove in his squad car across town to a small house in the middle of a row of other small houses, none of which seemed particularly well cared for.

"Do we know anything else about this guy?" Elaine asked as the deputy pulled the car to a stop.

"Just that he did time for fencing stolen antiquities and has been suspected in a number of others. A link to Harrison Ellerby could be the proof we need to put him away for a lot longer. If the two have been working together to steal and sell antiques, they could both see some serious time."

"It certainly seems suspicious," Jan said. "James Dawson could be just the proof we've been looking for to connect Ellerby to the vase."

"*If* he'll talk to us," the deputy said. "He really has no reason to cooperate."

"Should've brought more croissants." Jan chuckled to herself.

Her mood quickly turned somber as they headed up the sidewalk toward the small white house. It all felt so serious, and they'd never accompanied the police anywhere before.

It really was very kind of the deputy to allow it. He certainly didn't have to.

They waited behind Deputy Sheffield as he rang the doorbell. Moments later, a plump woman with cropped white hair opened the door.

"What's he done this time?" she barked before they had a chance to say a word.

"Mrs. Dawson? I'm Deputy Arnie Sheffield, and these are my..."

"It's Jimmy, right? What'd he do?" The woman cut him off before he had to make up an awkward excuse for Elaine and Jan's presence at his side.

"Maybe nothing, ma'am," he said. "Is James here? We'd like to ask him a couple of questions about a friend of his."

"Which friend?"

"I'd really prefer to talk to your son, ma'am." Deputy Sheffield certainly was official. Jan preferred a softer approach. She would've chatted with James Dawson's mother for a few minutes about living here on this block in Lancaster and probably asked about the little dog that had appeared at the large picture window at the front of the house.

But Deputy Sheffield was much more to the point when he spoke to people. It was a little bit intimidating.

James Dawson's mother frowned up at him. "He's out back in the garage. Tell him I told you where he was so he knows I'm done covering for him." She slammed the door, leaving the three of them wearing the same bewildered expression.

"I guess that's that. Maybe you two should wait in the car."

"Why?" Jan asked. "Do you think he's dangerous?"

"There's no way to know for sure."

"We'll be careful," Elaine promised.

"You're going to stay outside and behind me until I assess the situation," Deputy Sheffield said.

Jan and Elaine nodded in unison.

As they walked back toward the one-car, detached garage behind the house, Jan's pulse quickened and the nerves danced in her belly.

She wasn't used to dealing with the likes of James Dawson—not up close and personal. And while he could be a perfectly harmless man, there was always the chance he was exactly the opposite. She'd read too many stories to naively walk into a situation with a known criminal and not be at least a little worried.

As Deputy Sheffield knocked on the door, Jan said a silent prayer for their safety, wishing—not for the first time—that her overactive imagination would calm down a little.

CHAPTER TWENTY-THREE

Elaine tried—but failed—not to cower behind Deputy Sheffield as the door to the small garage opened, revealing a disheveled man with a beer belly, a longish beard, and a tattoo of a skull on his forearm.

He'd instructed them to stand behind him, but she was certain she looked as scared as she felt.

"Yeah?" the man asked, his voice gruff.

Jan folded herself in closer behind Elaine, turning them into descending stair steps behind the taller Deputy Sheffield. Maybe this was a mistake.

Deputy Sheffield appeared unruffled by James Dawson's rough exterior. "James Dawson?"

"I didn't do it." James did nothing to hide his irritation.

"Do what?" Deputy Sheffield asked.

"Whatever it is you're here to tell me I did." He slammed the door.

Deputy Sheffield straightened. "You two sure you don't want to go back to the car?"

"Do you think we should?" Jan asked, most likely ready to run at the first sight of danger.

"My gut says he's harmless. There's nothing in his file about violence, despite the way he looks. But I'm happy to question him and fill you in."

"We're fine." Elaine looked at her cousin. "Aren't we, Jan?"

Jan nodded, though the look on her face gave her concern away.

"You can go to the car," Elaine whispered. "You look green."

"I'll just stand over here." Jan stepped off the small sidewalk in front of the side garage door.

Once Jan was carefully hidden in her little corner, Deputy Sheffield knocked on the door again. They listened to the movement inside. Had James Dawson really expected them to go away?

The door opened, and the man stared at them, this time saying nothing.

"Mr. Dawson, I'm Deputy Sheffield. We'd like to ask you a few questions."

"Who are they?" James glanced at Elaine, then at Jan, whose hiding place, it turned out, wasn't very good.

"These are my associates, Mrs. Cook and Mrs. Blake."

"Did you draw the short straw or something?" James laughed.

Elaine leveled his gaze with a reprimanding look she'd perfected on her own children, and he quickly straightened.

"Sorry. Bad joke."

Hmm. Maybe Mr. Dawson wasn't so scary after all.

"Mr. Dawson." The deputy's tone demanded his attention.

James frowned. "I told you. I didn't do it. I'm clean. Walking the straight and narrow these days."

"It's about one of your associates. Harrison Ellerby."

Recognition splashed across James's face, but he said, "Never heard of him."

Deputy Sheffield put his hands on his hips. "Don't play games, Mr. Dawson."

The other man stroked his long beard while he studied them, as if making a decision.

"May we come in?" At the sound of the deputy's question, Jan recoiled, tucking herself behind a bush next to the garage.

"*Mi casa* is your casa." James left the door open as he walked away.

Deputy Sheffield looked at Elaine, then Jan, and walked through the door. Elaine followed, aware of Jan close behind her.

The small garage served as something else for James Dawson, as evidenced by the lack of car, lawn mower, or power tools. Instead, a thin rug was spread across the center of the floor. On one side was a shabby brown couch that looked far too soft to be comfortable, and on the other, a makeshift entertainment center comprised of two beat-up crates and a large television.

Off to one side was a small refrigerator and, hanging on the wall, an old radio with two antennae pulled all the way out in the form of a large *V*.

The last light of the day streamed through five small windows in the front door of the garage, highlighting the dust particles that danced in the air. Elaine supposed it was as close to his own place as James Dawson was going to get while still living with his mother.

"Did my ma tell you I was out here?" James asked.

"She did," Deputy Sheffield said.

"What do you want with Harrison?"

"How well do you know him?" Deputy Sheffield asked.

"Known him for years." James sat on the couch.

"Have you worked with him before?" the deputy asked.

James eyed the deputy. "I assume you've read my file."

Deputy Sheffield nodded.

"So you want to know if he's ever, uh, purchased any of my goods." As James leaned back, Elaine thought the plush couch might swallow him whole.

Deputy Sheffield shifted where he stood. "I suppose that's one way to put it."

"What are you looking for, Deputy Sheffield?" James overenunciated the last two words of his sentence. "This will go a lot quicker if you can be specific."

The deputy pulled a photo from his inside coat pocket and showed it to James. "Ever seen this?"

James gave the photo a passing glance, then shrugged. "Never seen it." But the way his eye twitched when he said it made Elaine wonder if he was lying.

The deputy must've picked up on it too. He waved the photo in the air. "Look again."

"I haven't seen it," James said. "Swear."

The sound of a cell phone buzzing cut through the air, pulling their attention. Deputy Sheffield fished his phone from his coat pocket. He checked the text message, then tucked it away.

"I suppose we could go search your little storage unit down by the river," the deputy said, clearly having received a new piece of information about James Dawson. At the mention of the unit, the burly man stiffened and looked away.

The deputy waited a few long seconds, then turned toward the door. "Have it your way. Unit 305 will be tossed within the hour."

James stood. "Wait."

All eyes settled on him.

"I have worked with Ellerby in the past, but it's been a long time."

"And you recognized the vase," Elaine said.

James nodded. "I've seen it before."

Deputy Sheffield ran a hand over his chin. "Where is the vase now?"

"I don't know." James's eyes darted from the deputy to Elaine to Jan and back again. "Honest." A funny word coming from a man who'd lied to them twice in as many minutes.

"You don't remember who you sold it to? Or Harrison hasn't given it to you yet?" Elaine had refrained from talking for far too long.

"What? No, you've got it all wrong," James said.

"So explain it to us," the deputy said.

"Ellerby's a collector," James said. "Not a thief."

"But the vase was stolen," Jan said.

"And he wants it. No doubt about it." James put his hands on his hips. "But he didn't steal it. He's trying to buy it."

Elaine shook her head. "That can't be right."

"Look, a guy like Ellerby, he's all about—how'd he put it?—preserving the integrity of a piece. Yeah, that's what he said. If he thinks he can do that, even if the piece is stolen, he will. But something like this vase—if he got his hands on it—there's no way he'd let it go."

"When did you last talk to Mr. Ellerby?" Jan asked.

James shrugged. "Few days after the vase went missing, I guess. He found out about it and said he wanted it for his collection. Said he'd increase my cut if I found it."

"Even though it's stolen?" Elaine asked.

"Part of the rush, I guess," James said. "He saw an opportunity, and he jumped at it, but he wouldn't go into someone else's home and *steal* something, no matter how much he wanted it."

"No, but he has no problem buying it on the black market."

"Sounds about right," James said.

"How do we know he didn't set you on its trail to throw us off?" Elaine asked.

"Huh?" James stared blankly.

"She means if Harrison Ellerby *did* steal that vase, he had to know we'd eventually link the two of you. Perhaps this is all an elaborate ploy to throw us off his trail." Deputy Sheffield stood up straighter, again hands on his hips in the most official way.

Elaine hugged her purse to her chest.

It would've been a smart ploy too, Elaine thought, for Harrison Ellerby to convince James Dawson he wanted the piece even though he already had it in his possession.

"Why would he do that?"

"It would give you plausible deniability and make Harrison look innocent." Elaine finished up her thoughts out loud.

"I guess that's one way to look at it," James said. "But in all my years of business, Harrison Ellerby has never once brought me a piece to be sold. He's always on the other side of the deal."

Unfortunately for their theory, Elaine believed him.

"What have you turned up about the vase so far?" Deputy Sheffield asked.

James lifted his shoulder. "Not much." He shook his head. "It's almost like whoever stole it has no plans to sell it. At least not through any of the normal channels."

"If you weren't going to sell it, then why would you steal it at all?" Deputy Sheffield asked.

The question hung in the air, unanswered. It seemed to be the missing piece of this whole puzzle, and Elaine had started to wonder if they'd ever know the truth.

"Deputy," Elaine said quietly, "if you think you've got enough, Jan and I really do need to get back to the tearoom."

The deputy gave James a once-over. "You hear anything about this vase, I expect you to give me a call." He fished a business card out of his wallet and handed it to the man.

James flicked it out of the officer's fingers, then slid it into his back pocket.

And while Elaine knew it might be beneficial to rehash the entire conversation with the deputy one more time, both she and Jan stayed silent the whole ride home.

CHAPTER TWENTY-FOUR

When the squad car pulled up in front of the tearoom, Deputy Sheffield finally broke the silence that had accompanied them on their ride home from James Dawson's garage.

"It seems like we're at a dead end," he said.

"It sure feels that way." Elaine sighed. "Harrison Ellerby seemed so guilty."

"There's still a chance he is," Deputy Sheffield said to Elaine. "Your theory that he set this whole thing up to make it look like he was innocent is a good one. I'm going to pay him a visit and find out where he was the day of the fire. I want to make sure we follow that lead all the way through."

Jan appreciated his persistence. Harrison Ellerby had been maddeningly coy about answering their questions. She supposed the deputy would have better luck compelling him to speak up, but as they walked up the sidewalk toward their front door, neither she nor Elaine was very hopeful.

Elaine headed straight for the kitchen and took the cheesecake bites out of the refrigerator. She glanced at Jan. "Brain food."

Jan smiled and fetched the plates, putting a kettle on for tea.

"I texted Sarah on the way home," Elaine said after she'd eaten two cheesecake bites.

"Oh? What about?"

"Well, she's the only one who can at least partially identify the man who was there that day. I sent her this." Elaine held up the photo she'd snapped of Harrison Ellerby from a distance wearing a coat that matched the description of the one on the man Sarah had seen. "She hasn't texted back yet."

The teakettle whistled for Jan's attention, and she moved it off the burner. "You really believe, after everything James Dawson told us, that Harrison Ellerby is our thief?"

Elaine clicked her phone off and set it on the counter. "It does seem unlikely, doesn't it? Although if he really is a collector, as James says, it would make sense that he hasn't tracked down the vase with any of his usual associates. Harrison stole the vase and added it to his personal collection. Case closed."

"Right. Case closed." Jan popped a cheesecake bite in her mouth, praying the little bit of brain food would work a miracle.

Before she had time to find out, though, there was a knock on the front door followed by the ring of the doorbell.

"Are you expecting someone?" Elaine asked.

"No." Jan walked toward the door. When she opened it, she found Sarah standing on the porch, a little boy clutching her hand.

"Sarah?" Jan glanced down at the boy. His face was adorably round and his big brown eyes stared up at her widely. Jan motioned for Elaine to join her.

Sarah held up her phone to reveal the photo Elaine had sent her. "I think this is him, the man I saw at the cottage the day of the fire."

"Why don't we all take a seat in the parlor?" Elaine led them inside and then to a table after taking their coats.

"This must be Dylan." Jan studied the boy as the three of them sat. The little boy gave her a nod and a shy smile. "It's good to see you both looking so well."

"Say hello, Dylan," Sarah prompted, and the little boy whispered a quiet "hello."

"Would you like a snack? You'd be doing us a favor. If you don't eat our cheesecake bites, Elaine and I will polish off the whole tray."

Sarah glanced down at her son, whose eyes begged without a single word. Sarah gave him a smile and mussed his dark-brown hair. "Maybe just one or two."

Jan fetched the tray of treats from the kitchen along with a pitcher of lemonade. "So you believe this is the man you saw?"

"I really think so." Sarah studied the image still pulled up on her phone. "He's tall, thin, and wearing the same coat and hat as he was the day I saw him. He's even carrying the same bag. The only thing that's different is the shoes."

Yes, the shoes. Jan's eyes fell to the image on her phone. According to Sarah, the man she saw wore blue cross trainers, and for the life of her, she couldn't fathom Harrison Ellerby in a pair of flashy sneakers.

"Who is this?" Sarah asked.

"It's Harrison Ellerby," Jan said. "The same man you saw at the antique store that day."

Sarah's forehead scrunched. "Maybe I just couldn't tell up close. But this"—she glanced down at the photo on the phone—"this makes it pretty clear."

"I see," Elaine said.

"So he stole the vase to sell it to some rich collector?" Sarah asked. "It fits, doesn't it?"

"Yes," Jan said. "In theory. Though if he stole the vase, there is a chance he has no intention of selling it at all, which would make catching him a lot more difficult."

"I think we should call Deputy Sheffield and tell him about this," Elaine said. "He may want to talk to you, Sarah. He's planning to see if he can find out where Mr. Ellerby was that morning, and if he knows someone spotted him at Green Glade, that's going to be very important."

The younger woman closed her eyes and let out a long breath. "Anything. Anything to put this whole misunderstanding behind me. I told Mrs. Atherton about my part in the fire."

"You did?" Jan wished she hadn't done that, but she understood why she did. Sarah was an honest person who had made a few thoughtless mistakes. She hoped Macy would be gracious.

"Yes," Sarah said. "I couldn't live with myself anymore. It was my carelessness that caused it. You both agree, don't you?"

Neither Jan nor Elaine responded. Sarah felt badly enough that she hadn't paid close enough attention to the loose knob on the stove. Still, it was an accident, and they really had no proof the fire wouldn't have started on its own, even if the knob hadn't been loose.

"What did Macy say?" Elaine asked.

"She said she needs a couple of days to figure out how to proceed," Sarah said, eyes falling to her folded hands in her lap. "I thought she was going to fire me right there on the spot."

"Would you like us to speak with her?" Elaine asked. "She does have a reasonable side."

Sarah shook her head. "Thank you, Mrs. Cook, but I'm ready to pay for my mistakes, even if it means finding another job."

"You have to find another job, Mommy?" Dylan looked at her with an anxious line of worry stretched across his forehead.

She pushed a tuft of hair out of his eyes. "I hope not, monkey. But Mommy made a couple of mistakes, and my boss has to decide what to do."

"But what will we do if you don't have a job?" He had a smear of cheesecake on his chin. Sarah reached over and wiped it away.

"God will help us, buddy."

Elaine smiled empathetically, a look of admiration on her face. It seemed they'd both grown a soft spot for Sarah Clayton.

"I should go," Sarah said. "Thank you for the treats."

"Of course," Jan said. "You and Dylan are welcome here anytime."

"You'll let me know if the deputy has questions?"

Jan nodded. "We'll be sure he has your number."

Jan saw them out, then returned to the parlor where Elaine was stacking their empty plates.

"That certainly changes things," she said.

Jan picked up her phone. "Let's call Arnie right away." She dialed, sitting back down at the table. When he answered, she filled him in on their conversation with Sarah, and he decided he would go question Mr. Ellerby the following morning.

"We could be there to help," Jan said.

"I'm not sure that's necessary," Deputy Sheffield said.

"Of course," Jan said. "Official police business." She hung up and turned to Elaine.

"He doesn't want our help?" her cousin asked.

Jan shrugged. "No, but he didn't say we couldn't go shopping."

Elaine's eyes widened. "Did he tell you what time he's going?"

"Bright and early. That's all he said."

"Then I suppose we'll have to go shopping bright and early too." Elaine's grin could only be described as mischievous, and as soon as she said the words, a ripple of nervousness shot straight through Jan. Were they finally going to catch their man?

THE E-MAIL HAD come in during the night, but Jan didn't see it until morning. She wasn't expecting to hear back from Jenna Kushman until after she and Elaine responded to her, something they planned to do as soon as they had more information on the vase's whereabouts.

The subject line read "Interesting coincidence regarding that vase." Jan clicked it open and started reading.

Dear Ms. Blake,

An e-mail that came to the museum was forwarded to me, and I thought it was a rather strange coincidence. The name attached to the e-mail was John Smith, which I'm assuming is a fake name, and while I can't be certain, it seems that the photo is of the very same vase you were inquiring about recently.

The sender is hoping to meet and discuss placing this priceless vase at the museum so it can go on display with the others, making the trio complete. Whoever wrote the e-mail seems to know a great deal about its history and seems to be very passionate about returning all Nazi plunder to its rightful owners, or, if that's not possible, putting them on display in a museum like ours so people are reminded of the tragedy of the Holocaust.

We've been searching for the vase for a very long time, as you can imagine, and now we have two separate leads as to its whereabouts. We are very excited, but can't help but wonder if it's possible your vase (or this one) is a forgery. I'm anxious to discuss the vase with you at your earliest convenience.

Sincerely,
Jenna Kushman

ELLERBY'S ANTIQUES OPENED at nine in the morning, but Jan and Elaine arrived a half an hour prior, hoping to beat the deputy there. They parked behind the building and down the street, and only moments later, his squad car pulled up.

He parked right behind them on the street, then got out of his car and sauntered over to theirs. He stood at the driver's side window and knocked on it, the way he would if he'd just pulled them over for speeding.

Elaine rolled down her window but kept her eyes forward. "Good morning, Deputy Sheffield."

"Fancy meeting you here, outside the very store where I'm going to question our suspect."

"We came to shop," Elaine said brightly. "There's this gorgeous English Rose tea set in there."

He leaned down and peeked inside the car. Jan pulled a brown paper bag from her purse. "I thought you might be hungry."

The deputy took the bag, and as he opened it, the smell of Jan's freshly baked cinnamon rolls filled the car.

"We can go in as soon as I finish one of these." He pulled one out and bit into it.

Elaine's expression told Jan her cousin was impressed at her foresight. She had a feeling those cinnamon rolls would go a long way with Arnie Sheffield.

"We received an e-mail from someone at the Holocaust museum. She said someone reached out about the vase," Elaine said.

"Oh?" The deputy squinted up at them, shielding his eyes from the morning sun.

"Apparently someone named John Smith is in possession of the vase and wants to meet with her about placing it in the museum. What that means in terms of finances, I don't know."

"John Smith? Sounds like a fake name to me," Deputy Sheffield said.

"I thought so too," Elaine said.

"You didn't bring any backup?" Jan asked, scanning the deputy's empty squad car.

"I hardly think this guy is dangerous," Deputy Sheffield said. "Besides, we're just here to ask a few questions." He popped the last bite into his mouth.

"I'm surprised you tasted that cinnamon roll at all." Elaine sounded equal parts concerned and impressed. "You practically inhaled it."

He swallowed. "Oh, I tasted it. Believe me." He held the brown paper bag up and shook it. "I'm just glad there are two more in here for later."

Jan shook her head. "It's a wonder you're not three hundred pounds."

"I have a fast metabolism." Deputy Sheffield grinned. "You girls ready?"

They got out of the car, but as they crossed their street and made their way around the front of the building, he made it clear they were not to speak to the suspect. They nodded as he gave them their instructions, fully aware he could've sent them home. They'd taken a risk coming there at all. They reached the front of the store, but when Deputy Sheffield tried to push open the front door, he found it locked. He knocked—hard—until finally Harrison Ellerby appeared on the other side of the door.

The man strode toward the front door and pulled it open. "We're closed."

"We just have a few questions." The deputy held Harrison's gaze for several long seconds, until finally the man opened the door. He took a few steps back to allow them room to enter.

"We're not open yet," he said coldly.

The deputy glanced at his watch. "We're two minutes early. Do you want us to go back outside and wait?"

Harrison only glared. "What's this about? I told you I had nothing to do with that missing vase."

Jan didn't want to be picky, but technically, Mr. Ellerby hadn't exactly said he had nothing to do with the missing vase. If anything, he avoided the question altogether. But she didn't think now was a good time to say so.

"Where were you on October third?" Deputy Sheffield cut right to the chase.

"Who can remember?" Mr. Ellerby turned and started walking toward the back of the store. "I hardly remember where I was yesterday." He thought for a moment. "Ah, yes, of course. I was here all day. Should I call my lawyer?"

"That depends," Deputy Sheffield said. "Do you have something to hide?"

Mr. Ellerby shook his head as if he couldn't be bothered to answer the question at all. Jan wondered how long the deputy's patience would last.

"Have you sold the English Rose tea set yet?" Elaine asked, and while her question came out of the blue, it was a welcome diversion. The air in the store had grown thick and tense. Harrison Ellerby certainly was, as Nathan had described him to Elaine, a "prickly fellow."

He raised a brow, turning toward Elaine, and though he looked down on her, his chin jutted upward. It was quite a thing to see, really.

"Perhaps we'll just look around a little bit." Elaine motioned for Jan to follow her. They walked a few steps to the left, down an aisle with two shelves of milk glass, both pretending to be interested but still listening to the conversation.

"Do you want to tell me what this is all about?" Ellerby asked. "I'm getting irritated and I have work to do."

"We have a witness who puts you out at Green Glade the day of the fire," the deputy said.

Mr. Ellerby frowned. "Who would say such a thing?"

"We aren't saying you're guilty," the deputy said. "But I'm sure you can see it would be to your benefit to cooperate. We just need to know where you were that day."

Harrison stiffened even more than usual. "Excuse me while I call my lawyer."

The deputy waited while Mr. Ellerby placed the call. When he was finished, he set the phone down on the counter and turned back to Deputy Sheffield. "He's coming right over. I simply don't think I have to answer your questions if I don't want to. I've done nothing wrong."

"Oh, Mr. Ellerby, we met a friend of yours. James Dawson." Jan moved back out into the main aisle and stood next to the deputy. "He's an interesting fellow."

Ellerby's eyes drifted back toward the counter, where George Newsome stood watching with wide eyes.

Poor George. Jan suspected he wouldn't be working at Ellerby's Antiques very much longer.

"Are you responsible for this?" Ellerby glared at George.

"They must've found something to link you to Dawson in your ledger," George said, remaining calm, but still standing safely behind the counter. "I'm sorry, Mr. Ellerby."

That wasn't exactly honest of George, Jan thought. He'd showed them the ledger and pointed out the names of James Dawson and a few other unsavory characters associated with Mr. Ellerby. She watched George for several seconds, but he didn't move or flinch.

"I have nothing criminal to hide," Harrison said. "I just don't like being told what to do."

"Then maybe you wouldn't mind if we looked around a little bit?"

"It's a store," Ellerby said. "You can browse all you want. At least until my lawyer gets here."

The deputy began moving through shelves of cluttered antiques, but Jan and Elaine stayed near the counter, busying themselves with a display of Hummel figurines, tiny little glass sculptures whose price tags nearly made Jan gasp.

She picked one up and turned it over in her hands.

"Be careful with that," Harrison said through what seemed like clenched teeth.

"I remember my grandmother had a shelf of these in her living room," Jan said. "They're very expensive."

"They're not what they used to be." Ellerby reached out and took the figurine from Jan, holding it carefully with his long, slender fingers. "Though it's something of a shame. To me, and to many people, they are symbolic of a very important time in our country's history—a time when we were bouncing back after World War II."

Jan watched as he studied the piece for a few long seconds before placing it cautiously back on the shelf. She had begun to believe James Dawson. This man was a collector—but he didn't seem to be a thief. It was something about the look in his eyes. While he was, in fact, prickly, he cared about these antiques and what they represented. It was the stories behind them, their history, that he regarded.

If he was in possession of Macy's vase, he wouldn't part with it. It wouldn't go to a museum and it definitely wouldn't go to the highest bidder. Someone had e-mailed Jenna Kushman about the vase, but it wasn't Harrison Ellerby.

"I believe you didn't take the vase," Jan said quietly.

His eyebrow shot up as he peered down at her. "You do, do you?"

She nodded. "But the deputy isn't going to leave until you tell him where you were."

Harrison shifted, refusing to meet her eyes, but before he could say anything the front door opened and a man wearing a trench coat and carrying a briefcase burst in.

"Deputy Sheffield!" he called out, drawing the attention of everyone in the little shop.

The deputy turned toward the voice and they all gathered near the center of the store.

The man rushed back behind the counter. "Maxwell Mundy." He handed Deputy Sheffield a card. "Attorney. Would you mind telling me what it is you're looking for and how my client is involved?"

Deputy Sheffield explained the situation to the lawyer, who listened intently, while Harrison crossed his arms, an annoyed sort of glower on his face. George disappeared into the back room, leaving Jan standing at the counter alone.

"Harrison, a word." The lawyer motioned for Mr. Ellerby to join him a few yards away where they huddled behind a shelf of glass knickknacks. They whispered back and forth for a few moments, and Jan wondered why Harrison hadn't been forthcoming with them in the first place. What did he have to hide?

While they waited, her eyes fell to the front counter where a black ledger, not unlike the "memoir" Mr. Ellerby kept, sat. It looked very official. She slowly looked around the store, and when she realized no one was paying attention, she opened the cover of the book, just far enough that she could peek inside. It was some sort of journal with nothing written in it but numbers. Dates? Some sort of filing system for stolen goods? Or maybe just Harrison Ellerby's method for keeping track of the pieces he restored.

She glanced around again, thankful for at least a few more seconds to try and decipher what this journal was. As she let one of the pages fall, she saw more numbers and a folded sheet of paper caught her eye. The paper had been folded so the logo at the top of the letterhead was showing—the United States Holocaust Memorial Museum in Washington, DC.

The same museum Jenna Kushman worked for.

She glanced back at Harrison Ellerby, studying him. Sarah was sure he was the man in the photo. Tall, thin, dark coat and hat along with a pair of sunglasses.

But the shoes weren't a match, and based on what she'd observed, James Dawson's assessment of the man seemed more likely.

Something wasn't adding up, but what was it?

Jan's thoughts were interrupted as his lawyer cleared his throat—loudly—and the two men rejoined the rest of them near the front counter.

"Mr. Ellerby hasn't been completely honest with you," Mundy said. "But I've advised him that it's time to swallow his pride and tell you the truth."

"Not that I owe you any kind of explanation," Harrison said. "After all, it's not like you have a warrant."

He was a stickler for the rules, obviously.

"But we both agree it would save us all a lot of headache if we got everything out in the open," the lawyer said. "And Mr. Ellerby has an airtight alibi for the day of the fire."

Jan glanced at Mr. Ellerby, who had a blank look on his face.

"Why don't you tell them what you told me?" Mundy suggested with a nod toward Mr. Ellerby.

"There is no way I could've been at Green Glade on October the third, because I was..." Ellerby glanced up and found Mundy's eyes encouraging him to continue. "I was at a morning mixer."

A collective frown wound its way around the circle.

"A morning mixer?" Elaine asked. "Like, for single people?"

Mr. Ellerby rolled his eyes. "Yes. Like, for single people. It's very upscale and respectable. Nothing cheap or sleazy about it."

"Of course," Jan said. "What a lovely thought."

He looked surprised by her approval, but it seemed to give him the courage to continue. "I go every week. It's a standing appointment. We have lunch and tea and wonderful conversation with the most delightful, intelligent people."

Was he blushing?

"It sounds like a wonderful event," Jan said. "There's no shame in tea and conversation." She smiled.

"Can you imagine? A man like *me* at a singles' event?" He waved his hand from his shoulder to his waist, as if the rest of them were supposed to drink in his glorious beauty. "I am not exactly the picture of desperation."

"Oh brother." Deputy Sheffield rolled his eyes.

"I've met some wonderful women at this mixer over the past few months, but that day—I remember it well—that day I met Marjorie Clincher." He pulled his phone from his pocket. After tapping around on it for a few moments, he set it on the counter to reveal an image of himself and a tall, thin, dark-haired woman with bright-red lips. "Isn't she stunning?"

Never mind that the resemblance between the two of them was uncanny. They reminded Jan of Morticia and Gomez Addams.

"She's special to you." Elaine's comment sounded like a realization.

Harrison scoffed, took the phone back, and stared at the photo. "She's not just special, Mrs. Cook. She's *the one*."

"How do we know this photo was taken on that exact day?" Jan hated to interject reality into romance, but they had no proof his story was true.

"You can check the date on the photo." Harrison tapped on the photo again. "There, October third. You can even see the time on the photo—1:35 p.m."

Jan studied the photo a little more closely. Harrison wore a black suit coat over a crisp white button-down shirt. "Was it particularly cold that day, Mr. Ellerby?"

Harrison shrugged. "Actually, no. It was unseasonably warm for October. I remember because I took Marjorie for ice cream when we finished at the mixer. Have you ever had ice cream for lunch? It's a wonderful treat."

"We're all very happy for you, Mr. Ellerby." Elaine's eyes were still on the photo and she was still in shock that this, of all things, was his alibi. "I'm curious why you didn't tell us this before. Surely you want the world to know this beautiful woman is a part of your life?"

Harrison's face turned smug. "I've always maintained that someone like Macy Atherton should not be in possession of something as priceless as that vase. I saw no reason to help you find it. After all, it's not my job to save you time."

Jan felt her jaw go slack at his admission. Harrison Ellerby may not be a thief, but there was a side to him that wasn't very nice. She wondered what Marjorie saw in him. She supposed that everyone was somebody's cup of tea.

"What about James Dawson?" Deputy Sheffield piped up.

Harrison rolled his eyes. "Oh yes, what did Dawson tell you about me?"

"He said you asked him to track down the vase."

"Did he?" Mr. Ellerby crossed his arms over his thin chest. "Interesting."

"Harrison," Mundy said. "No more games."

"Fine, yes, I asked him to track it down, but how do you know my plan wasn't to return it to its rightful owner?"

"Because you just told us you didn't think she deserved to have it," Deputy Sheffield said.

Mundy shrugged. "You have no proof as to what he may or may not have done had the vase turned up. That is merely speculation."

A door behind the counter slammed, pulling all eyes back to the doorway, where George Newsome appeared.

"Sorry to interrupt," he said. "I just forgot something."

Jan watched him as he walked toward the counter, her eyes drawn down to his feet.

Bright-blue running shoes.

She glanced at Elaine, who seemed to notice the same thing at precisely the same time. They hadn't seen his feet earlier because he'd been standing directly behind the counter, but now, with some distance between them, they both saw it.

He picked up the black ledger off the counter and tucked it under his arm. "I have a quick errand to run, Mr. Ellerby, but I'll be back in about an hour."

They watched him go.

And just like that, Jan knew exactly who had stolen that vase. The question was—how were they going to get it back?

CHAPTER TWENTY-FIVE

W hat an interesting morning," Elaine said as she and Jan drove back to the tearoom in Lancaster. She and Jan had both noticed George Newsome's shoes, and more importantly, Jan had explained she'd seen a letter from the very museum where Jenna Kushman worked—in the ledger George claimed as his own.

"Should we have said something as soon as we knew?" Jan asked.

Elaine shook her head. "I don't think so. If we had, we could've scared him, and there's no guarantee he would've returned that vase."

"I wonder where he was going." Jan's brow knit into one thin, worried line. "I hope we're not too late."

"From the sounds of Jenna's e-mail, we still have time," Elaine said. "But I'm not sure how much."

"I have an idea." Jan turned toward her, a glow of excitement dancing in her eyes. "But we're going to have to enlist a bit of help."

"And Deputy Sheffield?" Elaine asked.

Jan's face fell. "We'll tell him the very moment we can."

Later that evening, the doorbell rang and Elaine found Sarah standing on the porch with Dylan at her side.

"Good evening," Elaine said, welcoming them in. She took their jackets and hung them in the front closet. "We're in here."

She led them all into the east parlor, where Jan waited for them. Her cousin had explained her entire plan, and Elaine had to admit—it was a good one. If Sarah was on board, it just might work.

"I made some cookies for you all," Jan said as they took their seats around the table. "I hope you like snickerdoodles."

Dylan's eyes lit up. "Can I have one, Mom?"

Sarah smiled at her son, then glanced up at Jan. "Sorry I couldn't find a sitter on short notice."

"Oh, don't be silly. We love having Dylan here. I have a box of coloring books and some crayons that my grandchildren play with when they're here. Let me go get them."

Dylan reached over to the tray and took a cookie, one eye glued to his mother. He pulled it carefully toward himself, waiting for her approval. Finally, she gave him a nod and he took a bite.

"What do you say?" Sarah whispered.

"Thanks," Dylan said with his mouth full just as Jan walked back in the room. She set a stack of coloring books and a box of crayons in front of him with a smile.

"So I assume this has something to do with the vase? Did you figure out who took it?" Sarah asked.

"We think so." Jan caught Sarah up to speed, then laid out her entire plan for not only catching the real thief, but for also getting the vase back.

"So what do you think? Will you help us?" Elaine turned to Sarah.

"Help them, Mom. They make good cookies." Dylan slid another snickerdoodle from the tray on to his plate.

Sarah shook her head, a slight smile playing at the corners of her mouth, but then her face fell. "Of course I'll help. I feel responsible for this whole thing."

"Sarah, you should know that if the fire hadn't started that day, there's a good chance the theft of the vase would've gone unnoticed," Elaine explained.

Sarah met Elaine's eyes, hopeful. "What do you mean?"

"Macy doesn't inspect each cottage every single day, does she?"

"Surprisingly, no," Sarah said.

"It could've been weeks before anyone discovered the vase was gone," Elaine said. "And by then, we would've had more guests to eliminate as suspects and no real idea when the vase went missing at all."

"What are you saying? That it was a good thing the fire happened?" Sarah's voice was quiet, her eyes glassy. The weight of this seemed to be almost more than she could handle.

All things work for good... Elaine thought. She covered the young woman's hand with her own. "Not a good thing, but maybe not all bad. I was sure to point that out to Macy too," Elaine said.

"Thanks, Mrs. Cook." Sarah's eyes fell to the table. "I'm still very happy to help if you need me."

"In that case..." Jan slid a small slip of paper across the table to Sarah. "Are you ready?"

Sarah picked up the paper, then glanced at Dylan. "Maybe we should go into the other room. I think this whole thing would confuse him."

Jan and Elaine both nodded, then led Sarah into the kitchen after she told Dylan that Mommy and the nice ladies would be right back. He barely looked up from his coloring book.

"Here goes nothing," Sarah said as the door to the parlor closed. She sat down on one of the stools at the kitchen island, took out her phone, dialed, and waited. When she got an answer, she held up one finger, as if to warn them all to be quiet. "Yes, hello. My name is"—she glanced down at the piece of paper—"Jenna Kushman, the research assistant to Daniel Kingston, director of the United States Holocaust..." Sarah glanced around the room, listening intently to whoever was on the other end of the line.

"I see, sir. So you're anxious to make sure we get this piece quickly." Sarah's eyes widened at whatever he was saying. "Yes, it's very good timing in fact, because I happen to be coming through Lancaster tomorrow...yes, a last-minute trip. I should be there around..." She glanced at Jan, who mouthed the words "9:00 a.m." to her.

"Nine in the morning," Sarah said. "I'm afraid I won't have more than a half an hour." She shrugged as if to let them know she was making this whole thing up as she went along. "I'm not familiar with it, but I'm sure I can find it. It's down by the lake?...Very good. I will be there tomorrow at nine."

Sarah clicked the phone off and dropped it on to the counter. "I've never been so nervous in my life."

"You did great." Jan reached over and squeezed her hand. "The hard part comes tomorrow."

"When we meet him face to face," Sarah said, a new wave of visible panic washing over her. "Do you really think we can pull this off?"

Jan gave a deliberate nod. "I really do."

Elaine could only hope her cousin was right. They were so close to retrieving Macy's vase.

CHAPTER TWENTY-SIX

Morning came swiftly, and though Jan was sure she'd slept at least some of the night, it had not been a restful sleep. She awoke on edge, thoughts of the day ahead percolating in the forefront of her mind.

After she'd showered and dressed, she made her way to the kitchen, where she prepped the refreshments for the tearoom that morning. There was a good chance Archie and Rose would have to handle this one on their own, and while she was more than confident they would be fine, a part of her still felt like it was wrong to leave them again.

Rose wafted through the kitchen, light and airy like a gentle breeze. She stopped when she saw Jan. "Are you okay? You have that look on your face."

"I don't know what makes me more nervous, leaving you two to fend for yourselves or actually catching this criminal in the act of trying to unload Macy's vase."

Rose stared at her from the other side of the island. "I hope these two things don't give you the same level of anxiety."

Jan glanced up from the batter in her mixing bowl and laughed. "No, you're right. I'm sure you and Archie will be just fine."

"We'll take good care of everything for you, Jan," Rose said with a smile.

Jan was thankful they'd had the good sense to hire Rose and make her a part of their family. She had become invaluable to them, and Archie was well on his way to becoming the same. "I know you will."

"Then you just finish whatever delectable thing you're baking today, and let us handle the rest." She flashed a smile and strolled out of the room just as Elaine entered from the other door, wearing a nervous expression.

"What is it?" Jan clapped the flour from her hands.

But seconds later, when Macy entered the room, Jan had her answer.

"You two really are terrible with the updates," Macy said. "I expected to be kept in the loop and here I find out you have some big sting operation planned for this morning, and you didn't even tell me."

Elaine put the kettle on. "Why don't I make you some tea, Macy?"

"So you can try to convince me of all the reasons I shouldn't join you on your little fishing expedition?" Macy propped herself up on a stool, clinging to the purse in her lap.

"Of course not," Jan said.

"Actually, yes," Elaine corrected. "I don't think it's a good idea for you to come along."

"But Sarah said you know who did it," Macy said. "I believe I deserve to be clued in."

Sarah. That girl's conscience must have gotten the better of her. That, or Macy had badgered her into spilling everything she knew.

"Of course you do, Macy," Elaine said. "After we've got your vase back, we'll tell you everything."

Macy grimaced. "Unacceptable."

Jan glanced at the clock. She had to keep mixing if she had any hope of pulling her muffins from the oven before they left for their meeting. She understood Macy's insistence on being there when they recovered her vase, but she also understood Elaine's hesitation in allowing her to do so.

She filled the hollow parts of the mini muffin tin with batter.

"I'm coming along." Macy sipped her tea as if she were a proper Englishwoman.

Elaine sighed.

"I will sit in the back and be so quiet you'll never even know I'm there." Macy held her hand up as if taking an oath. "Promise."

Jan did a slow turn toward Elaine, who stared at Macy as if making up her mind. They both knew better, and yet how could they say no? It was Macy's vase. She did have a right to know who took it and why.

Besides, Jan wasn't convinced they could stop the woman if they wanted to.

"Well?" Macy tapped her fingers on the counter.

"You cannot say a word," Elaine said.

Macy let out a sigh of relief. "Promise. I'll be the best little ride-along you've ever had."

Elaine left the kitchen, shaking her head the whole way.

About an hour later, it was time for them to leave for the meeting. They would drive separately, Sarah in one car and Jan, Elaine, and now Macy in another.

"Remember," Jan said, going over the details, "we need to get him to show you the vase."

Sarah nodded. "I'll call you when I'm on my way in and put the phone in my pocket so you can hear the whole conversation. Also, look." She reached into her coat pocket and pulled out a small white business card. On it was printed the name of the museum above her name and phony contact information. "I made it up yesterday."

Jan turned the card over in her hand. "Very nice touch."

"Couldn't I pretend to be something?" Macy asked. "The appraiser or something?"

"It's unlikely, but possible, that George Newsome would recognize you, Macy," Elaine said. "It's important for the three of us to stay completely out of sight."

Macy didn't hide her disappointment.

"Once you have the vase in your sight, say the words *It's even more beautiful in person,* and we'll know we can come in and catch him."

"And when the time is right, we'll call Deputy Sheffield."

"He might be upset with you two," Macy said. "Shouldn't he be handling this little sting operation you've concocted?"

"It's hardly a 'sting operation,'" Jan said with a laugh. But as the words slipped out, she said a silent prayer that her plan would work.

Macy walked off toward Elaine's Malibu. "We're going to be late if you all keep gabbing."

The rest of them took a moment to set their resolve, then dispersed toward their respective vehicles.

"I'm sorry about telling Mrs. Atherton," Sarah said as they trudged back to their cars. "She started asking me questions, and after everything that's happened, I didn't feel like I could hide anything else from her."

"I understand." Jan watched Macy open the front door of Elaine's car, but her cousin quickly shooed her to the back. "Macy is harmless, really, and she has a good heart."

"She hasn't fired me," Sarah said. "I'd say I have to agree."

Jan wound her arm through Sarah's. "At some point you're going to have to stop beating yourself up over this whole mess."

Sarah gave her a sad look. "I know. Maybe once the vase is returned and the real thief is behind bars, it'll be easier, though I don't think I can ever pay for the damage to that cottage."

"I don't think Macy would ever allow you to, no matter how loud her bark." Jan patted Sarah on the arm as she broke away from her and took her place in Elaine's front seat.

The drive to the storage unit down by the lake was uneventful, but Macy didn't stop talking the entire way. She ran through her theories of who could possibly be responsible for the theft of her vase, as Jan and Elaine hadn't filled her in on their theory yet. Next, she detailed a litany of ideas of what she was going to do when she found out for sure who it was.

"The nerve of some people," she said. "Stealing a priceless heirloom just for their own personal gain."

"I'm not so sure about that, Macy," Jan said. "Seems to me that this person has other motives."

Macy scoffed. "Like what? What other possible explanation could there be than greed?"

"The thief stands to make a lot more money by selling it through someone like James Dawson." Jan folded her hands in her lap and stared out the window as Elaine led them to an alley where they could hide, but still see the storage unit where the meeting had been arranged to take place.

Sarah pulled in, parking in front of the storage unit.

Jan's phone rang.

"Can you hear me okay?" Sarah asked on the other end of the call.

Jan put her on speakerphone and turned up the volume. "Yes, I think we'll be fine. Just be careful."

"Do you think I need to be worried?" Sarah asked.

"I think you'll be just fine," Jan said in her most reassuring tone.

From where they sat, they kept their eyes on Sarah's car, parked in front of the unit that resembled a garage. Moments later, another car pulled into the slot right beside it.

"Here I go." Sarah got out of the car and Jan pushed the mute button on her phone, giving them the freedom to talk without worrying about the man overhearing them.

"Who is it?" Macy asked, leaning forward for a better look. "Ellerby? Did you finally get proof?"

"Harrison Ellerby has an airtight alibi, as Deputy Sheffield would say." Elaine squinted toward the storage unit as the door to the second car opened. They all watched as a man emerged from the driver's seat. He wore a knee-length black coat, a black scarf, and a pair of sunglasses. Slung across his shoulder was a familiar messenger bag.

"See? Harrison Ellerby," Macy said victoriously.

Jan leaned forward, trying to get a better look. From this distance, it certainly appeared to be Mr. Ellerby. Had he made up his alibi and somehow figured out a way to change the date stamp on his photo?

"But it can't be..." Elaine's voice trailed off. "We eliminated Mr. Ellerby as a suspect."

"We certainly did," Jan agreed.

From where they sat, they watched the man approach the door to the storage unit, unlock the padlock, and go inside. Sarah joined him in front of the unit, waiting outside to draw the man back out so the others could witness whatever deal was about to take place. Smart thinking, Jan thought.

He emerged from the unit without his bag and extended a hand toward Sarah. "Miss Kushman," he said, shaking her hand, "good of you to come. I'm leaving town soon, so it's good we made this connection when we did."

"Thank you, Mr. ...?"

"Ellerby," the man said. "Harrison Ellerby."

Sarah hesitated but quickly recovered. "I'm glad you could see me on such short notice. Do you have the vase? I'd love to take a look at it."

"Of course," he said. "Follow me." Before he disappeared into the storage unit, Jan spotted the flash of blue at his feet.

"It's not Ellerby," Jan said.

Macy harrumphed in the back seat. "He just said it was. Besides, it looks just like him."

"That's his hat, coat, and bag, but those are definitely not his shoes. We were right, Elaine."

"Right about what?" Macy practically whined the question.

"Here it is," they heard the man say through the phone. "Please be careful with it."

A few long seconds of silence.

"Wow, it's even more beautiful in person," Sarah said.

Quickly, Elaine took out her phone and dialed the deputy, asking him to please come down to the storage units by the lake. From the sound of Elaine's end of the phone call, Deputy Sheffield wasn't exactly happy with them, but Jan had a home-made cheesecake drizzled with raspberry sauce with his name on it. She hoped he would be understanding.

"It's the real thing," the man said. "It was stolen from a Jewish family in Poland during World War II."

Macy gasped. "I still don't believe it."

"How do you know?" Sarah asked.

"Because I've been researching Nazi plunder since I was twelve. It started as a hobby when I found out my own great-grandfather's work had been stolen during the war.

But once I recovered that, I saw it was only the tip of the iceberg."

"It's unlikely we'll ever recover everything that was stolen," Sarah said. "But we're thankful for anything we can put on display. These pieces keep those victims and all they suffered alive to a new generation."

The man was quiet.

"May I ask where you acquired this piece?" Sarah asked in his silence.

"A local woman," the man said. "I'm not sure she realized exactly what she had when she sold it to me."

"Sold it?" Macy shouted. "What a crook!"

Elaine shushed her.

"What are your expectations for a reward?" Sarah asked carefully.

After a short pause, the man cleared his throat. "I'm not looking for financial compensation."

Another pause, then Sarah went on. "This vase is very valuable, as you know. Generally our policy has been to honor a donor with a monetary gift."

"I don't want any money, Miss Kushman. I can't return the piece to its rightful owner, but I can at least do it the service of putting it on display somewhere where it will be remembered for what it is. A critical piece of history. A reminder of the tragedy and injustice that should never be forgotten."

Macy slowly leaned back in her seat.

"Are you sure?" Sarah asked. "That's awfully generous of you."

"Yes, awfully generous." A new voice came across the phone.

"Who is that?" Elaine whispered.

"We were all watching the phone too intently," Jan said. "I didn't even see anyone else go in."

Elaine pointed just right of the storage unit. "I didn't either, but I recognize that car." Jan looked up and saw Harrison Ellerby's black sedan parked in the other spot next to Sarah's car.

"We should go in," Elaine said. "Deputy Sheffield will be here any minute."

"Don't you think we should wait for him?" Jan asked.

"Not this time," Elaine said. She turned around to the backseat where Macy sat. "You stay here."

She and Jan got out of the car and hurried toward the storage unit as Jan tried to figure out if Harrison Ellerby was involved in this whole mess. When they reached the unit, they waited a moment before entering.

"I'm telling you there's been some sort of mix-up," Ellerby was saying. "I have documented evidence that this vase belongs to me. I'm the rightful owner. This man has no business attempting to sell it to you. Why else would he come in here impersonating me? Because he knows that vase is mine."

"Mr. Ellerby, you know that's not true," the other man said.

"Do I? Can you *honestly* tell me you bought this vase?"

Silence from the other man.

"Now if you'll kindly hand it over," Mr. Ellerby said.

"Actually..." Elaine barged into the room with Jan at her heels. "Wait just a moment before you do that."

"*What* are you doing here?" Harrison glared at them.

George Newsome, dressed in a coat identical to the one Harrison Ellerby wore, met Jan's eyes, then quickly looked away. "I'm sorry." His voice was quiet, and Jan thought there was something rather sad about him.

"You two have caused an awful lot of trouble lately," Elaine said.

Harrison shook a bony finger in the air. "I had nothing to do with this, as you well know."

"There wasn't supposed to be a fire," George said. "It should've been weeks before anyone realized that vase was missing in the first place."

"And once there was a fire?"

"I knew I didn't have much time," George said. "I'm not a thief, really. But you have to agree this vase belongs in a museum. It never should've been in Green Glade in the first place."

"How did you even find out it was there?" Elaine asked. "Mr. Ellerby said he restored the vase several years ago, but you didn't work for him then."

"I studied the ledger too. Mr. Ellerby keeps records of everything he's ever restored. Photos. Details. I've been search-ing for missing artifacts for years—and I've recovered several pieces. When I saw that vase, I knew what it was. It was one of three, and the other two are already in the museum where they belong. I thought if I could put them all back together, then somehow it would right a wrong."

"It's noble what you tried to do, even if your methods were faulty." Jan reached over and squeezed the man's shoulder. "But some wrongs can't be righted so easily."

"Especially not by impersonating your boss," Harrison spat. "It's dreadful you tried to pin this whole thing on me. And even worse that you didn't really appreciate the vase for what it is. How small-minded of you to think everything should be in a museum behind glass. This piece is better in the collection of someone who can really appreciate it." Harrison's sentence was punctuated with a flourish.

"The families of those artists and the families who originally owned those pieces deserve to either have them back in their possession or know they are safe in a place where they will be respected. Putting this collection of vases back together would go a very long way in doing that." George's passion was admirable, though Jan didn't make a habit of sympathizing with criminals.

"I couldn't agree more." The voice, which came from behind, belonged to Macy, who had obviously disregarded their instructions to stay put in the car. "In this case, *I* am the family who deserves to have her stolen antique back in her possession."

"Mrs. Atherton, with all due respect, you are not the rightful owner of this vase." George spoke with passion but not anger, and at his tone Macy seemed to soften ever so slightly. "My great-grandfather was an artist in Poland during the war. He wasn't famous by any means, but the Nazis still stole his work," George said. "I spent years trying to track it down, and I had a certain degree of success, but what it showed me was that there were so many people just like my great-grandfather, who would never recover what was rightfully theirs."

George only spoke to Macy now, as if trying to appeal to her humanity. "I know what I did was wrong, and I'm willing to accept responsibility for that, but you have an opportunity. There are two other vases identical to this one at the museum.

They were given to three Jewish brothers who were very prominent leaders of the day. Putting the collection back together is the right thing to do."

Macy stiffened. "And what about *my* family? You honestly believe they plundered the Jewish people during the war?"

"I don't presume to know how the vase came to be part of your family's story. I only know, from my research, that it shouldn't have been," George said quietly.

Macy stilled, but before she could respond, a squad car pulled up in front of the storage unit and Deputy Sheffield exited the car along with another officer. Judging by the look on his face, he was none too happy with their decision to go in before he arrived.

"What have we got here?" He glanced at Jan and Elaine, then around the room, sizing up who all had turned up for this interesting display.

"We found the vase," Jan said meekly.

"I see that." The deputy nodded at his fellow officer, who relieved Sarah of the vase.

"Be careful!" Macy and George spoke the words at the same time, stopping short when they realized it.

"We'll be careful with it," Deputy Sheffield said. "Now does someone want to tell me how all this"—he waved his hands around in a circle—"happened?"

Jan quickly caught Deputy Sheffield up to speed. He then loaded both Harrison and George into the back of the squad car. Before he hauled them away, he turned to Jan and Elaine.

"I have to hand it to the two of you," he said. "You've got great instincts. How did you know it was George?"

"The shoes." Jan glanced at George, sitting in the back of the squad car, a sad look on his face. "The shoes gave him away."

"What will happen to them?" Macy asked.

"Hard to say," the deputy said. "I'm sure the prosecutor will want to talk to you."

Macy hugged her purse to her chest. "What if I don't cooperate?"

All eyes shot to Macy.

The deputy lifted his chin as he crossed his arms over his chest. "Now, why wouldn't you cooperate?"

"Yes, Macy." Elaine turned to her. "You were right when you said you were the victim in all of this."

Macy's eyes fell on George Newsome, who watched her through the glass of the squad car window. "Maybe not the real victim after all."

CHAPTER TWENTY-SEVEN

The following day, with the mystery of Macy's vase safely behind them, Elaine decided to visit her mother at the Millpond Senior Community in Augusta. She enjoyed visiting Millpond. The bungalows the residents stayed in were well kept and clean, and a nurse was on call twenty-four hours a day. Her mother Virginia was in good health, but it made Elaine feel better knowing she would be well attended to if anything went wrong. Elaine parked in front of her mother's house and stepped up the path toward the door and rang the bell.

"Hello, Elaine. Come on in. Richard and I have been waiting for you." Her mother smiled and moved out of the way, gesturing for Elaine to step inside. She'd already met her mother's friend Richard once before, and given her recent findings about Jameson Wood, the fire that destroyed his business, and the possibility of a local rivalry, she wondered if he might have more information for her. So she'd asked her mother to invite Richard over, too, for their visit.

Today her mother was dressed in a comfortable pair of tailored slacks and a cashmere royal-blue cardigan. No matter the weather, her mother always wore long sleeves, because she was perennially cold.

The walked to the kitchen table, where Virginia had set out some cookies and a water pitcher. Richard stood to greet Elaine.

"Looking almost as beautiful as your mother," he said, kissing her hand.

"Hello, Richard," Elaine said with a laugh. "I choose to take that as a compliment."

"It was meant as one." Richard winked at her. "So how's life in the old Gardner house?" Richard asked.

"Better than ever, thank you." Elaine poured some water in a tall glass. "But I'm still working on figuring out more of the history of the place. Mind if I pick your brain again?"

"Pick away," Richard turned his mug around in his hand.

"I've been able to determine a number of people who lived there, but it seems there are a few missing links."

"Well sure," he said. "That makes sense with so many people in and out of there for so long."

Elaine was confused. "Was the Gardner family very large?"

"No, no. But for a time, the house was a boarding home. I'm sure I told you that the last time you were here."

"I can't say I remember that," Elaine said, her heart starting to beat faster. A boarding house? Surely she would have remembered him saying that. "Are you sure it was the Gardner house?" Maybe Richard was confused.

"Yes, that's right." Richard nodded. "Mike Gardener's parents opened up the house. It was the Depression, you understand, so everyone was very worried about money. I assume that's what happened with the Gardners." He took a bite of a cookie and took a moment to chew. "I don't think Mr. Gardner liked the fact that they had to take in boarders. I got the sense they felt like they'd come down in the world."

"When was this?" Elaine's mind was spinning. If the Gardners had taken in boarders, many different people would have come through the house. Could that have anything to do with how the ring had ended up in the wall of the house?

"Oh, goodness. This must have been the late 1930s, I would imagine?"

Elaine tried to imagine how the house could have been configured to allow for boarders. She knew walls had been moved around at some point, but she hadn't imagined this.

"Do you remember anything about any of the boarders?" she asked.

"I'm afraid not. This was, what, seventy years ago?" He laughed, as if he couldn't believe it had been so long."

Elaine was a little stunned. It felt like a breakthrough and like hitting a brick wall at the same time.

Now all she needed to do was figure out all the people who had lived in the house while it was a boarding house. And she had no idea how to do that.

AFTER HER VISIT with her mother and Richard, Elaine headed back to the tearoom and was now preparing for morning service. She finished setting the last table in the parlor, ready for a new group of customers to arrive at Tea for Two that morning, and she couldn't wait to tell everyone who came in about her latest exotic tea import—a peach cobbler Guayusa from the rainforest of Ecuador.

She'd sampled it yesterday, and while the caffeine had been a bit more than she bargained for, the taste was divine. She knew it would be a hit, especially when paired with the truffles and tea cakes Jan had prepared.

The crisp white linens had been freshly pressed, and Elaine had brought out her favorite china. The new autumn-inspired centerpieces had been delivered the night before. Elaine took a moment to admire the way the yellow orchids hugged red roses. Each vase was filled with the perfect amount of greenery to make the arrangement pop. She picked up one of the centerpieces and inhaled the fresh aroma just as she heard the front door open.

Were the guests arriving already?

Rose entered from the kitchen carrying a tray of freshly pressed napkins.

"Do you mind finishing the centerpieces? I think we've already got customers arriving." Elaine would never tire of the excitement of welcoming friends—new and old—into the tearoom.

Rose nodded, took the centerpiece from Elaine, and got to work. Elaine turned toward the entryway and found

Macy standing in the doorway, holding a box wrapped like a gift.

"Macy? I didn't expect you today," Elaine said. "I thought you'd be out celebrating your victory."

"Is Jan here?" Macy asked. "I'd like to speak with you both before your crowd arrives."

"Oh, I don't know how much of a crowd we'll have," Elaine said, hoping the day proved her wrong. "Rose, can you let Jan know we need her out here?"

The younger woman nodded, then disappeared into the kitchen.

Macy raised a brow. "I hope you're prepared for a crowd."

"Oh? Have you convinced half of Lancaster to sample our tea this morning?" Elaine laughed, but Macy's only reply was a silent stare.

Jan rushed in from the kitchen, a line of worry woven across her forehead. "I'm right in the middle of finishing the tea cakes." She looked at Elaine. "Is everything okay?"

"I think so," Elaine said. "Macy wanted to talk to us both."

Jan's eyes darted over to the other woman. "Oh. Is everything okay, Macy?"

Macy moved into the parlor and sat down at the table, seemingly in no hurry at all. Elaine could see Jan doing her best not to fret over the ticking clock that told them they only had a few minutes before they should be opening their doors.

"I've been thinking a lot about this whole mystery," Macy said, eyes darting from Jan to Elaine and back again. "It was the right decision to bring it to you."

There was something different about the way Macy spoke, something rather professional and pointed. It must've made Jan nervous because she moved over to the table and sat down next to Macy, then motioned for Elaine to do the same. It would seem the other woman had something important to say.

"I appreciate you taking so much time to help me find my vase," Macy said. "But I appreciate even more that you helped me realize it wasn't my vase at all."

Elaine and Jan exchanged a look, but neither said a word.

"I got you something." Macy nodded at the wrapped box she'd plunked down on the table, shifting the place setting as she did. "As a thank-you."

"Macy, you didn't have to…"

"I wanted to," Macy said, cutting Jan off midsentence. "Go ahead. Open it."

Jan looked at Elaine, who gave a nod of permission, then tugged at the ribbon until she shimmied it off the box. She pushed it between them so Elaine could help her open it.

Gently, they tugged on the lid, lifting it away from the bottom of the box, revealing neatly positioned white tissue paper with gold flecks of glitter in it. As Elaine moved the tissue paper out of the way, she and Jan came face to face with the gorgeous English Rose tea set they'd been admiring since the day she walked into Ellerby's Antiques.

"Macy, this is too much," Jan said.

Her cousin was right. They'd looked at the price tag more than once. This was far too much—much more valuable than they would've spent on themselves.

"I wanted you to have something to remember our little adventure by," Macy said with a smile that faded as quickly as it had appeared. "And to thank you for all your hard work helping track down the vase. I know I'm not the easiest person to put up with, so it means a lot to me that you didn't quit." She nodded sternly.

"Of course," Elaine said. "But we were happy to help. No gift necessary."

The front door opened again.

"Don't panic," Macy said, standing. "That is not your crowd. It's just for me." She rushed off to greet whoever had just come through the door. When she returned, she was accompanied by a young woman wearing a pair of sharp black pants, a crisp white dress shirt with thin black pinstripes on it and a pair of pointy black heels. She carried a large black bag, and a pair of black-rimmed glasses framed shockingly blue eyes.

"Miss Kushman," Macy said. "These are the women responsible for recovering the vase: Elaine Cook and Jan Blake."

Elaine and Jan both stood as the woman extended a hand in Elaine's direction. She shook it and then reached for Jan's hand. "It's wonderful to meet you both in person."

"*Jenna* Kushman?" Jan asked. "From the museum?"

"That's me," she said with a nod.

"How wonderful to meet you!" Elaine couldn't help giving her a hug.

"You too." Jenna smiled at them. "Mrs. Atherton filled me in on everything. It would seem we owe you a debt of gratitude."

"I can promise you, Jenna, nobody owes us anything. We're happy to help our friends." Elaine glanced at Macy.

Still, her affection for Macy didn't explain why Jenna Kushman had traveled from Washington, DC, to Lancaster, Maine—or why she was here at Tea for Two.

"Oh, where are our manners? Come in and let us get you a cup of tea." Jan led them all back to the table where they'd been sitting before Jenna's arrival.

"I shouldn't stay long," Jenna said. "But a cup of tea would be very nice."

"What brings you all the way to Lancaster, Miss Kushman?" Elaine asked as Jan went to fetch the tea.

She glanced at Macy, then back at Elaine. "I've come to retrieve Mrs. Atherton's vase."

Macy folded her hands on the table but said nothing. Jan returned and set the tray down on the table. "What did I miss?"

"Miss Kushman is here to retrieve Macy's vase," Elaine told her.

"I don't understand." Jan slowly sat back down in her chair.

"I've decided that while I don't agree with Mr Newsome's methods, I can appreciate his passion." Macy paused for a long moment. "I've decided that he was right. If my family was not the rightful owner of that vase, and I can't determine who that person was, then it should be in a museum, where it will be part of a larger story. A reminder of a tragedy that should never be forgotten."

Macy had surprised Elaine many times over the last few months, but she had to say, this might be the biggest surprise of all. After a few quiet seconds, she asked, "What about your family's stories, Macy?"

Macy lifted her chin proudly. "I've got plenty of photos to remember my family by. I'm choosing to believe they didn't realize where the vase came from when they first acquired it."

"That is likely, but unfortunately we will probably never know." Jenna looked at the thin silver watch on her wrist. "I'm sorry to rush, Mrs. Atherton, but I do have another engagement while I'm out here. It would appear the police uncovered quite a stockpile in Mr. Newsome's storage unit. I'm going to help them sort through it all."

"Of course. I understand." Macy pushed her chair away from the table and stood as Jenna did the same.

"We never did settle on a price." Jenna reached inside her large bag, presumably to retrieve her checkbook, but Macy's uplifted hand stopped her.

"This is a donation, Miss Kushman," she said. "And one I am happy to give."

Jenna froze, as if taken aback by the gesture. "Well, the museum is grateful, Mrs. Atherton. We'll be sure to put your name on the plaque when we put it on display."

Macy shook Jenna's outstretched hand. "That won't be necessary. I'd prefer to remain anonymous. Nothing should take away from the collection of vases being brought back together."

They made a plan for Jenna to pick up the vase, which Macy had retrieved from the police station earlier that day, then the three of them saw her out the front door.

"Macy, I'm proud of you," Elaine said after Jenna had driven off.

"It was the right thing to do," Macy said with a shrug. "Now, where are the tea cakes?"

ABOUT THE AUTHOR

Rebecca Adams is a small-town Midwestern girl who loves coffee (sorry, tea drinkers!), live theater, and various forms of art. Rebecca is a pastor's wife, business owner, and mother of three who lives in Illinois. She's allergic to Earl Grey.

From the Tea for Two Kitchen

JAN'S FAMOUS PUMPKIN MUFFINS

1¾ cups all purpose flour

1 cup sugar

½ cup dark brown sugar

1 teaspoon baking soda

½ teaspoon salt

2 teaspoons cinnamon

¼ teaspoon ground cloves

¼ teaspoon nutmeg

2 eggs

1 15-ounce can pure
    pumpkin puree

½ cup coconut oil, melted

1 teaspoon vanilla extract.

Preheat oven to 375 degrees. Prepare your twelve-place muffin pan by inserting liners or putting baking spray in each well.

Whisk together flour, sugars, baking soda, salt, and spices in a medium bowl and set aside. Whisk together the eggs, pumpkin puree, coconut oil, and vanilla extract in another bowl. Pour the wet ingredients into the dry ingredients and blend, just until everything is incorporated into the batter. (Avoid overmixing.)

Evenly distribute the batter among the twelve lined wells. They should be nearly full. Bake for twenty to twenty-two minutes or until a toothpick inserted into the center of a muffin comes out clean.

READ ON FOR AN EXCITING SNEAK PEEK
INTO THE NEXT VOLUME OF TEAROOM MYSTERIES!

O Christmas Tea

BY KRISTIN ECKHARDT

Morning fog was just beginning to lift from its perch atop Chickadee Lake as Jan Blake sipped the last drops of tea from her cup, closing her eyes to savor a quiet moment as the liquid warmed her within. Thick, gray clouds hung low in the sky, but Jan, who had lived in Central Maine all her life, did not need those to sense the probability of oncoming snow.

"It won't warm up much today, Earl Gray," she warned the large, longhaired cat at her side.

Earl Grey opened one green eye, briefly acknowledging his human companion before returning to the all-important task of napping away the day tucked snugly in his chair inside Jan's and her cousin, Elaine Cook's, screened-in porch. The stray cat had made his home at their Victorian tearoom, Tea for Two, since they arrived, and the cousins had taken to setting out blankets on the porch in the winter to keep their outdoor feline tenant warm, since he wasn't allowed inside due to food-service laws.

Jan grinned and stood up, stretching her arms before collecting her teacup and saucer. She pushed her glasses up higher on her nose. "All right, sir," she said, nodding at the now sleeping tomcat. "It's back to work for me. Stick to the porch today and you'll stay warm."

Earl Gray tucked his tail in tighter, encircling all four limbs, and continued to snooze as Jan headed back inside to check progress on the morning baking.

Most mornings at Tea for Two were pleasantly busy, thanks to word-of-mouth recommendations to tourists and a handful of faithful locals, but that day was particularly so as they awaited the arrival of a special guest: a Miss Clara Hill, renowned food critic of Portland's most circulated newspaper. Reviews from Clara were known to elevate the popularity of up-and-coming eateries, and though business was going well for Tea for Two, Jan couldn't help the excited nervousness that had begun to tickle her stomach like butterfly wings upon waking that morning.

Jan took a steadying breath of crisp December air, then pushed open the kitchen door, welcoming the rich scents of maple syrup, butter, and flour that greeted her. The kitchen was her favorite spot in the house. It boasted granite countertops, a work island with built-in storage, gleaming appliances, and rich walnut cupboards. Over time, she'd decorated it with old kitchen utensils and tins, and a blue Fiesta bowl filled with lemons near the coffeemaker added a bright splash of color.

Their server, Rose Young, looked up at Jan, hand pausing over a mixing bowl. "How's the weather out there?" Rose asked.

Jan smiled at the question as she removed her hat and then gloves, stuffing one into each coat pocket before hanging up her outerwear. "If I had to guess, I'd say there's a good chance it's going to snow this afternoon."

"Oh, don't mind the *guess* part of that statement," Elaine's voice carried from the pantry. "Jan's too humble to point out that she never guesses and her forecasts are more reliable than the weather girl on the news."

Rose laughed, the pleasant sound reminding Jan how thankful she was that they'd hired the young woman, whose temperament was as golden as the wheat-colored hair she usually wore in a braid. The past few months had been hard on Rose since the death of her mother, and on occasion Jan sensed her vulnerability. Yes, Rose was a grown woman, but she had still needed her mother, and the loss had taken its toll.

Jan supposed that was part of the reason she'd taken Rose under her wing recently, and had begun teaching her how to bake all of the pastries that customers so loved ordering to accompany their tea.

But that day, Rose was nothing but smiles as she continued stirring the wet ingredients for Jan's favorite maple croissants. Jan stopped to wash her hands at the sink, then walked over to join Rose at the counter.

"I'm just about ready to mix this in with the dry ingredients," Rose said.

"Wonderful," Jan answered, rubbing her hands together. "We're right on time."

Rose nodded rapidly, betraying a little of the tension she must have been feeling.

"Don't you worry, Rose," Jan said. "You're doing great."

The younger woman sighed. "I still can't believe you're letting me make your special recipe," she said, chuckling nervously.

"Nonsense. You've been practicing for months now and these croissants will be just the thing for Miss Hill to try," Jan responded.

"Absolutely," Elaine said, joining Jan and Rose in the main part of the kitchen. Elaine's blue eyes sparkled above her cerulean sweater as she set a can of diced tomatoes and an onion on the counter before pulling a slow cooker down from an upper cabinet. "They're all the rage with the regulars, so if our food critic wants a taste of local flavor, she's certainly come to the right place."

"I sure hope so," said Rose, carefully adding a little of the wet ingredients at a time to the dry already in a spinning stand mixer. "Though I still wish you would have made today's batch, Jan. I'm so nervous I'm afraid I might forget something and ruin our chances at a good write-up."

Jan gave Rose's shoulder a gentle squeeze. "I have complete faith in you, Rose. Besides, if you're thinking about enrolling in culinary courses to become a grand pastry chef someday, you'll need to experience what it's like to cook for a famous foodie." She'd meant to encourage Rose, but the young woman's cheeks suddenly lost their rosy shade.

"You're scaring her, Jan," Elaine teased. "Why don't you let her handle the croissants while you come on over and help me with this stew?"

"All right, but let me know if you need me, Rose."

"Will do," Rose called, her voice sounding a little less anxious than before.

Jan and Elaine had decided to put together a beef stew that morning and let it cook all day, as they were certain time would fly with their visitor and they'd both be hungry and too worn out to put something together by the time dinner rolled around. Taking a quick glance at the inventory Elaine had already gathered, Jan pulled a pound of round steak from the fridge, along with carrots and celery. She grabbed an onion and a couple of potatoes from the pantry and began washing the vegetables while Elaine rubbed the meat with olive oil, salt, and pepper.

The cousins worked so well together, both in tasks related to the teashop and at life in general, Jan thought, tickled. When Elaine had first approached her with the idea of buying a large house on Chickadee Lake and turning it into a tearoom, Jan, having lived as a widow for a decade by that time, had not been able to envision such a different lifestyle.

But now she wouldn't trade it for anything. It was nice to come home to a warm house where she knew she wouldn't have to be alone very often. And baking for her community brought a new kind of joy into her world; she found satisfaction in comforting and nourishing the locals, many of whom she'd come to think of as extended family.

Though, never in her wildest dreams would she have imagined that Tea for Two would draw the attention of a food critic as well known and regarded as Clara Hill.

When Elaine had first gotten the telephone call from Clara's assistant, asking if they would entertain a review of their tearoom, Jan had given in to her curiosity and done a little research of her own. What she'd found had both pleased her and served to make her more nervous at the idea than she already had been, as Miss Hill's articles were exceptionally detailed, well-written, and seemed to be very fair. The critic's write-ups were never unkind, but always extremely honest, making the reader, at least in Jan's experience, either excited to try out the eatery in question, or very, very certain he or she was not missing anything by passing it up.

In other words, Jan mused with a deep sigh, a review from Clara Hill had the power to potentially make or break a budding establishment like Tea for Two.

Silently, she passed her worries on to God, praying that He would be by her side as He had been every day of her life, a reminder that, like a balm, soothed her instantly.

When she and Elaine finished preparing the vegetables and meat for stew, Jan turned the slow cooker to low and went to check on Rose.

"All set," Rose said, brushing floured hands against her apron. She picked up an empty banana peel from the counter and tossed it in the garbage can before washing her hands. "The croissants are in the oven and Miss Hill should be here in—" she glanced at the wall clock "—less than an hour."

Jan nodded and glanced around anxiously, wishing for something to occupy her hands. She'd risen early to get some of the baking out of the way before Rose came in, and she and Elaine had already completed their morning routine of checking that each table in the parlor was set to receive customers. Evidently they had just been too efficient for their own good that morning. Finally, she settled for wiping down the counters. By the time she'd finished, they were squeaky clean, and

Elaine had made a pot of oolong tea for the three of them and set out a jar of honey at the kitchen table.

"Everything is ready for Miss Hill." Elaine brushed a loose strand of brown hair from her eyes as she slid into a chair. "Don't worry," she said as Rose eyed her mug. "I made decaf. I didn't think any of us needed any help waking up, seeing as how we're already just bundles of nerves."

The three women broke into laughter, and Jan felt the tension in the room dissipate as they all managed to relax a little.

"Truer words have never been spoken," Rose added, sipping her tea. "I suppose all we can do now is wait."

"Wait and pray," Jan said. "But no use worrying ourselves too much."

Rose and Elaine nodded, and Jan noticed the apples of Rose's cheeks had returned to their usual pretty pink.

"We serve tea and pastries to so many people every day, and if the regulars' constant return is any indication, I think we're doing well enough," Jan said.

"Exactly," Elaine agreed. "We'll give Clara the very best treats we have to offer. If she enjoys our tearoom, that will be lovely. If not, we'll still get up the next day and get to work." She added a teaspoon of sugar to her cup and stirred. "Besides, it's a simple breakfast. What could possibly go wrong?"

An hour later, the tearoom was bustling with activity as Rose served croissants, scones, muffins, and the cookie of the day, a chocolate shortbread, while Jan wandered the parlor, chatting with locals and guests and pouring tea.

Suddenly, the parlor door opened, bringing a gust of frigid wind. "She's here," Jan whispered discreetly as she passed Rose on her way to greet Clara Hill, whose shoulder-length dark, wavy hair, green eyes, and slim stature she recognized from the photo that always accompanied the food critic's byline in the Portland paper.

Jan brushed imaginary crumbs off of her apron as she approached. "Good morning and welcome to Tea for Two," she said holding out an arm. "May I seat you?"

The woman smiled warmly and Jan was pleased to see that the smile reached her eyes. "Good morning to you as well. I'm Clara Hill from the *Portland Pelican,*" Clara answered, offering a hand. "I believe I spoke with your cousin Elaine on the phone."

Jan nodded, shaking Clara's outstretched hand. "Jan Blake. It's so nice to have you with us today. And, yes, a seat would be lovely."

Jan smiled, hoping her features didn't betray her nervousness. "Right this way." She took a deep breath as she led Clara further into the parlor, stopping at a cozy table for two near the fireplace. "How is this?" she asked.

"Wonderful." Clara wrapped her purse strap around the back of the chair and sat down, picking up a menu.

Jan hovered, suddenly unsure of what to do with herself. Normally, she would give a customer a few minutes to peruse the menu before she asked about an order, but in that moment, she froze.

Clara smiled up at Jan, her green eyes friendly. "Please don't be nervous. I'm just like any other guest," she said, reaching out a hand. "I know it probably feels a little strange, knowing I'll write about my experience here, but I'd love it if you'd try not to let that bother you too much."

Relief flooded through Jan and the two women giggled at the same time. "I'm so glad you said that. For a second there, I'd almost forgotten what I'm meant to be doing, but you've put me more at ease."

Clara grinned. "How about this?" she suggested, folding her menu and placing it neatly on the table. "Why don't you tell me your favorite things on the menu, and I'll start there?"

"Well, a lot of our customers have fallen in love with the cinnamon spice tea we're carrying over the fall and winter seasons. It's a nice blend of nutmeg, cinnamon, orange peel, and sweet cloves." As she spoke, Jan's apprehension began to fade and she felt a little more like her usual self. "The aroma just makes me think of Christmastime."

"Sold," Clara said. "I'd love a cup of that. Now, I haven't had breakfast and I'm famished. What can you recommend to eat along with it? I'd be thrilled to have something sweet."

Jan hesitated, not wanting to toot her own horn about her maple croissants. But, she had to admit they were a customer favorite, and Clara did not need to know who'd created the recipe to enjoy them, after all.

"Our mini maple croissants are popular with the regular customers, and they would definitely fix your sweet tooth right up. How does that sound?" Jan clasped her hands together in front of her apron, surprised to discover that she looked forward to reading the critic's commentary on her specialty. Perhaps, if Miss Hill didn't enjoy the treats, she might give insight into how they could be made even better. Jan was happy with the recipe, and the croissants had a growing fan base in Lancaster, but she believed there was always room for improvement.

"Mini maple croissants it is, then," Clara ordered, her voice cheerful and enthusiastic.

There was something open and discerning about the young woman that made a person want to please her palate, and Jan could see why Clara had gained her reputation for being honest and fair, but also a little intimidating.

"I'll have that right out." Jan gave a little nod and turned toward the kitchen to put together Clara's order. Out of the corner of her eye, she saw Rose chatting with a couple who appeared to be in their late thirties or early forties. She and Rose had served the regulars quickly and everyone seemed to be at ease, enjoying their orders. Confident that all was going smoothly, Jan left the parlor and passed through the entrance hall and into the kitchen.

"How's it going out there?" Elaine asked, busy at the stove with a large kettle.

"So far, so good. Miss Hill arrived a few minutes ago and ordered the cinnamon spice tea and maple croissants. Rose has everything else under control at the moment, so I'm going to gather Clara's tea and food and bring it on out."

Elaine turned off one of the burners and lifted a kettle, settling it on a trivet. She disappeared into the pantry, returning a moment later with the cinnamon spice tea tin. "So what was she like? Did she seem nice?"

"Yes, very nice, actually. She's kind and has a pretty face to go with her personality, and she seemed relaxed and happy to be here."

"Not at all what I was expecting," Elaine said. "For some reason, I'd pictured her with a very stern expression and a pad and pen out, taking notes."

Jan gave a little chuckle. "It is an interesting job, isn't it?" she mused, placing loose tealeaves into a steeper ball and pouring water over them in an individual pot. She'd chosen her favorite, a white ceramic one with little hand painted bluebells—not an antique, but sweet and pretty nonetheless. "It can't be easy to have restaurateurs so nervous around you all the time. I know I was. She called weeks ago to schedule a time to stop by, and still I had goose bumps covering my arms."

Elaine laughed. "Just remember, it's all in God's hands. Whatever happens, we'll make the best of it."

While the tea steeped, Jan arranged two maple croissants on a plate that matched the teapot, placing a tiny jar of fresh maple syrup next to everything else on a silver tray. As soon as the tea was ready, she added it along with a cup and saucer, then stood back to survey the arrangement. Pleased, she set off toward the parlor, almost bumping into Rose as she passed through the door.

"*Oof!*" Rose said, moving quickly out of the way. "That was a close one. Sorry, Jan, I had my mind on Miss Hill out there."

She smiled. "The couple I was chatting with ordered green tea, so I'm on my way in to get that ready and I'll be right back out there to help you. Is that her order?" she asked. "I hope she likes the croissants. I tried a nibble of one myself—just to make sure the batch came up okay—and it was divine, as ever."

"Yes, this is it." Jan clutched the tray tighter, easing carefully past Rose into the hallway. "Just a little while longer and we can rest easy."

Jan sent up another silent prayer and braced herself before returning to the parlor. Clara had gotten up from the table and was busy admiring the antique tea sets on display in a cabinet in a corner of the parlor. As soon as she saw Jan approaching with a tray, she returned to her table near the fire.

"You have a beautiful collection here, Miss Blake," Clara complimented, turning to face Jan. "It must have taken a great deal of work to put all this together."

"It's a hobby of mine and Elaine's. I suppose it is work in a way, but it's something we both enjoy." Jan placed the tray carefully on the table, setting the teacup and saucer at Clara's place just as she sat down.

"This looks fabulous," Clara commented, spreading a napkin in her lap.

Jan finished up and stood, her hands curled nervously at her sides. "And here we have everything you might need in the way of sweetening," she said, motioning to a lazy Susan at the center of the table. "If you like."

Clara smiled. "I think I'll try a sip plain first so I can get an unhindered taste of all the flavors."

"I'll leave you to it, then," Jan said. "Please let us know if there's anything else you need."

"Absolutely."

"Enjoy."

Though her instinct was to hurry, Jan tried her best to walk away at a normal pace. She checked on the regulars, and noticed a few new customers among them. Emmaline Cribbs and Pearl Trexler were there, enjoying a cup of tea together. Maureen Oakley had brought her youngest grandson and was giving him tiny nibbles from her cranberry scone.

As Jan walked through the parlor she smiled at Dr. Tyson McInnes and his wife, Claudia, as they sat at a corner table working on a crossword puzzle together.

Then she stopped a table where a young couple, Marisa and Sven, sat. They told her they were traveling through Maine on their honeymoon. She chatted with them about local sites to see, such as the lighthouses and the preserved granite fort in nearby Prospect, before moving on.

Jan waved to two tourists whose names she learned were Irene Kelly and Scott Landon—Rose had already served them—then took an order from River White before making her way back to the kitchen. Once again, she and Rose passed each other, the younger woman carrying a full tray this time.

"Did it go all right?" Rose asked, eyes wide in anticipation of Jan's answer.

"I think so," Jan lowered the empty silver tray to her side. "It remains to be seen how she likes everything. She said to think of her like any other customer, so I'm doing my best not to give her any special treatment."

"Well, I'll stop by her table and check on her once I drop off these orders."

"Sounds great."

Once she'd entered the kitchen, Jan released an audible sigh of relief. Elaine came in from her office next to the kitchen.

"Unless our famous critic has left so soon, that sigh's a little premature, don't you think?" Elaine teased.

"I'm just celebrating the fact I didn't drop the tray into Miss Hill's lap."

Elaine giggled. "Oh, come now. I'm sure you did just fine. She'll be finished in no time, and on her way to write us a positive review. I'm certain of it. It's out of our hands now."

"And thank goodness for that."

Jan was just about to grab a pitcher of water from the refrigerator when she heard a loud noise, like feet pounding on the wood floor outside the kitchen. Her heart lurched into her throat, knowing Rose wouldn't run down the hallway unless something wasn't right.

A few seconds later, her concern was validated, as Rose rushed in, pink-cheeked, her tray hanging listlessly at her side.

"Call an ambulance and come quick!" Rose gasped, the words rushing from her in a panicked jolt. "Something terrible has happened."

Jan bolted from where she'd stood in front of the fridge, letting the door slam loudly shut. "What is it?" she asked, rushing to Rose's side.

The younger woman's eyes swam back and forth as she worked to calm herself and gather her thoughts. "It's the food critic, Miss Hill," Rose blurted. "She's passed out!"

FROM THE
GUIDEPOSTS ARCHIVE

This story, by Rhonda Lowther of Ridgeland, South Carolina, originally appeared in *Guideposts*.

Mom's red vase sits in my curio cabinet, and sometimes the sunlight hits it just the way it did the day I first saw it. I was eight and visiting my grandparents for the weekend. I cleaned my plate at Friday dinner. Granddaddy pressed a quarter into my hand as a reward.

Oh, the things I could buy with that quarter! Pixie Sticks, little wax Coke bottles, the tiny dot candies on paper. Saturday morning we headed for the little grocery store at the strip mall across the street. We were about to go inside when my eye caught a flash of red in the window of a second-hand store. Red like the lamps in our living room and the stemware glasses and candleholders my mom used for special occasions. Mom's red, I thought, suddenly excited. I have to get it for her.

"Can I look in this store?" I asked Granddaddy.

"Sure, Rhonda. I'll be in the grocery."

I slipped inside the shop. "Howdy, young lady," the man behind the cash register said. I put my quarter on the glass-top counter.

"I'd like that red vase in the window," I said.

The man smiled and shook his head. "I'm afraid it'll take more than that."

I stared at the red vase, afraid to ask the price of a treasure like that, then slunk out of the store. That night Granddaddy and Nannie watched Lawrence Welk on TV. I sat on the couch between them, dreaming of the red vase that I knew Mom would love. I saved my allowance, returned bottles for pennies and put aside every cent I could. Next time I visited my grandparents, my pink beaded purse was so heavy I was afraid the handle would break. Again Granddaddy gave me a quarter for cleaning my plate. The next morning I marched into the secondhand shop. The red vase was still there!

I dumped all the coins on the counter. "Is this enough?"

The man looked at me and looked at the dimes, quarters, nickels and pennies—mostly pennies. Finally he nodded. "It's just the right amount," he said.

Mom loved the vase. She put it into her china cabinet and took it out for special occasions. Later, she moved in with my husband and me, and the vase came with her. Then she got the cancer diagnosis.

She fought a valiant battle. I put the vase with flowers in it by her bedside to cheer her up. Or I put it on the table if she felt strong enough to join us at mealtime. Then one awful day she was gone. The vase went into the cabinet. I didn't want to look at it. It made me miss Mom too much. How will I face life without her? I asked in my prayers.

One day a friend was visiting. An antiques dealer. I caught him admiring the vase. "It belonged to my mother," I said.

"May I?" He picked it up. "I haven't seen something like this in years. It's a special glass, a technique that's rarely done anymore. It's called ruby glass."

I felt my breath go. For one brief moment I was back at the strip mall, staring into the secondhand store and seeing the vase for the first time. And feeling the wonderment of a divine hand. For you see, my mother's name was Ruby.

A NOTE FROM THE EDITORS

We hope you enjoyed Tearoom Mysteries, published by the Books and Inspirational Media Division of Guideposts, a nonprofit organization that touches millions of lives every day through products and services that inspire, encourage, help you grow in your faith, and celebrate God's love.

Thank you for making a difference with your purchase of this book, which helps fund our many outreach programs to military personnel, prisons, hospitals, nursing homes, and educational institutions.

We also create many useful and uplifting online resources. Visit Guideposts.org to read true stories of hope and inspiration, access OurPrayer network, sign up for free newsletters, download free e-books, join our Facebook community, and follow our stimulating blogs.

To learn about other Guideposts publications, including the best-selling devotional *Daily Guideposts*, go to Guideposts.org/Shop, call (800) 932-2145, or write to Guideposts, PO Box 5815, Harlan, Iowa 51593.

Sign up for the
Guideposts Fiction Newsletter

and stay up-to-date on
the fiction you love!

You'll get sneak peeks of new releases, recommendations from other Guideposts readers, and special offers just for you . . .

And it's FREE!

Just go to Guideposts.org/Newsletters
today to sign up.

Guideposts

Visit Guideposts.org/Shop
or call (800) 932-2145

Find more inspiring fiction in these best-loved Guideposts series!

Sugarcreek Amish Mysteries
Be intrigued by the suspense and joyful "aha" moments in these delightful stories. Each book in the series brings together two women of vastly different backgrounds and traditions, who realize there's much more to the "simple life" than meets the eye.

Miracles of Marble Cove
Follow four women who are drawn together to face life's challenges, support one another in faith, and experience God's amazing grace as they encounter mysterious events in the small town of Marble Cove.

Secrets of Mary's Bookshop
Delve into a cozy mystery where Mary, the owner of Mary's Mystery Bookshop, finds herself using sleuthing skills that she didn't realize she had. There are quirky characters and lots of unexpected twists and turns.

Patchwork Mysteries
Discover that life's little mysteries often have a common thread in a series where every novel contains an intriguing mystery centered around a quilt located in a beautiful New England town.

Mysteries of Silver Peak
Escape to the historic mining town of Silver Peak, Colorado, and discover how one woman's love of antiques helps her solve mysteries buried deep in the town's checkered past.

To learn more about these books, visit Guideposts.org/Shop